DANCE

OF THE

MONGOOSE

DANCE
OF THE
MONGOOSE

◆

T. J. Phillips

BERKLEY PRIME CRIME, NEW YORK

A Berkley Prime Crime Book
Published by The Berkley Publishing Group
200 Madison Avenue, New York, New York 10016

Book design by Stanley S. Drate/Folio Graphics, Inc.

First edition: August 1995

Library of Congress Cataloging-in-Publication Data

Phillips, T. J.
    Dance of the mongoose / T. J. Phillips. — 1st ed.
      p. cm.
    ISBN 0-425-14786-X (hardcover)
    ISBN 0-425-14921-8 (trade)
    I. Title.
    PS3566.H523D36   1995
    813'.54—dc20   94-24524
                                          CIP

Printed in the United States of America

10 9 8 7 6 5 4 3 2 1

DANCE

OF THE

MONGOOSE

WARM-UP FOR THE ORCHESTRA

I 've been trying to imagine the murder scene. It probably went something like this:

Somewhere around two o'clock, in the middle of that cool tropical night, the moon came out from behind a cloud and shone brightly down on the tiny smudge of land in the Caribbean. In St. Thomas, the moon sees everything: I know that for a fact. On this particular night in July, the moon beamed beneficently down on the mountains rising dramatically from the sea; on the long strips of pure white beach at the water's edge, muted now in darkness; and on the sleeping, crescent-shaped seaside town of Charlotte Amalie. Its rays highlighted the roofs of the town, of the houses in the hills above, and of the large resort hotels next to the water outside the city limits. It watched the boats bobbing gently in the harbor; the palms, hibiscus, and frangipani waving slightly in the moist trade wind; and the occasional small nocturnal ani-

mal creeping furtively from shadow to shadow. The island was still, silent, at rest, bathed in a wash of blue.

The moon chased itself up the winding hillside road
across the harbor from the town, through the huge
wrought iron gates flanked by solid stone walls, and
around the curved gravel driveway to Haven View. It
dazzled the corrugated tin roof of the massive, pillared
plantation manor. It glowed on the surfaces of the dark
red walls and formed ghostly, ice-blue outlines on the
thick jungle of trees and bushes that engulfed house, veranda, and patio. At last, it competed angrily with the
yellow beams of artificial light emanating from the shut-
ter-framed doors and windows of one downstairs room.

In that room the Honorable Hubert Jensen sat at his
desk, writing. There was a manila folder opened in front
of him, and a few typed pages of facts and figures were
scattered about. In another, closed folder were several
glossy photographs. Stapled to each photo were sheets of
memo paper with more facts and figures scrawled, earlier
in the evening, in the judge's cramped, nearly illegible
hand. Now, however, neither of these files commanded
his attention: he was working on a speech to be given
the following week at a meeting of the local Chamber of
Commerce. A large brandy snifter and a bottle stood off
to the side on the mahogany desk, away from the clutter.

Judge Jensen paused in his writing. Lifting the glass,
he sat back in his padded leather chair and sighed. The
campaign was going well, or so his supporters kept telling
him. These past few weeks had been a cavalcade of parties, fund-raisers, and speeches like the one he was now
composing. He was popular; he was rich; he was one of
the island's most powerful men. In the first week of No-

vember, he fully expected to be voted governor of the Virgin Islands.

He was sixty-two years old. He was tall, handsome, a bit portly (perhaps he giggled as he sipped the cognac), and his full head of hair was still black—well, almost: his sideburns were getting lighter, and he touched up his temples now and then with dye. But what the voters didn't know wouldn't hurt them. Hubert Jensen was a proud man.

To his way of thinking, he had every reason to be proud. He had utilized his legendary charm and magnetism to become the leading Republican candidate for governor—on an island that had never seen a white elected governor—and where charisma hadn't worked, he had resorted to newer, more exciting tactics. (He probably smiled when he reflected on this, and perhaps he reached out his fingers to caress the closed folder of facts and photographs on his desk.) Charm, magnetism, bribery, and blackmail: he already had one foot in the governor's mansion. He would not live there, of course: he would rule the three United States Virgin Islands from his beloved Haven View. Not bad for a man who had arrived here forty years ago, a penniless, recently orphaned merchant sailor on a rusty freighter that had reeked of diesel and stale fish, with nothing but a keen intelligence and a burning desire to be Somebody.

Now, so many years later, he closed his eyes, sipped his drink, and smiled. Being in charge was easy; what was difficult was *not* being in charge. Working, moving, responding to the commands of others: these were the talents that Hubert Jensen had never mastered. And now, of course, they would never again be necessary. He had seen to that.

Still with his eyes closed, he leaned forward and listened for sounds elsewhere in the house. No, nothing. His wife, Helen, would be asleep by now, aided in her quest for oblivion by her nightly ritual of liquor and barbiturates. (Stupid woman! But he wouldn't have to put up with her idiocies for much longer, thank God!) The servants had all retired for the night in their cottage elsewhere on the grounds of the estate. And Frank—no. Frank, his only child, no longer lived in this house. (Here, I think, the judge would have rapped the shiny surface of the desk with his fist.) He had been betrayed, countermanded: he had lost his son. Frank was dead—no, *better* than dead. Disinherited. He had not spoken to Frank for more than a month.

Until tonight.

In the light from the desk lamp and the chandelier above, he reflected on the evening's activities. Over the past few weeks, His Honor had made a few decisions concerning his gubernatorial future. Tonight he had begun to act on those decisions.

At the dinner table on the veranda, at approximately seven-thirty, he had informed his silent, only slightly drunk wife that she would be leaving St. Thomas. As soon as he had been sworn in, and shortly after the Inaugural Ball, he would send Helen back to the States, to a very exclusive, very expensive sanitarium. As governor, he would no longer be able to afford the embarrassment of an alcoholic, pill-popping consort. She would not be allowed to return to the island until she had learned to control her self-destructive tendencies. Without a word, Helen had risen and wandered from the veranda to her room upstairs, to the bottles she always kept on her night table.

Hubert had finished his meal and retired to this room, his office. While the servants cleared the table on the veranda outside, he had picked up the telephone and called his son. Frank had been informed in a brief, cold speech that Hubert was disinheriting him. Papers to that effect would be drawn up in the next few days. The judge had made it clear that he never wanted to see his son again. With a harsh Anglo-Saxon expletive, Frank had slammed down the receiver.

Vitelco, the Virgin Islands Telephone Company, would later produce a bill proving that Hubert had made several more calls during the next two hours. As he had hung up on each party, he had reached into his blackmail file and scribbled furiously (he was probably smiling). From about ten-fifteen, when the last call was completed, until two in the morning, he had worked on his notes, on a new budget proposal, and on the speech for the Chamber of Commerce.

Even if he had made a conscious effort to set the stage for his own murder, he could not have done so with more precision. It is difficult, in retrospect, to understand why he didn't at least suspect what was obviously going to happen. Arrogance, perhaps. Or simply the feeling we all share that such things don't really happen—not to us, at any rate. For whatever reason, Judge Jensen worked on into the night, oblivious, never anticipating his imminent danger.

As the clock in the living room across the hall announced the second hour of the morning, he put down the snifter, rose, and walked over to the open French doors that led to the veranda. He stood in the doorway, gazing out at the patio, at the shadowy trees, and at the distant lights of the city. It really is a magnificent view, he probably thought, the finest on the island. He must have noticed the moon: it is possible that he even went so far as to look up at the full moon and smile.

He returned to his desk and sat. It was now a few moments after two o'clock. As he reached for his pen, he heard a slight noise, a rustling from somewhere outside. He was still for a moment, listening, wondering what it could be. The breeze, the faraway surf, the tree frogs, the song of the moon: otherwise, nothing. Silence. With a shrug, he picked up the pen.

"Wind," he said aloud. "Or something-or-other dancing." What was it that danced under the full moon? Some native folklore, very quaint and charming. Big with the tourists. Oh, yes . . . "Mongoose!" he cried, triumphant, and he began to write.

He felt the eyes before he saw them. In one sudden, chilling instant, he knew that he was no longer alone in the room. Startled, he looked up. His eyes met those of the figure standing quite still in the doorway that had been empty only seconds before. When he saw who it was, his momentary shock was quickly replaced by anger. This is really too much, he undoubtedly thought.

"What the hell do *you* want at this hour of the morning?" he demanded of the figure in the doorway.

Without a sound, the intruder began to advance across the room. Hubert started to rise, to protest.

"I thought I made myself clear earlier—" He stopped in mid-sentence when he noticed the machete.

There was no time. An arm was raised. The blade flashed. Instinctively, the judge brought up his hands to protect himself. In that last wild moment, he may have wondered at how quickly it comes. There was no time to scream, no time for anything. He would never be heard.

He would never be saved. The Honorable Hubert Jensen would never be governor of the Virgin Islands.

With a soft whistle, the machete came down.

The moon saw everything. It stared down from the dark Atlantic sky, omniscient yet indifferent. Its function was to illuminate, not to explain. If anyone had been able to question it, the events of subsequent months would never have taken place, and several other people would still be alive.

But nobody asked the moon.

That, for what it's worth, is my interpretation of what happened that night. The rest is documented.

The housekeeper found him at eight o'clock the next morning. Coming over from the servants' cottage to start breakfast, she had noticed the light still shining from the windows of the office, and she had gone to investigate.

He was sitting in the leather chair. There was blood everywhere, soaking the front of his suit and splattered across the various folders on the desk. There were even dark red specks on the white stucco wall behind him. Flies were buzzing lazily around his head, which rested in a sticky, congealing pool on the floor, several yards from the body in the chair.

The housekeeper, whose name is Eunice, remembers the flies. She remembers the look in the eyes staring up at her from the head on the floor. And she distinctly remembers it was at that moment, when she first entered the stinking, bloodstained, fly-infested study, just before she began to scream, that she heard, on the patio and foliage outside, the first tentative drops of rain.

1

INVITATION
TO THE DANCE

The first tentative flakes of snow had fallen thirty minutes before. Now, outside on Hudson Street, a blizzard was raging. I watched from the warmth of my fourth floor apartment as the last-minute Christmas shoppers trudged and skidded, heads bent forward over their laden arms, through the ever-rising mountain of powdered ice. Now and then they slalomed to the curb to search the oncoming traffic for empty taxis. No such luck: it was December twenty-third, and it was snowing, and every cab in Manhattan was occupied.

I stood at my window, sipping coffee and gazing down at the unfortunates. I had for once had the common sense to buy my presents early. I would be spared this storm, at least. It was a comforting thought, my first in several weeks. The approach of the holiday had only exacerbated the boredom, the depression, the restlessness I had been experiencing for the past few months.

It had been some September. Three days after my latest play had ended its brief, floundering, Off-Broadway run, I had come across a stack of copies of my latest novel in the marked-down section at Barnes and Noble. Breakdown, Part One. Part Two: I found the just-released paperback edition of the book not in the "New and Noteworthy" section but in "Recent Fiction." ("Oh, don't be so silly," my mother said when I told her of the slight. "At least it wasn't in 'Games and Amusements.'" I love my mother, so I'll stop there.)

Ah, yes: September. My thirtieth birthday, the failure of my second play (a hit, compared to the first), and the remaindering of my second novel (the first had been a "critical success," which means it was read by several reviewers, one or two college English professors, and my immediate family). Now, here I was, two days before Christmas, thirty years old. Two (flop) plays, two (dull) novels, a beautiful (ex-) girlfriend, one or two (busy) friends, and a charming (scattered) family. Joe Wilder: Recent Fiction.

The snow was doing nothing for my mood. I was bored, listless, and very, very tired. Unhappiness is draining. A good four-month slump uses up so much of one's energies. I had begun no fewer than three (dull) third novels since October, but I had immediately abandoned them. I was restless, restive; I wanted something to do. I wanted *something* to happen.

Something happened: the telephone rang. It was Bonnie, my beautiful (ex-) girlfriend. Merry Christmas, Joe, and I'm getting married. In that order.

Back at the window, I was toying with the idea of crawling out on the ledge and accompanying the flurry on its graceful descent to Hudson Street ("Recent Fiction Joins Recent Snowfall!" the *New York Post* would undoubtedly scream, if they bothered to mention it at all, which they wouldn't, because my plays were flops and my novels were remaindered at Barnes and —). . . .

The phone rang again.

"Mr. Joseph Wilder, please. Person-to-person from Lee in St. Thomas."

"Yes."

"Is this Mr. Wilder?"

"Yes, it is."

"Go ahead, please." Click.

"Joe?"

"Hi, Lee." My sister in the Virgin Islands.

"God, Joe, I didn't recognize your voice. Are you okay?"

"I'm fine. Hang on a minute, I gotta close the window." I looked around for my cigarettes, lit one, and picked up the receiver. "Hi. How's the sunny V.I.?"

"Sunny. In fact, that's why I'm calling. Have you thought about my invitation?"

Oh, boy, I thought, here it comes. Lee was always inviting me to St. Thomas. Not that I minded: I love my sister, and since she and Marla and I were born and raised in St. Thomas, it was definitely my second favorite place in the world, after New York. Lee is the only member of the family who still lives in the Islands, with her husband, Paul. Marla was in Upstate New York with her young family, Mom had a penthouse on Fifth Avenue, and I was in Greenwich Village, writing bad plays and dull novels.

Lee and Paul own a ship-to-shore radio station at Mountaintop, the highest point on St. Thomas, and they live in a lovely old Danish house on Blackbeard's Hill in Charlotte Amalie. Paul works twenty-six hours a day with his computerized radio equipment, which is—after Lee—the love of his life. At that time, my sister enjoyed entertaining family members from New York. She took a break from her own work in the station's front office to take us to the beach, to brunch, and to nightclubs.

As Marla was raising two children and Mom had an ear disorder that prevented her from flying, I was the one who took the most advantage of Lee and Paul's hospitality, usually once every couple of years. All of which was fine with me—usually. But after the ennui of the last few months and the frustration of trying to start a new writing project, I just didn't feel like making the effort. My lack of movement had rendered me immobile.

Back on the phone:

"Uh, yeah, sure—I've thought about going down there after Christmas, but—"

"Look, Joe, I know this mood. Mom told me you're in one of your famous declines, and you've been looking for something to do. So do something. Come on down, as they say on the game shows."

"I don't know, Lee—"

"Besides, it's not just Paul and I who'd like to see you. You may be able to do a good deed here."

"What? What are you talking about?"

"I'm talking about Frank Jensen. Remember him? Only your best friend in the world . . ."

Frank? That was a surprise. "What about him?"

"Well, I saw him downtown last week, and he looked terrible. He's looked like that ever since his father was—well, you know, last July."

"Any news about that?"

"No. It hasn't been solved, and I don't know if it ever will be, Joe. There's no real evidence against anybody, and on this island nobody asks who wanted to kill the judge. The question is, who didn't? But that's not what I'm getting at. I'm talking about Frank's wife. You've never met her, have you? Well, she's really beautiful, and very nice, I guess. She called me last night and asked for your address. She said she's going to write to you."

"To me? Why?"

"How should I know? Oh, Joe, I don't know those people. You do. You and Frank and that other one, Dennis Grey. The Three Musketeers, remember? You were all pests when we were kids—"

"We were *not* pests—"

"As I said, *pests*, and now—well, anyway, you should be getting a letter from her shortly. That's as much as I know. Incidentally, Dennis said to say hi, and some other people did, too, I forget who all—"

"Okay, Lee. Say hi to them for me. Mom and I are going to Saugerties on Christmas Day. Why don't you call the whole family there?"

"Why don't *you* call *me*? This call is costing me a fortune. I'll talk to you later. Merry Christmas, and, Joe—"

"Yes?"

"Make up your mind. Come see us. You're a writer: you can write anywhere."

"I'll let you know. Merry Christmas, Lee."

The letter from Frank's wife arrived two days after Christmas.

December 23
Haven View

Dear Mr. Wilder,

I am writing to you regarding my husband, your friend, Frank Jensen. As we have never been intro-

duced, I have chosen not to call you, but to communicate to you more formally. Your sister, Lee, whom I know slightly, has been so kind as to provide me with your address. Frank has it, of course, but I have decided, for reasons that should soon be clear, not to let him know that I have approached you.

You know that Frank and I were married in secret eighteen months ago, and why (I thank you again for your beautiful flowers). You are probably also familiar with the circumstances surrounding the family's recent tragedy. You are Frank's oldest friend, and you will forgive me for being direct.

Ever since his father's death, Frank has been behaving most peculiarly. Naturally, the horrible way in which Judge Jensen was killed would upset anyone who loved him. But it's more than that. Some awful sadness, or guilt, has altered his very personality. And this strange behavior is also apparent in his mother.

I am not being clear. I do not mean to imply that Frank and his mother were in any way responsible for the judge's death. I am certain that they are as mystified as everyone else, and I can assure you that their grief is genuine. But there are secrets here, secrets between Frank and his mother, to which I am not a party.

I am a stranger in this place, Mr. Wilder. I have lived in this house a mere five months, since the tragedy occurred. Frank thought it best, then, to come home and take care of his mother, and I agreed. She was distraught, and this condition was complicated by other illnesses. I think you know to what I refer. Nevertheless, I barely know Helen Jensen. *It is not for her that I ask my favor of you, but for Frank.*

Please come to St. Thomas, and soon. I cannot explain, or even convey, my anxieties in a letter. I can only tell you this, briefly: something is very wrong at Haven View. If you would only come here, I could explain what I know and feel much more clearly. Frank speaks of you so often that it seems I already know you. I trust that, when we meet, we will be friends. I know that you can help him now, better than I, and better than anyone else here.

I can tell you this much: it is not fear or imagination, but certainty. If the situation I see around me is not altered, something dreadful is going to happen. I repeat that I am not imagining things: I know.

I realize that my request could be regarded as an imposition. It was only after Lee mentioned the possibility of your coming to visit her in the near future that I decided to write to you. However, it is your decision.

My regards to you and your family in this holiday season.

Sincerely,
Tangera Jensen

PS: Please forgive any errors of grammar or punctuation herein. I am from the island of Martinique, and my native tongue is French.

Tangera Jensen. So. My oldest friend had been married for a year and a half, and I had not until that moment known his wife's name. Her stationery was a pale, creamy orange color, and in the upper left corner of the first page was a tiny bright orange circle. From the top of the circle grew one minuscule green leaf. I sniffed· citrus. Tangera. Of course.

We all have old friends who make us feel guilty, through no fault of their own. I had two, Frank Jensen and Dennis Grey, and they both lived in St. Thomas. The Three Musketeers, as everyone had called us, had been children together. We had played, swum, sailed, gone to school, and hated girls and arithmetic. Later, in high school, we had been on all the teams, swum, sailed, chased girls and hated algebra. For the first eighteen years of our lives we had been inseparable. Each of us had three sets of parents: when anyone's mother planned a family function, she simply counted on two extra children, and we always obliged. Servants in all three households grew used to extracting unfamiliar clothes and towels from their washing machines. It was a good thing that our families were rich, as the cost of feeding us must have been prohibitive. We had been an exclusive club: Dennis, the tall, powerfully built, scowling black boy; Joe, the big, chunky comedian with nice blondish-brown hair and enormous feet; and Frank, the slight, pale, black-eyed, black-haired, astonishingly handsome judge's son.

Then, after high school, the inevitable had occurred. Dennis, scion of one of the island's oldest, wealthiest native families, followed in the footsteps of his father and grandfather by attending Howard University. For Frank, it had been Harvard and Harvard Law. I had my own family tradition: I was going to be in show business.

My mother had been an actress, director, and producer before marrying and moving to St. Thomas. Once there, she had helped to introduce to the island the con-

cept of television. After she and my father were divorced
and Lee, Marla, and I had gone to the States to college,
she returned to New York and her erstwhile profession
as a theatrical producer. Marla opted for marriage and
children, nipping a promising acting career in the bud,
and Lee had other interests, but Joe Wilder would follow
Linda Wilder to the footlights. That was the plan,
anyway. . . .

So the Musketeers disbanded and went their separate
ways into the world of adulthood. Dennis majored in political science, graduated with honors, and returned to
the island of his ancestors to work in—and ultimately to
head—the Virgin Islands Department of Conservation
and Cultural Affairs. I majored in drama at a respectable
university near New York, where I soon realized that I
would never cause Olivier to tremble with envy, and concentrated on writing, rather than performing in, plays.
And Frank . . .

Frank had always been a dull student. He never
seemed to be interested in learning. Dennis had rail-
roaded him through science and history, and I had been
the true author of more than a few of his English assign-
ments. Of course, all three of us had met our Waterloo
on the field of cosines and isosceles triangles, but Frank's
math scores were particularly bad. It was therefore
astounding to all of us when he performed splendidly on
his college board exams and was actually accepted into
Harvard. The men on his mother's side of the family had
attended Harvard for generations, and Hubert was a
graduate of Harvard Law School, and these were certainly considerations in his favor. Still, it was after he arrived there that the true miracle occurred.

He loved it. He became one of the top students in his

class, and he continued his brilliance at Harvard Law. He received several offers of a junior partnership before he had so much as passed the Bar exam. One of the offers was from Austin Hammond, a highly regarded attorney in St. Thomas. This, naturally, was the position Frank accepted. He aced the exam, returned to the island, and went to work.

Hubert Jensen was ecstatic. For four years, Frank's father watched his progress with delight. My son, he must have been thinking. My heir.

Then, eighteen months ago, I had been awakened by a phone call at four o'clock in the morning. Frank—nervous, giggling, and roaring drunk—had informed me that he had been secretly married a week before to a beautiful, wonderful, incredible girl, a student at the University of the Virgin Islands. He went on to say that he had left Haven View to live in town with her, and that "everything's finished between me and His Lordship. I finally told the old poop to go jump in the ocean. Took me twenty-eight years, but I actually did it!"

When I'd asked him what had happened with his father, Frank had changed the subject. Three days later, Lee had informed me that the beautiful, wonderful, incredible young woman was black.

Now I had received a letter from the woman and learned that her name was Tangera.

In the past twelve years, since we had all left for college, I had fallen out of touch with my friends. Of course, the main reason for this was that I had not returned to the island to live: I had gone from school to New York and the theater. I had visited the island three times in seven years, the last time being more than two years ago, and on these visits I had seen Frank and Dennis only briefly, both of them being preoccupied with their professions. When Frank had told me of his marriage, I had wired flowers and received a note of thanks from "Mrs. Frank Jensen."

My recent flop play was in rehearsal when news of the murder reached me. I immediately called Frank, who remained very quiet as I murmured sympathies. He thanked me perfunctorily and hung up.

That had been five months ago: we hadn't communicated since then. That's why I felt so guilty when Tangera's letter arrived.

Why did I go to St. Thomas?

I could be cavalier and say I don't remember now. I could be jaded and say there wasn't much going on that week. Or I could be weird and philosophical and say I was trying to find something—anything—that would put some sort of meaning in my life. I could say any of these things, but they wouldn't be the truth. The truth is, there was a moment in which I realized that something would have to be done, and that I was the one to do it. It was something my mother said; something I'd avoided saying, or even thinking about. I remember the moment clearly: it occurred later that day, a few hours after I received the letter from Frank's wife.

It snowed again on the evening of December twenty-seven. I remember sitting at my mother's dinner table, watching the flakes blowing by outside the glass doors that led out to the terrace from the dining room of her apartment on Fifth Avenue, high above Central Park. The conversation over the meal was dominated by news of the play my mother was producing on Broadway. I smiled vacantly as I ate, only half-listening to the talk of

the director she'd hired and the actors he wanted and
everybody's ideas for the second act and how much
money it was all going to cost. I nodded and made appropriate noises, but all the while I was distracted, preoccupied by the creamy orange stationery that was all but
burning a hole in my jacket pocket. It was an effort to
focus on my mother.

Linda Wilder is a lovely woman; tall, blond, and
graceful. The decor of her penthouse bears witness to her
many years in the West Indies: vivid colors, potted tropical plants, naive paintings of island scenes, wicker furniture—and animals. Everywhere there are animals. Our
meal was closely monitored from the floor around us by
eleven pairs of hungry eyes. There were, at that moment,
four poodles, one German shepherd, and six cats of various breeds and one lazy temperament. When we at last
rose from the table and repaired to the living room, we
were accompanied by the troops.

"Take a look at this," I said when she had settled on
a couch. I pulled out the letter, handed it to her, and
went to the kitchen to make coffee.

My mother had been one of the island's leading citi-
zens, first as a television personality and later as the
owner of a large shopping center in the middle of town.
She had lived there for twenty-five years, and even now,
after ten years back in New York, the *Virgin Islands Daily
News* was delivered to her door every afternoon. She was
constantly in touch with her daughter and her many
friends on the island. If anyone would know all about the
Jensens, it would be Linda.

When I returned with the coffee, she was standing at
the huge picture window that runs the length of one wall,
gazing out at the thousands of lights that make up the

nighttime cityscape. The letter lay on the coffee table. Her pose was familiar: I knew better than to say anything, to disrupt her train of thought. I put down the cups, found a spot on a couch that was not already occupied, and sat. We waited, the zoo and I, for Mom to tell us a story. When she finally spoke, her voice was full of memory.

"You know, he really was a dreadful man. I was worried for a while, when you and Frank became such fast friends. I was relieved to discover that he didn't take after Hubert."

She paused, letting that sink in.

"I don't really know anything about him," I confessed. "I guess I was too young. To me, he was just Frank's father."

"Yes," she said. "Well, let me see. . . . His family had been poor. He worked his way through college, then he joined the Merchant Marines. When he arrived in St. Thomas, he hadn't a penny to his name. He apparently fell in love with the place at first sight. The island was then growing at a rapid rate, and Hubert realized that anyone with half a brain could make a fortune there. He wanted to be a lawyer, and lawyers usually do well in boomtowns. Naturally, he decided to stay.

"He won some money in a dockside poker game and bought Haven View, which was nothing but ruins. He went to work for the only architect on the island at the time, a man named Hoffer, and he saved every cent he made for law school. He was very charming, I gather. He coerced Hoffer into rebuilding Haven View—restoring it to its former glory, and all that. The architect took it as an artistic challenge and reconstructed the mansion for free, only charging Hubert for materials.

"Then, when his dream house was completed, Hubert went to Boston for three years. Harvard Law: Hoffer and some of his powerful buddies on the island helped him get in. It was there that he met Helen. She was young and beautiful and very Back Bay. Just piles of money they had, the Bennett family. Well, you know the rest. Hubert courted her, not to mention her family—he always had an eye out for the main chance. And they all fell in love with Hubert. You have to hand it to him: he certainly could magnetize people. He was a complete nobody, and yet he somehow talked the daughter of a famous house into marrying him. When he passed the Bar he married Helen and her millions, and they sailed away to the island, to Haven View.

"By the time Frank was born, Hubert was the hottest lawyer in the Virgin Islands. Everything was going up fast at the time; a lot of people were moving there. So Hubert bought real estate cheap and sold it at enormous profit. Helen's parents died, leaving her a huge fortune. Somewhere in there, Hubert became a municipal judge, then he went on to district court. He was big pals with all the governors: every time a new one was appointed, there was Hubert, slapping him on the back. When the territory won the right to elect its own governors—you remember that?—he got all sorts of ideas. Like the fisherman's wife in the story: why be king when you could be pope?" She gazed out at the Manhattan skyline. "Why, indeed?"

She came over and sat across from me. We sipped our coffee. I lit a cigarette and put the pack and the lighter down on the orange paper, the letter from Frank's wife, trying to form a picture in my mind of Hubert and Helen as young people. People my age, or even younger . . .

"He never loved Helen," Mom said. "He loved her money, and it took her all of five minutes to realize it. He tossed Frank on his knee a couple of times and took off to become The Great Hubert Jensen. You can imagine poor Helen, alone in that house with a baby and a bunch of maids, so far from Beacon Hill. She was a very private woman; she didn't make friends easily. We all invited her around, but she never got into the swing of things. And then there was Hubert. . . ."

I stopped, the cigarette poised inches from my lips. "What do you mean?"

She shrugged. "I think you were too young to realize it, Joe, but your father and I wouldn't have him in the house. Nobody else would, either. It wasn't that he was loud and vulgar—hell, half the island is loud and vulgar!—but he was just so *mean*. He really lost his chance to crash St. Thomas society, such as it was, at a dinner party at Letitia Stewart's house. I remember: your father and I were there."

Letitia Stewart is the head of the Virgin Islands Council on the Arts. She is a very sweet old widow who lives in a big house near Mountaintop. I remember that she always smelled like roses, and she always wore little white gloves outdoors, even in summer.

"He got into an argument with someone else at the table," my mother was saying, "about the local natives. I've forgotten the particulars, but suddenly he jumped up and started yelling at all of us, all sorts of things about 'niggers' and 'nigger lovers.' He'd been drinking, naturally, but it was then that we all saw what kind of a man he was. The 'niggers,' as he called them, were morons, too stupid to run their own lives. They had to be supervised, he said, and you had to watch them every minute or they'd rob you blind. He went on and on, and here's the killer: four of the twelve people at that table were black! John and Caroline Grey, Dennis's parents, and are you ready for this?—Clay and Iris Hughes! Imagine; there was Hubert, screaming about the 'niggers' to Clayton Hughes! It was too much!"

My mother laughed. She threw back her head and shook with merriment until tears came to her eyes. I was laughing, too: there was something perfect, symmetrical, about the irony of it.

Clayton Hughes was now the governor of the Virgin Islands.

When we settled down, she continued. "Well, Letitia threw him out of her house, of course. And poor Helen, who hadn't said a word, got up and left with him. That was twenty-some-odd years ago, and he was never invited anywhere again. Not by our group, at any rate. But there were other groups.

"He still had a lot of powerful friends—lawyers and judges and people in the government. And a lot of them were black, believe it or not. They paid no attention to the dinner-party story. He was drunk, they'd say, which made sense: half of them were drunks, too. Anyway, he kept on going, and he was actually running for governor when he was killed. The majority of the island didn't know what a creep he was. They only knew him as the rich, flamboyant judge who lived at Haven View with his lovely wife. They thought he was just great. He would have won the primary easily, and he probably would have beaten Clay Hughes in the election. Ugh."

Something was puzzling me. "Lee says everyone on the island wanted to kill him."

"She must mean everyone who knew what he was

really like. Not many people, actually. It's so cliquey down there. I presume whoever killed him had a very good reason. Someone in the know."

We sat there for a while, thinking about that. Then I drew us back to my initial intent. "What do you think of the letter?"

She reached out and stroked the nose of the shepherd.

"Tangera," she said. "What a name! I heard about her. She told someone—who told me—that her mother was going to name her Tangerine, but then decided it would be too much. Tangera, apparently, was not. I hear she's very pretty. There's a lot of speculation about why she married Frank, but with his money that's to be expected. It's quite a letter. If English is her second language, I'd like to see her French! 'Something is wrong at Haven View.' Sounds like Daphne du Maurier, doesn't it?"

"You think she's overreacting?" I asked.

"I have no idea. I don't know the girl. She hasn't had an easy time, you can bet on that! I don't think Helen would have been pleased, having a black daughter-in-law, and Hubert must have hit high C. No, she and Frank have been through quite an ordeal. And that's what puzzles me: Frank. You wouldn't think he had it in him, to stand up to all that pressure."

"No," I agreed. It was the truth: Frank had always been thin and pale, in spirit as well as body. "Frank was always crazy about his mother. I think he loved his father, too, but I also seem to remember a lot of animosity."

"I can understand that," Mom drawled, scratching the ears of the Persian in her lap.

Then it happened.

My mother suddenly shuddered and opened her eyes wide. The cat, disturbed by the abrupt movement, leaped to the floor.

"You don't suppose," she whispered, raising her startled eyes to meet mine, "that Frank killed his father, do you?"

I stared at her, fighting my own automatic reaction, the first thing that entered my mind.

Of course he did.

No. I couldn't believe that. I wouldn't even think such a—

And I know it. I simply won't admit it to myself.

The words came, unbidden, into my head.

Lee: "*I saw him downtown. He looked terrible. He's looked like that ever since . . .*"

The letter: "*Some awful sadness, or guilt, has altered his very personality. . . .*"

Frank himself: "*I finally told the old poop to go . . .*"

It all added up to one thing, could only mean one thing: Frank Jensen, my oldest friend, was in trouble. Big trouble. And I knew what he needed. Dennis was there, and I would be there, too. Frank needed the Musketeers.

It is an odd fact of human nature that when we reach a turning point in our lives, we seldom stop to consider. Enormous events simply occur, and it is often only much later that we look back and realize what has happened. That was the moment, we will say, or that, or that. At the time, however, the moment is unremarkable.

I picked up my mother's phone and called American Airlines.

2

---◆---

ARRIVALS

The thing you always noticed first was the heat. You would emerge from the crisp, dry, air-conditioned cabin onto a mobile stairway that descended to the tarmac, and you were smacked by a wave of warm, wet air. You'd look around to see the lush, dark green hills in the distance, a backdrop for the long stretches of runway shimmering in the sunlight, your first sight of the island.

You'd follow a smiling hostess down the stairs, across an open expanse of concrete, and into a makeshift wooden corridor. As you walked down this seemingly endless gangway, you became aware of the beads and trickles of perspiration on your forehead and under your too-thick continental clothes. At last you passed the garish stenciled sign WELCOME TO THE U.S. VIRGIN ISLANDS, and arrived at the gigantic hangar that was the main building of Cyril E. King Airport.

Inside the terminal, the temperature dropped a good

twenty degrees and you were plunged into blissfully cool
darkness. Enormous, colorful advertisements predomi-
nated: try this local rum, stay at that resort hotel, don't
forget the other jewelry shop on Main Street. You passed
a sinister-looking cocktail lounge, an overcrowded sandwich shop of dubious cleanliness, and a seedy duty-free
store stocking everything from Coppertone to Courvoi-
sier. Ancient speakers piped in muffled Calypso music.
Your fifteen-minute walk ended at a wheezing, hopelessly
outmoded contraption that aspired to be a luggage ca-
rousel. Here you would wait for your bags to be whisked
from the cargo hold and rushed across a few yards of
runway, during which time you could translate *David
Copperfield* into a language you'd never learned.

It was absolutely charming. How appropriate that
your first experience in St. Thomas served to shift your
inner gears, to slow you from the brisk clip of mainland
cities to the laid-back, lackadaisical crawl of paradise.

If you were not a tourist, staring and pointing and
delighting in the photogenic backwardness of it all, it was
best to be met by someone. I was therefore always
pleased, at the end of the endless passageway to the terminal, to find that Lee was waiting for me.

As we joined my fellow travelers in the baggage claim
area, I took a good look at my sister. She is a small
woman, what the fashion magazines call petite. Little
hands, little heart-shaped face from which stare two
enormous dark eyes, dainty little feet. Topping off all of
this small prettiness is a dramatic cascade of long dark
hair.

"Tired, Joe?"

"No."

"Good. We can check in at the house, and then we're going to Haven View."

I looked at my watch: two thirty-five.

"Dinner?"

"No, just for a drink. We're meeting Paul at the station after that, and he and I are taking you to dinner. She wants to meet you this afternoon."

"Who?"

"Tamarinda."

"Tangera," I corrected.

"Right. Damn! Why can't I remember that? Anyway, she made me promise you'd go over and see Frank first thing."

I nodded. The crowd around the inert luggage belt had grown in size and restlessness. December twenty-ninth, I thought. Everybody got plane tickets for Christmas. Where did these people come from? Where was the baggage? Why did Tangera Jensen want to see me the minute I arrived on the island? Urgency . . .

Lee laughed at my perplexed expression. "Your bags will be here soon."

" 'Chapter One: I Am Born,' " I replied. "How do you say that in Spanish?"

She looked at me, rolled her eyes, and, being Lee, said nothing.

At last the luggage arrived, and I claimed my suitcase. This and the laptop computer I was carrying were placed in the back of Lee's tiny, powerful foreign car, and off we drove.

Imagine a long, thin fish, mouth agape, arching its back, and you have a pretty good idea of the general shape of St. Thomas. The island is approximately thirteen miles long and five miles wide. The harbor of Charlotte Amalie is the underbelly of the curved fish; the town rises from the harbor into the hills above. The airport is to the west of the town, and to the east are hills and valleys referred to by residents with a sense of humor as "the countryside." Signal Hill is the dominant central image, rising some fifteen hundred feet above the city to its peak, known familiarly as Mountaintop, the island's highest point. This is flanked by several lesser hills, forming a chain that runs almost the entire length of the island. Around its edges lie many gorgeous white beaches; the longest of these is Magens Bay, on the north side across the mountains from town, which has been designated one of the five most beautiful beaches in the Western Hemisphere. Three miles east of St. Thomas is St. John, the smallest of the three U.S. Virgin Islands: it is a national park. Forty miles south is St. Croix, the largest and flattest island. These three tiny dots on the map lie some fifty miles east of Puerto Rico. Small, compact, beautiful; they float, almost unnoticed by the rest of the world, where the Caribbean Sea meets the Atlantic Ocean.

We rode slowly in the dense afternoon traffic along the main Waterfront highway into town. Everywhere I looked was vibrant green. All travelers returning home after several years are met by the odd incongruity of the familiar and the unexpected. The topography was the same, as were most of the buildings, but I noticed several new structures—and more were on the way, apparently, judging from the proliferation of construction sites we had passed.

In front of one as-yet-uncompleted building I noticed a large sign: Brandt Construction Company. Along the way from the airport we had passed quite a few signs reading: For Sale—Brandt Real Estate.

"Brandt," I said, pointing to one such sign. "Is that Abel Brandt?"

My sister followed my gaze and nodded.

"The construction company is," she said, inching the car forward in the congestion along Harwood Highway. "The real estate company is his wife, Abby. You don't know her, do you? Well, you'll meet them both soon enough. We're going to their house on New Year's Eve. They give a big party every year, and Paul and I have gone to the last few. You'll feel right at home, Joe. Architects, artists, show biz people. They're fun."

"Can't wait," I murmured, smiling insincerely. I'd had my fill of artist parties in New York, thank you very much, and I certainly hadn't anticipated attending one in St. Thomas.

Lee chuckled and glanced maliciously over at me. "You're on vacation, Joe. You're supposed to go to parties and have a good time. Adjust, *capisce?*"

I laughed. "Yes, ma'am."

I relaxed back in the seat, accepting the idea of a New Year's Eve artist party. Of course, I had no way of knowing, then, that I wouldn't just be meeting a room full of artist types. As it turned out, it was a room full of suspects. Neither of us knew that: if we had, I would have asked her to turn around right there and then and take me back to the airport.

The car finally made its way across the Waterfront before the town and turned left. The traffic in the town itself was not as bad as on the highway. In a relatively short time, Lee had driven through the eastern edge of the downtown area and up Blackbeard's Hill. Another left turn led us into the long loop that circled the old sugar mill known—capriciously and erroneously—as Blackbeard's Castle. This drive just above the main part of town is dotted with large houses ringing it and descending in tiers to Main Street, one block in from the Waterfront. This residential hillside enclave is known variously as Blackbeard's Hill, after the mill (allegedly once a pirate stronghold, now a guest house and restaurant), or Government Hill, after Government House, the other notable building in the area, in the tier just below Lee.

Lee's house was as I remembered it; a large, square structure at the top of the Ninety-nine Steps, which descend into town. An enormous living room is in the center, running the length of the house, with doors leading from it to the kitchen and three bedrooms. There is a large, wooden-railed suspended porch at the farthest end from the entrance, from which one may look down at the town and the harbor below.

We were greeted by a pack of friendly dogs (Lee has inherited our mother's penchant for animals). I put my suitcase and laptop in the guest room while Lee went to change her clothes. I washed my face and went out onto the porch, the dogs yapping at my heels.

I was home again. The fact hit me at that moment as I stared delightedly around me, breathing in the fresh, salt air. The brilliant sunshine poured down on the town at my feet, enhancing every vivid color. Amazingly green hills and impossibly blue water stretched away in all directions. There below me was Main Street, and over there the way to the airport from which we had come. On the hill to my left were the red roofs and white walls of Bluebeard's Castle Hotel (even less appropriate an allusion than that of Blackbeard's Castle up the hill behind me: at least there actually *was* a Blackbeard!). Yacht Haven, in the harbor before me, seemed to have grown: I could not remember ever seeing so many boats moored there. At the West Indian Company docks beyond Yacht Haven, three cruise ships were tied, and a fourth, larger, vessel was anchored farther out, in the center of the harbor, white against blue. In the far distance, on a point of land across the bay, was the Frenchman's Reef Holiday Inn; enormous, imposing, settled on its cliff just beyond—

A cloud passed in front of the sun and a long, dark shadow fell across the town. An unaccountably chilly breeze sliced through the hot, tropical air. I shivered. There, on the hill across the harbor, just visible through the trees, was the silver corrugated tin roof of Haven View.

I folded my arms in front of me, hugging myself. Why was it suddenly so cold? I thought I had left winter behind me when I'd boarded the plane in New York that morning. I stared across the bay at the roof among the trees. The chill washed over me; piercing, permeating, insistent.

That house, so familiar from my childhood, stood before me, waiting.

There was a footstep behind me. I gasped and whirled around. Lee stood there, staring, surprised by my sudden, violent movement. She almost remarked on my action, but then she apparently thought better of it.

After a moment she said, "Ready?"

"Yes," I lied.

By the time we had driven around the harbor and up the winding road to the gates of Haven View, the sun had completely disappeared behind a bank of clouds. It was not yet four o'clock, but already twilight had fallen on St. Thomas.

He was standing in the shadows under the trees by the patio, watching as we got out of the car. Though I could see only a dark silhouette, I recognized him immediately. He was thinner, and when he stepped forward into the light I saw that he was paler, too. He did not look well.

"Hey! If it isn't the missing Musketeer!" he called as I came toward him. I reached out to shake his hand, but he was having none of that: immediately, his arms were around my neck. "God, it's great to see you!"

I stood there for a moment, embraced, awkward, vaguely embarrassed. Then, instinctively, I pulled away. I smiled to cover my action. "Hello, Frank."

When he grinned at me, I noticed that there was no light in his black eyes. It was just a grin, a facial expression. I wondered what had happened to the old, familiar glint, hoping that I would never have to find out. His handsome face was haggard and lined, and his once jet black hair was streaked with gray.

The house loomed up behind him. My gaze traveled from his dark, haunted eyes to the dark, haunted edifice in the background. Bloodred walls and bone white pillars, shutters and storm windows composed the facade that rose to meet the thick press of trees around and above. The shadows of the clouded afternoon stretched across the walls, giving me the fleeting, fanciful impression of a red-and-white child's building block clutched tightly in a ghostly, bony fist. I felt an inexorable pull drawing me toward its waiting silence. Even from across the harbor I had been aware of the phenomenon: at close range it was almost palpable. This oppressive, secret place was summoning me, beckoning to me, demanding—

Frank's arm went around my shoulders. He greeted Lee, took her by the arm and led us across the patio and up the steps to the veranda.

"This is a nice surprise," he said as we sat down in the white wicker chairs near the entrance to the house. "My wife only told me about your visit this morning. She loves secrets. So, how the hell are you, Kiddo?"

Kiddo. I had never been called that by anyone else. I assured him that I was fine and asked after his mother.

"Oh, she'll be out in a moment, and you can see for yourself." Had he emphasized that secondary phrase? "My wife will be here soon, I expect. I guess she's caught in traffic. She wanted to be here when you arrived. Oh, well." The odd smile again. "You look terrific! Doesn't he look great, Lee? New York seems to agree with you."

I asked, as diplomatically as possible, about his own health.

He stared at me for a moment and opened his mouth to speak, then he apparently changed his mind. He glanced at Lee, who sat smiling on the other side of the glass-topped wicker patio table, and back to me. I knew that look: I waited for the lie.

"Oh, can't complain. Business is good—everybody needs a lawyer these days! I'm usually pretty busy—" He stopped, staring at me for a moment. Then the false smile vanished and his voice dropped to a hoarse whisper. "What the hell am I babbling about? You know what's happened here. Nothing's been the same around here since—"

A low, smoky voice cut through his sentence.

"Joe! How marvelous to see you. Hello, Lee."

The three of us rose and turned in the direction of the entrance. Helen Jensen stood, one hand on the doorframe, the other to her chest; a tall, regal brunette beauty in a flowing pink gown. I watched as she walked, or floated, toward me. I felt the soft brush of her cool, dry lips on my cheek. She extended a hand to Lee.

"Sit down, everyone," she commanded with a smile. She wafted down into the empty chair next to her son. She paused briefly to accept our greetings, then pressed on in a rush of words.

"Eunice will be serving tea in a few minutes. Don't you just love tea? I don't mean the drink, I mean the concept. So civilized. It isn't often we have a chance to entertain anymore here at Haven View. I've been *so* looking forward to . . ."

She droned on. Her speech seemed almost prepared, so charming, so appropriate. I stared, the dread from across the bay returning. Here was my oldest friend, strained and prematurely aged, watching silently as his mother made hostess noises on the veranda of their gracious, ominous mansion. Lee sat, attentive, hands in lap, a polite smile freezing over on her face. Everywhere there was artifice, unreality.

Helen Jensen was drunk. What I had at first taken to be an affected lilt was in fact a slight slurring of her words. She was a handsome woman, probably in her mid-fifties, and her manner and carriage bespoke the training of great wealth and privilege. But behind the dark eyes and immaculately rouged and powdered cheeks were all the signs. She was pale—too pale for a resident of a tropical island. The tip of her nose, despite cosmetics, glowed pink against the surrounding pallor. I looked closer: her pupils were slightly dilated. Alcohol, probably mixed with something else. There were blue shadows under her eyes, which, like her son's, appeared to have been extinguished. This was the face of a woman who had lived with unhappiness for a very long time, yet there were no signs of recent improvement. If Hubert had been the cause of her sorrow, why had his death six months before not brought a new bloom to the rose? The woman before me was, if anything, nearly dead with grief.

I watched them, mother and son. They chatted and joked, but now and then they caught each other's attention and something unspoken was communicated. I thought of the letter that had brought me here: *"There are secrets here, secrets between Frank and his mother . . . something is terribly wrong . . . I am not imagining things. I know . . ."* I shook my head. What on earth had been going on in this house?

I saw Lee glance at her watch, and it suddenly occurred to me what we had been doing. We, all of us, were waiting. I should have recognized the scene: I've certainly written enough of them. Act One usually begins like this, with a gathering of people being introduced. They laugh and chatter their way through the obligatory exposition, but what they are really doing is paving the way for the star. Tea is often served, to help them in their labor.

As if on cue, the tray arrived. Eunice greeted me with a warm smile. Enormous, despite her medium stature; friendly and efficient in her starched white apron; she was a welcome, all too brief respite from the playacting. Her beautiful, musical Calypso washed over me.

"Joe, how you does be? Ya loose sum weht! Iss good ah mehk me chacklut chip brahnees fo' you. De moment ah heah you was comin', ah gets out de Toll House chips!"

Indeed she had. The Three Musketeers had been raised on her brownies, and here they were, once again before me. I glanced at Frank: he had not even noticed them. Eunice was a widow with a small boy who would be—ten?—by now. I couldn't remember his name, but I asked after him.

"Geahge? Oh, he be gettin' so big! You won't even regnize him. De good Lahd watch out fo' him."

George: that was it. With another smile for me and a brief, nervous glance at her mistress, Eunice bustled back into the house. It struck me then that it had been she who had found the judge's decapitated remains. I had never, up to that time, seen a dead body. It was difficult to imagine what one looked like without a head. I glanced at my hosts, hoping they would not offer me a brownie. Not for a few moments, at any rate.

Helen smiled as she poured the tea. "Have a brownie, Joe."

I sighed and took one, a prop, something to do with my hands. On we went for several more minutes, carefully keeping the talk small, not mentioning what was uppermost in all our minds. "Oh, yes, Frank," I imagined myself saying, "the brownies are delicious. By the way, I understand you murdered your father. How exciting!"

Shortly into Act One, when there is a lull in the action, it is time for the star to make an appearance. A light laugh is heard, or a breathless line from offstage. The actors then turn and stare at a door. After a moment the door flies open and somebody wonderful arrives— Hepburn, perhaps, or Vanessa Redgrave. Thunderous applause.

The entrance was not through a door. One moment all was peaceful; the next was filled with the roar of a powerful engine. A flash of silver, a streak of motion, and the screech of tires displacing loose gravel: a small, expensive sports car shrieked up the driveway and shuddered to a halt. A tall, slim black girl emerged and dashed across the patio toward us.

"Hello, hello!" she called as she approached. "So sorry I am late. The traffic was unbearable. I swear, one more car on this rock and it is going to sink! There should be some sort of quota. Hello, darling." She arrived behind Frank's chair, leaned over, and kissed the top of his head. "Hello, Lee." She shook my sister's hand and came over to stand before me. I rose. "And you must be Joseph Wilder. How glad I am to meet you, at last!"

She stood grinning at me; young, vital, glowing copper skin, flashing brown eyes, bright orange dress, exuding the scent of citrus fruit. Tangera Jensen came in, and Life came with her. She was the most beautiful woman I had ever seen, and not the least of her beauty was her apparently unlimited energy. Even the air around her seemed to vibrate. The feeling I got from her was in dramatic contrast to my impression of the other occupants of this house, and of the house itself. Drops of water glistened in her dark brown hair, and her orange dress was damp. It had obviously been thrown on over a wet bathing suit.

"I lose all sense of time at the beach," she was saying in her lovely, carefully articulated, vaguely foreign-sounding speech. "I just flew back here—as much as one can, of course. I did not even say good-bye to my friends. They are probably wondering where I have got to."

She laughed, and her dark eyes twinkled. I wondered who her friends were, and if they really were fazed by her abrupt disappearances. I doubted it: this volatile beauty was capable of anything at slightly less than a moment's notice.

I saw, on her dress just above her left breast where alligators and foxes were usually found, a small, dark orange circle and a green leaf, identical to that of the stationery. Her paper and her person even bore the same scent; Essence of Tangerine, or some such nonsense. I stood staring, falling for the whole bag of tricks, instantly in thrall.

As if she didn't know. "I see you have all had tea. I would like a glass of wine, myself." She sank into the chair next to mine, picked up a small silver bell from the tray, and rang it.

At the same moment, Helen Jensen rose. "Joe, Lee, you must excuse me. I do hope you will visit us again soon. I'm expecting—a rather important call. From the States," she added, as if to qualify its importance.

With a smile, she floated away into the house. She and her daughter-in-law had not exchanged a single word.

Tangera waited until Helen had gone, but only just. Immediately, she leaned forward and took my hand in hers.

"Good," she sighed with obvious relief. "Now we can really talk. I bet you want to know all about the murder."

Frank shot up from his seat, nearly toppling it. "Tangera! Really, I don't think they—"

"Of course they do!" she cried. She looked from Lee to me: *This child is impossible*, her expression seemed to say. "I have a nickel that says they have been sitting here being very polite, and all the while just burning with curiosity. I think we should tell your friends everything. I am sure Joseph is very concerned."

"Everybody calls me Joe," I offered, not knowing quite what else to say.

Tangera laughed as she stood up from her chair.

"Then I," she whispered, staring into my eyes, "shall call you Joseph."

Of course. It went with the insignia and the perfume, right in character. Calculated magnificence. She would call me Joseph.

Frank sighed. "You'd better come into the house. We might as well start where it happened, in my father's office. Tangera can tell you more about it than I can."

Lee rose, unsure of how to take all this. My sister and I both turned to look at the beautiful girl who stood grinning at us, an adventurous glint in her eyes.

"You know that much about it?" Lee asked her.

Tangera nodded, delighted. "Oh, my dear, of course. I saw it happen!"

3

THE GUESTS ASSEMBLE

The house was waiting for me. I stared at the white-shuttered entrance; it stared back. This was the moment I had been dreading. The twin doors were wide open, the cavern between them yawning pitch-black. The others were already moving toward it, and I would have to go with them.

Frank was still chuckling from Tangera's last comment. "She says that every now and then. Her little joke, you know."

"I did not mean that I actually saw it," Tangera said, leading the way inside. "I just knew it was going to happen—that *something* was going to happen. All day before that night I had my feeling."

Lee was confused. "Your—feeling?"

"She has them quite often," Frank explained. "You see, Tangera is clairvoyant. Has been all her life. Some doctors even tested her, or whatever, in Martinique."

"Yes!" She seemed to take a childish pleasure in her gift. "I have *l'oeil extraordinaire*, the, um, extra sensitive protection.".

I grinned, indulging her. It had not been a mistake: she had mastered English. She all but skipped into the house, followed by Frank and Lee. As they moved away through the front hall, they were swallowed by the darkness.

I hesitated on the threshold. What was it? Why the dread, the tightening in my chest? This was silly. It was just a house, and yet . . . I looked down. My hands were rigid at my sides, clenched tightly into fists. Oh, come on. . . .

"Joe?" Lee's voice came from the shadows ahead.

"Coming," I called, and I stepped forward into Haven View.

It was like going back in time. Everything was the same. The hallway stretched away before me, running almost the entire length of the house. Halfway down it was the staircase leading to the bedrooms on the second floor. To my right, through a huge archway, was the living room: light blue stucco walls and darker blue upholstery on couches and chairs. The wood furniture was of the same deep cordovan mahogany as the floor. Down the hall was a formal dining room (seldom used, as the veranda was a more pleasant setting for meals), a library/music room, and the enormous kitchen at the back of the house.

To my left, directly across the hall from the living room, was the judge's office. In all my life I had never set foot in that room: it had been off limits, particularly to children. The door to the room was open. The voices of the others came from there.

The air was cool and smelled of furniture polish. Even with all the doors and windows open, as they were in the living room, the interior of the house was shadowy. There was a lit chandelier above my head, and the lights in the living room were already on, as well. I took a deep breath.

Same house. I'd been here a hundred times in the past. Never before had I felt a sense of foreboding here. It had began to subside as I crossed the hall to the office door and entered the room.

The panic returned full force. The first thing I saw was the large mahogany desk where he had been sitting. I turned my eyes away, and my gaze now rested on the front wall of the house. The French doors leading out from there to the veranda were closed and shuttered. They had not been closed that night. Frank stood leaning against the desk. Two overstuffed chairs faced it; in these Tangera and Lee were seated. All three of them were looking at me, and on Lee's face I read an expression of concern. Rows of law books lined the walls. There was no furniture polish here: the air was close, dry, and tangible with dust. Everything in the room was rimed with a thin layer of gray powder. The servants did not clean this room, and the doors and windows were always closed and locked, to keep people out.

No. To keep him in.

I could not speak, but I could whisper. "I'm sorry," I breathed, backing swiftly, clumsily toward the hall behind me. "I have to get out of here."

"It seems that I am not the only one here who is psychic," Tangera said.

We were sitting in the living room. Tangera's wine

had been brought, and Frank had asked for the bottle and another glass. I was on my second glass of wine and my third cigarette since I had staggered across the hall and collapsed onto the dark blue couch. The panic had gone, leaving me shaken and mortified.

"I don't think I'm psychic," I said. "I've never had an episode of that in my life—until now, that is. I don't know what came over me. I just knew I couldn't stay in that room. I'm fine now."

Tangera seemed to understand. "It happens, especially in places where something like that has occurred. Even to people who do not usually have the power." She smiled at me. "You are very sensitive. I have no problem with that room. My feelings come before events, not after. Perhaps we should not discuss what happened to Hubert at present."

"No, please," I said. "I really do want to hear about it."

No, I didn't, but I wanted to get it over with. I looked at Frank, wondering what fiction he would provide for us, how he would describe it without giving himself away.

He was looking back at me. I had just told him that I had never experienced clairvoyance. That was not exactly true: the Musketeers had usually been able to read each other's minds. Once.

Still. Without taking his eyes from me, Frank said, "I didn't kill him. You think I did, but I didn't."

There were no gasps of surprise, no heated denials, no protestations. Nobody moved. There was a moment of silence; then, with a long sigh, Frank began.

"It was a Friday night, actually Saturday morning. The police place the time between one and three. Mother was in her room upstairs, asleep. Eunice and her son and the two other servants were in their house out back. The maid and the gardener are relatively new, and they're both born-again Christians. Eunice, of course, is above suspicion. The gates were locked, but anyone can climb over the walls.

"They killed Prince. I guess you know that."

Prince and Princess had been the Jensens' most recent brace of Dobermans. Hubert had always had Dobermans; King and Queen, when we were small, then Duke and Duchess. Princess, Frank explained, had died earlier in the year, and Prince had deteriorated as a guard dog, apparently in mourning. On that Friday night last July, the murderer had tossed a poisoned steak over the wall of the estate. It had landed directly in front of the dog-house in the backyard, next to the servants' cottage. No one heard barking: Prince was found there by the police searching the grounds on the following morning.

"Whoever it was knew the house," Frank continued. "They knew where the doghouse was, and where the tools were kept. It was our machete, from the crawl space under the kitchen. Lucien—that's the gardener—had last used it that afternoon, so it was taken that night when they—he?—came here. It was never found. It's probably at the bottom of the ocean somewhere. They killed the dog, climbed over the wall, got the machete, went around to the front of the house, and in by the French doors. It must have happened very fast: if Father had yelled, someone would have heard. He must not have had time."

Frank paused. He rose and went to look out at the patio, his back to the rest of us. The sun was setting, and shadows were growing longer. Soon all would be darkness. When Frank resumed the story, still with his back to us, I realized from his voice that he was weeping.

"The killer presumably left the way he came. There were no footprints, or anything like that. It rained the next morning. Any evidence there might have been was washed away."

Now we could hear the sobs, see his shoulders as they rose and fell involuntarily. Tangera walked up behind him, and her arms encircled his chest. She pressed her cheek against his back. I looked over at Lee, who was staring at the carpet in front of her.

The silence of the room was shattered by Frank's furious, anguished cry. "Who would do that? What kind of twisted mind would even think of it? What sort of—of *freak?* They cut his head off, for Christ's sake! Whoever did that is obviously—damaged. Inside."

Two things happened simultaneously. Frank reached up to detach himself from his wife's grasp: she, in the same instant, pulled away and took a tiny step backward. Frank turned to face her.

"You must not upset yourself," Tangera said, her voice low and surprisingly unanimated. "Remember what Dr. Deveaux said."

After a moment, he nodded and resumed his seat on the sofa across from me.

"What did Dr. Deveaux say?" I asked, watching Frank's face.

He shrugged. "Oh, he's over here all the time, fussing about us. It's really just an excuse to be here. Everybody knows he's—"

"Frank!" Tangera came over and sat next to me. "The doctor has been very kind. He says that Frank has high blood pressure, and that he must be very careful. Do you know him, Joseph?"

I nodded. "He was our family doctor as well as theirs." I indicated Frank.

Her lovely smile reappeared. "Then perhaps you also know that he has a special interest in Helen."

"He's in love with her," Frank said. "Has been for years. Even Father knew about it. No," he added, as I must have registered astonishment, "it wasn't anything like that. Mother was always faithful to Father. But now that she's a widow, you see . . . I don't know. Maybe it's not such a bad thing."

I remembered the doctor clearly. He was a widower; tall, good-looking, about Helen's age, and he spoke with a thick French accent. My mother had mentioned once that she thought he was sexy. There weren't that many doctors on St. Thomas: Deveaux had treated just about everyone I knew. In addition to his private practice as an internist, he was a surgeon on the staff of St. Thomas Hospital. But Dr. Deveaux and his alleged romance with Mrs. Jensen were none of my business.

"Did the police have any leads?" I asked. "I mean, there must have been—"

I broke off, embarrassed. What had made me ask that? Of course there had been a suspect. He sat, now, facing me. I felt the blood rush to my face.

It was Tangera who saved the moment, although not in the way I was expecting. She merely answered the question.

"You mean suspects. Actually, there were several. First the family was considered, having the most to gain. Hubert left everything to Helen and Frank. Well, almost: some bequests to friends, and the usual charitable donations. But I hardly think the Red Cross is desperate enough to kill someone, do you? At any rate, Helen was asleep. Dr. Deveaux and the police doctor agreed that she had ingested—well, definitely asleep at the time. And Frank was home with me. The others were questioned, but it led to nothing."

"What others?" I asked.

Frank took up the story. "When they found him, there were some papers on his desk. He'd apparently been keeping files on certain people, and he had called them earlier in the evening. Two local senators and a congressman. A newspaper publisher. Abel Brandt, the land developer—he was in the will. Father left him and his wife a lot of money." He paused a moment, then went on. "There were four other phone calls, but there were no files on those people. Clayton Hughes, the Democratic front runner; he's the governor now, of course. A local beach bum named Willie Whitney. Belle Court— you know her as Biff."

Biff Court had been a local character since we were children; a big, friendly lesbian who ran the island's principal gay night club, called, appropriately, Biff's Bar.

"Wait a minute." I was becoming confused. "What was his business with all these people?"

Frank sighed. "Pressure. I guess you could call it blackmail. Not for money, but to get things done his way. The senators and the congressman and the newspaperman were loudly opposed to his policies, and to his becoming the Republican candidate. In his files he had amassed certain secrets about all of them. I think those phone calls were just to remind the opposition who was boss. But they weren't serious suspects. He only got through to one of them. Two weren't on the island, and the senator who was here was at a party until after three in the morning. Only the publisher was home, and he gave Father short shrift. According to him, Father mentioned that he knew all about his mistress, and he laughed and said, 'So does my wife,' or something like that, and he hung up. That wasn't going to stop his editorials."

"What did your father have on the others?" I asked.

"Oh, the usual. A teenage girlfriend, a secret bank account; things like that. But they aren't the type of people to be pressured. They didn't take him very seriously. Anyway, he didn't speak to them that night, and they're all accounted for."

"The usual?" I shook my head. "Those things sound pretty serious to me."

Frank shrugged. "This is St. Thomas." End of subject.

I looked around. Lee sat quietly, listening, but she was not looking at Frank and me. She was watching Tangera, who wandered about the room in her bright orange dress. Tangera seemed to be paying little attention to the conversation, finding more of interest in the knicknacks on various tables and in the large breakfront against one wall. She inspected each ashtray, bowl, and figurine as if committing it to memory for future inventory. As she arrived at a beautiful pink Oriental vase in its own glass case in one corner, I turned back to Frank.

"What was in your father's file on Abel Brandt?" I asked.

"Oh, that wasn't blackmail," Frank said. "In fact, Father and Abel were friends. The file was just detailed accounts of some development deals Abel was trying to make with the local government: two shopping centers, a resort hotel, and some condominiums. Abel says Father called him that night to check some figures. He and his wife used to be over here a lot for dinner. Abby helped

Father with some lucrative real estate deals. I guess that's why he remembered them in his will. No, they had no reason to kill him, because Frank planned to support the development proposals, and to make them realities as soon as he took office. It would have made them millions."

"Would have?" I asked.

"Yes. It's no secret that Governor Hughes is very much opposed to Abel's plans. He maintains that the island is being built up much too quickly. He intends to keep things on a more even keel. I don't think Abel's deals will go through now."

"What did your father say to Hughes and the others on the telephone?"

Frank shook his head. "I don't know. The police questioned everyone who had been called, but they didn't pursue it. Everybody has alibis. I guess the detectives felt that the subjects of the calls were not important."

"Somebody killed him," I said. "Isn't that important?"

He sighed and shook his head again. Tangera turned from her inspection of the vase to look intently at me for a moment, then she turned back to it. Lee consulted her watch and rose.

"I wonder," she said, "if I might use your phone? My husband is expecting Joe and me soon for dinner."

"Of course," Frank said, rising.

I had one more question. "You said that, other than the people with files, your father called four people. Governor Hughes, a beach bum named—Whitney?—and Biff Court. That's only three. Who was the other one?"

Frank paused on his way to the door. He looked from me to Lee, who waited beside him to be shown to a telephone. It was then that I realized my sister already knew everything he had been telling me. The local newspapers had probably written of little else at the time, and gossip would have supplied the unprinted details. I looked at her. She nodded to Frank.

He avoided my eyes, and his voice was barely more than a whisper.

"The fourth phone call was to Elsa Tremayne."

"What do you know about the mongoose?" Tangera Jensen asked me.

I looked up, disoriented. Frank, his exit line completed, had ushered Lee from the room. I had sat—for seconds? minutes?—staring ahead of me, remembering. Tangera had apparently stood silently by, waiting for me to come back to shore.

Elsa. I couldn't think about that now. Later.

"I beg your pardon?" I stammered.

"The mongoose." She laughed, flashing even white teeth as she shook her head in mock exasperation. "Oh, my, Joseph! I think you have seen another ghost. Come outside with me. There is a breeze now; it may be just what you need."

I followed her through the French doors—the opposites of the doors in the office across the hall—to the veranda. She was right: the cool evening air brought me comfortably back to the present. We descended to the patio and stood gazing at the town across the harbor, beyond the trees. It was dusk, and already tiny dots of light were transforming the distant city into a diamond necklace on black velvet.

After a while I said, "The mongoose is a small, furry mammal, much like a squirrel. The first ones arrived here on boats, where they were kept for killing rats. I believe they were first discovered by ships' captains in India—"

"I know all that," Tangera said. Her silver laughter floated off across the flagstones. "Why do they dance in the moonlight?"

"What? Oh, that. It's an old West Indian legend. You see, mongooses prey on snakes, and shortly after they arrived in the islands, most of the local snakes disappeared. To this day you hardly ever see a snake on St. Thomas. Anyway, the old wives, or whoever, came up with a story that the mongoose possesses mystical powers, that it can drive evil from a place. When the last snake was dead, they say, the mongooses celebrated their victory by dancing under a full moon."

The lights of Charlotte Amalie were reflected in the dark water of the bay. The trees around the patio rustled in the wind. Tangera strained nearer, drinking in every word. I had deliberately lowered my voice; the actor, the obeah woman, the native parent leaning over the bed, thrilling and delighting generations of St. Thomian children.

"And now, whenever the moon is full," I whispered, "somewhere deep in the island forests, they dance. You can't ever see them, of course. Their domain is not for human eyes. Just imagine: Evil is vanquished, and thousands of mongooses gather to celebrate under the moon."

After an appropriate moment of silence, I burst into laughter. I stopped when I looked at Tangera. She was gazing into the distance, knitting her brows. When she spoke, it was not to me but to something far away.

"So that is what it meant," she said, slowly nodding her head. Then, with another smile, she turned back to me. "I am glad you are here, Joseph. I have heard so much about you from Frank. You really care about him. He has not spoken of these things until now. He talks to you, and that is good. I think it is best for him to be open about it, instead of always festering."

It was my turn to look away. I gazed out over the harbor, knowing that the time had come to say what I had been thinking since my arrival here, wondering how to say it. She waited. Slowly, with difficulty, I began.

"I'm a writer, Tangera. Plays, novels, what have you: that's what I do, what I know. Six months ago a man was killed in this house, a man I hardly knew. We were children, and to me he was merely Frank's father. I haven't seen much of my friends on this island for nearly twelve years. You and Frank have told me about what happened. You've mentioned names of people I barely remember, and some I don't know at all. I live in New York now. I don't know what it is you want me to do."

She placed a hand on my arm, and the scent of citrus wafted toward me.

"I want you to tell Frank that it is time to go on," she said, staring into my eyes. "He has been sitting around for so long now, trying to figure this out. To solve it. He wants to know who killed his father, and I do not think he ever will. He has lost several clients recently; some days he does not go to work at all. He does not even leave the house." She paused for a moment, looking away, then she returned her gaze to my face. "He drinks. You know that is not good, given his family history."

"Where are his friends?" I asked. "Where's Dennis Grey? Does Frank ever see him?"

She shrugged and waved her hand in dismissal. "The

other Musketeer? Not much. Dennis is very busy these days."

Her clairvoyance was contagious. In this house today, I could feel things usually denied me.

"There's something else that's bothering you," I said.

She stared, then nodded. She had apparently made some sort of decision. "I suppose I should tell you. Someone; a stranger. They say it is easier to tell strangers. I am worried about myself, the way I am reacting to all this. We met two years ago, Frank and I, at a club in town. Instant crazy, as a friend of mine would say. I was at the university here, majoring in English. I was on a student visa. I had vague notions of returning to Martinique and teaching. Meeting Frank changed that future for me. His parents objected, of course. A Jensen with a black woman? Horrors! So we eloped. We rented a house downtown, and Frank went back to work with his firm. Hubert tried to talk Mr. Hammond into firing Frank, but Mr. Hammond paid no attention. Hubert was more successful with his other friends, with island society. Here I was, a new American citizen married to a wealthy lawyer I adored, and we were outcasts. I did not mind: Frank was enough for me. But then all this happened, and Frank withdrew into himself. We came to Haven View, to his mother who loathes me, and who has some strange power over him."

"And how are you reacting to it?" I asked.

She stared off at the early lights of the city across the bay. "How do you think? I am going mad. I get out of here whenever I can. I have found a group of people—the beach crowd, I suppose you could call them. Bored young people who have a lot of money and nothing to do. They are on the beach all the time, playing volleyball and windsurfing and sunbathing. Most of them are white, so I suppose they find me exotic. Drunks, dope fiends, failed artists—dropouts of one kind or another. My new friends: fellow outcasts. I am there every day now." She uttered a low, rueful laugh. "It gets me out of the house."

We were silent for a long time, watching dusk turn to evening. I was thinking how different this woman was from the one who had run, breathless, onto the veranda. From madcap to tragic heroine in little more than an hour. Or was it all a performance, a craving for the dramatic? The orange fetish, the sudden grin, *I shall call you Joseph.* I had no previous experience of this: by accident or design, she was unique.

I said, "So you decided it was time to do something."

She turned to face me. "Yes. I do not want to become a permanent member of the beach crowd. I want my husband back from—from wherever he has gone to."

"So," I said, "that's why you wrote me the letter?"

Her eyes widened. I could see, feel, the sudden panic, even as I heard the footsteps on the flagstones behind me. She was staring beyond me, past my shoulder. Her hand was on my arm again, and her long, coral-colored nails bit into my flesh.

"What letter?" Frank asked.

I turned around. He had joined us on the patio.

Tangera laughed. It was a light, untroubled sound, breaking the tension and restoring order.

"Oh, you remember, darling," she gushed as she took his arm in hers. "My thank you note to Joseph when he sent us the flowers. I was just telling him about our wedding."

"Oh, yes," he said. "Lee will be out in a moment, Joe, and she said to tell you that you have to leave immediately. You're meeting Paul and some other people for dinner."

"Thank you," I said. "I guess it is getting late. Please thank your mother for having us."

"Of course. You must come for dinner next week."

"Talk to Lee. She's my social director," I said, and we laughed. "I've already been told of a New Year's party, and I don't know what else she has planned."

This interested Tangera. "Oh? Which party is that?"

"The Brandts'."

"Ah," she said. "They give lovely ones. We went last year. We have been invited this year, as well." She glanced at her husband, and the excitement left her face. "I do not know if we will be able to attend. . . ."

Frank gave her a forced smile. "For a little while, perhaps. But we should be back by midnight." He turned to me. "Mother rarely goes out any more, since—"

"I understand," I said quickly to spare him awkward explanations. I did understand. She was a recent widow, and even on St. Thomas, appearances were important. Also, her condition this afternoon made me wonder how she behaved at parties, particularly New Year's parties. I suspected that this was Frank's chief concern.

Lee joined us, and Frank and Tangera walked us to the car. Frank and I walked ahead. Behind us, Tangera chatted with Lee. Frank put his arm around my shoulders and leaned closer, lowering his voice.

"I'm so glad you're here. I want to talk to you sometime. Alone. Please."

I nodded, smiling, choosing to ignore the urgency of his tone. I was suddenly very tired; the plane, this house, too many intimations. I could hardly wait for dinner with my own family, away from this place.

"Yes," I sang, patting his back. "And we should get together with Dennis, too. All for one and one for all!"

I laughed. Frank did not; he stopped and stared at me for a moment. I almost expected him to say, "Dennis who?"

What he said was, "Yes. Yes, we must."

As we arrived at the car, the front door of the house opened and a small black boy in a T-shirt and shorts ran lightly across the patio toward us. The last time I had seen him he had practically been in a carriage, but there was no doubt as to his identity.

"Hello, George," I said, extending my right hand.

He took it in a surprisingly firm grip. I looked down at his large hands and long, tapering fingers.

"Hullo, Mistuh Wilduh," he whispered, looking up at me with the gravest expression I'd ever seen on one so young. His enormous, serious eyes traveled from me to Lee and back. "Mistress Jensen say thank you fo' comin', and you is welcome again any time."

"Thank you," Lee said, grinning, "and thank her for us."

George, his carefully memorized message conveyed, turned to leave. He did not get away, however. Tangera knelt before him and placed her hands on his shoulders.

"That was very well done," she laughed. "Did you practice your new piano piece today?"

The child, shy, embarrassed, and speechless with delight, nodded an affirmative. Her beauty worked wonders on all men, apparently, regardless of age.

"And if your mother says it's all right," she continued, "will you play it for us after dinner?"

A breathless whisper this time: "Yes."

"Wonderful!" she cried, rising. George, released,

turned and fairly flew back into the house. Tangera laughed. "He is adorable."

As we drove away, I looked back at my friend and his wife. They stood, his arm around her shoulders, hers around his waist, waving from the patio. The house was behind them, lights now shining from every window. A perfect picture.

As soon as we had driven through the wrought iron gates, Lee shook her head dismissively. "House on Haunted Hill. That bit with the boy—I could almost like her for that."

I said nothing. Almost?

Tamarinda. His wife, the one with the exotic name . . .

Then, as we descended the winding road toward the Waterfront, I recalled that Lee has an uncanny memory for names. Only twice before, that I knew of, had she ever had trouble remembering one. In both cases, they had been people she despised.

"Very interesting," she mused, "that nobody bothered to mention the other phone call. . . ."

I stared: more intimations. "Another one? What was this call about?"

There was an edge of humor to her voice. "I don't know what about, but I know to whom."

I watched her as she drove. "I take it he didn't order a pizza."

Lee shook her head and gazed into the beam from the headlights as she maneuvered the car down the mountainside.

"He called Frank," she said.

4

PROMENADE

The party on Skyline Drive was in full swing when we arrived.

Abby Brandt met us at the front door of her spacious, ultramodern hillside residence. She was a glamorous honey-blonde in her early forties, as best as I could tell. Her white satin blouse and slit skirt revealed enticing amounts of her well-tanned, well-toned body. My first impression of her was a literal one. In the act of shaking hands she leaned forward and brushed her bosom against me. No citrus for this one: her scent was darker, musky, blatantly erotic. My brother-in-law had warned me about her, and I watched, amused, as he received the same greeting. She did not touch Lee, but merely smiled and nodded. She took my arm and led me through the throng to the bar. Lee and Paul followed.

"You are really handsome, Joe," she gushed as soon as we all had drinks in hand. "Much better than that photograph on the back of *Bridge of Sighs*, which, incidentally, I read twice and which, please please, you must autograph for me!"

Surprise. "Of course, I'd be glad to."

It was odd: somehow I couldn't imagine this woman taking the time to read a book. She seemed too wound up, too energetic; the sort of person who flutters constantly back and forth, rarely pausing to rest anywhere. She reminded me of Tangera Jensen in that respect.

"Such a marvelous story. So moving! You do know Venice. Doesn't he, Paul? And don't *you* look charming tonight! Lee, the men in your family. Heaven!" She giggled and fussed, receiving a forced smile from my sister and genuine ones from Paul and me. "I'm going to take you around the room, Joe. Just *everybody* is longing to meet you." She scanned the crowd, and suddenly she grabbed my arm. "Quick, put on your clothes. It's my husband!"

As she shrieked with amusement at her own witticism, I watched Abel Brandt approach us. He was rather short, with sandy hair and beard, and his immaculate white linen suit barely concealed the beginnings of a beer belly. I guessed he was about forty-five. His face was reddish, flushed; from sun and alcohol, I supposed. His overall appearance was one of softness, joviality: he did not look like the powerful maker of deals Frank had described. I'd met him once or twice when I was a teenager, but I had not been able to recall his face.

He remembered me, however. On closer inspection, I noticed that he was neither soft nor jovial. His voice was low-pitched, and there was something hard, cold, about it. He smiled perfunctorily as he shook my hand.

"Hello, Joe. It's been a while, hasn't it? You're look-

ing well. I trust my wife is making you at home?" There
was an awkward pause as he looked from me to Abby and
back.

"Yes, very much," I offered into the odd silence.

His mouth curved into another smile in which his
eyes did not join. "Good. A friend of yours over there
saw you come in, and he wants to say hello."

I looked in the direction he had indicated, searching
a sea of unfamiliar faces. Then my eyes met those of a
tall black man on the other side of the room. He grinned
and waved.

"Oh, my God! Please excuse me a moment," I said,
already crossing through the crowd.

The bear hug nearly crushed my ribs.

"Hello, Athos," he said.

I laughed. "How's it going, Aramis?"

I stepped back for a good look at Dennis Grey. He,
unlike our Porthos, was just as I remembered him. Large,
solid, serious, a smile temporarily replacing his usual
grave expression. As I watched, he placed his arm across
the shoulders of the pretty young woman next to him.

I knew her. We had attended different schools, and
she was a good deal younger than I, but I recognized the
governor's daughter immediately. "Hello, Ms. Hughes."

She smiled. "Please call me Jenny."

"I'm Joe," I said.

"He sure is!" Dennis beamed. "He's also not up on
the latest news. Jenny and I are engaged, Joe."

This island was full of surprises. "Congratulations!
How long has this been going on?"

"Quite a while," he said. "The wedding is on Valen-
tine's Day." He punched me lightly on the arm, as of old.

"Hey! We'd love to have you there. Will you be on the island that long?"

"I don't know—" I began.

"Well, no matter. We'll talk you into it later. Won't we, honey?"

Jenny Hughes nodded. She was lovely; small and slender, her red dress beautifully complementing her close-cropped Afro and deep ebony skin. Gold glittered at her throat and wrists; simple, elegant, valuable. Something in her manner made me decide instantly that she would be a perfect match for Dennis. What was it? Of course, they had a common background, both being from well-to-do, even aristocratic local families. No, it was something else. . . .

"This is terrific," I said. "I'd get us some champagne, but we'll have enough of that at midnight."

Dennis looked me over, still grinning uncharacteristically. "You're looking good, Wilder. Are you writing a new book, or something? You always looked better when you had a new idea."

"Uh, no, I'm not, really," I stammered, not wanting to be reminded. Best defense: offense. "How's the local government these days."

"Better than it might have been, since November," he replied, glancing at the governor's daughter. "But I guess you mean my department. Cultural Affairs are in order, but Conservation is a constant struggle. How long have you been back?"

"Two days."

"Well, even in that amount of time you've probably noticed all the construction and so-called modernization going on." He glanced around the room and lowered his voice. "If certain parties have their way, St. Thomas will soon be wall-to-wall concrete. Hotels, condos, co-ops, shopping malls—"

"Hush, Dennis," Jenny whispered.

He regarded her for a moment, then nodded. "Okay. I don't want to insult our hosts. . . ."

Jenny frowned at him. "Perhaps you didn't want to come to this party, but I had to."

"I know," he said.

I was confused. I looked from one to the other. "What are you two talking about—or is it personal?"

Dennis shook his head. Any onlookers would have thought us an odd trio, heads bent together and whispering despite the loud music and dancers nearby.

"I'm her escort," he explained, indicating Jenny. "Clay—the governor and Mrs. Hughes were invited to quite a few parties tonight. They'll put in an appearance at several, but there are still some they can't make. So they've sent ambassadors. Jenny opted for the Brandts." He placed his hands on my arms. "Actually, now I'm glad she did. It sure is great to see you. Are you on vacation?"

"Sort of," I mumbled, wondering just how to introduce the subject of the murder.

As it turned out, it wasn't necessary. Realization dawned on Dennis's face. "Oh. Frank asked you to come."

"Not exactly. Actually, it was his wife. She thought I might be of some help. He isn't very well, but I guess you know that."

I regretted my words instantly. Hadn't Tangera made quite a show of keeping her letter a secret? Dumb.

Dennis shook his head. "I rarely see him. In town, mostly, when we happen to have lunch in the same place, or go to the same parties."

"In that case, you'll see him tonight. He and Tangera are going to be here." I leaned closer to him. "What do you make of all that—what happened to the judge, I mean?"

He shrugged. "I'm really not interested. It's over, as far as I'm concerned. He was a disgusting man, and now he's dead. I'm sorry about Frank, but—"

Jenny Hughes interrupted him.

"Look," she said, pointing across the room.

The music had temporarily stopped, and with it all conversation. It seemed that everyone in the room had turned at the same instant. Tangera Jensen stood just inside the doorway, a vision in coral chiffon. Leave it to her to wear an evening dress, diaphanous and flowing, with diamond necklace and earrings flashing. Seconds passed before anyone could look beyond her to Frank, who slouched behind her in a navy blazer and white slacks, his hands casually buried in his pockets. They were dazzling, of course, but what I now remember best about the moment was the expression on Tangera's face. She surveyed the room, smiling disarmingly. But behind that smile, deep in her eyes, there was a hint of challenge, of defiance, and even of contempt. Frank's face, as nearly as I could see, revealed nothing but polite indifference. I wish I had a photograph of that brief tableau: it could explain so much. My vision of it becomes less vivid with each recalling.

Then Abby Brandt stepped forward to greet them, everyone else turned back to whatever they had been doing, music and voices resumed, and the moment was gone.

*   *   *

True to her word, Abby took me on a grand tour. I had joined her with Frank and Tangera just after their arrival, but I was barely able to say hello to them before she whisked me away.

She showed me the house ("We built it ourselves . . . I always wanted something hanging off a cliff overlooking the harbor . . . So much fun, so scenic . . . It's patterned after a little manse we rented one season in Monte Carlo. . . .") and the suspended, wraparound balcony ("It's held up by beams and cables, you know . . . There's absolutely nothing under us, just a fifty-foot drop!"). We ended up in the master bedroom ("Where the *real* work gets done, ha ha!"), with Abby offering me her copy of my first novel for signing. When it became apparent that she was about to offer me something else, I managed to lead her back to the living room.

The hour before midnight was a mixture of old and new faces. Not many old ones, really. Most of the people with whom I had grown up were no longer living on the island, or they were not friends of the Brandts. There were Frank and Dennis, of course, and two or three other acquaintances, but, for the most part, I was meeting people for the first time.

One familiar face belonged to Biff Court. Abby presented me to the nightclub owner, and she, in turn, introduced me to the pale, freckled redhead beside her, a squeaky-voiced slip of a thing named Honey, who giggled incessantly. I assumed that she was Biff's lover. I was right. We murmured amenities, and Biff extended an open invitation to visit them at her club on Back Street in town. I watched the large, masculine woman with the short, dark hair and the pleasant, friendly face, realizing as I did that she was one of the last people ever to speak with Hubert Jensen. I wondered again what could have been the subjects of those telephone calls.

I would not find out tonight. Abby and I moved from group to group, shaking hands and exchanging banal pleasantries. The many sections of St. Thomas society were well-represented: the old families from the Danish days, before the islands were purchased by the United States in 1917; the new Stateside group, Americans attracted by the booming tourist industry; and the local royalty, the native families who had once owned the islands, and who made huge fortunes selling their properties. They all knew each other, and, having known my parents, they were all very polite to me. Many asked after my mother, and several complimented me on my books.

At last the rounds came to an end, and Abby fluttered off to attend to other guests. I looked around me. Through the dancers I saw Lee and Paul talking to another couple. Dennis and Jenny were dancing. Frank was on a couch, deep in conversation with a man I didn't recognize. Tangera, in another part of the room, was holding court. I made my way over to her and the two men with whom she stood chatting.

"Joseph, do you know Bertram and Carlos? Boys, this is *the* Joseph Wilder!"

I laughed. "The only one at the party, at any rate."

The one called Bertram flashed a winning smile and winked.

"Don't be so modest, sir," he chirped. "This divine woman has been telling us all about your literary and theatrical exploits. How do you do?"

We shook hands. He was a slight man with a large, good-natured face and thick, curly brown hair. His lips were framed by a mustache and a small, impeccable goatee. A tiny diamond glistened on his left earlobe. The man next to him was his antithesis: a very tall, muscular, dark-skinned Hispanic with straight black hair in a shoulder-length ponytail. He nodded and shook my hand, nearly crushing it. Unlike Bertram, he was not even remotely effeminate. I thought of Biff and Honey and decided that these two were an item. Right again.

"Say hello to the man," Bertram encouraged.

"Hello," Carlos muttered.

His partner grinned. "A man of few words. So, you're in books. I'm in hair."

"Yes," Tangera added. "Bert has a salon downtown, Snips. He does everybody." She raised a hand to her own coiffure.

"One of my more inspired creations," Bertram said, indicating her. "I guess I've done every head in this room, including your sister." He gave my own hair a professional once-over. "I'd love to do yours."

"Sure," I said. "I'll call you for an appointment."

"Terrif! Carlos here is not in hair. He's in cement. He works for our host, don't you know, Brandt Construction. Strong, silent type. So, what brings you back to our little Caribbean hotbed of sin and vice?"

"Visiting Lee," I explained, "and this 'divine woman.' Her husband is an old friend of mine."

"Oh." The friendly grin slowly vanished from Bertram's face. He looked closely at me, into my eyes, and for a moment I thought he was about to say something else.

If he was going to speak, he never got the chance. Tangera chose that instant to grab his arm.

"Dance with me, darling," she cooed.

The grin returned immediately. *"Enchanté, madame!"*

The two of them moved off, and I was left alone with the large, frowning Carlos.

"So," I began, "you work for Abel Brandt."

He nodded.

"Have you done that for long?"

He shook his head.

"Do you like your work?"

He shrugged.

"I see," I said. "Well, uh, see you around. Nice talking to you."

He glanced at me then. His eyes crinkled at the corners, and I even saw a brief flash of teeth. Score one for me: that was apparently his monthly smile. I grinned and began to move away.

"Hello, Joe."

I froze. The music and voices faded from my consciousness. Carlos looked disinterestedly over my shoulder, in the direction of the voice we'd just heard. He shrugged again and walked away. I, on the other hand, could not move. I stood there, stupid, all movement arrested by that voice, by those two words.

A little boy sits in a tree in a school playground, watching a group of children play foursquare below him. He is not really observing all of them, just one: the pretty girl with long blond hair who has held the one-square position all afternoon. No one can bounce the ball past her and claim her court; she is too quick, too agile, too competent. The boy watches her closely, his face flushed, his heart aching against his ribs. At a break in the action another girl runs to her, whispers in her ear, and points up at the tree. The blond girl turns and peers up into the branches, her lovely, serious face a study in condescension.

"What are you looking at?" she demands.

Everyone on the playground turns to see the boy in the tree look quickly, guiltily away. He grabs a branch to keep from toppling to the ground and expiring at her feet, which is exactly, at that moment, what he wants to do. . . .

Three teenage boys—two white, one black—are running up and down a stretch of Morning Star Beach, tossing a red Frisbee between them under the glaring summer sun. At one point, the black boy flips the saucer to the larger of the other two, who misses the catch. The missile sails across the beach and lands, with a thump and a huge spray of sand, directly between two bikini-clad girls, supine on towels, tanning. One of the girls, brunette, shrieks in fury and sits up on her towel, shaking sand from oily limbs.

"Thanks a lot, stupid!" she cries at the tall boy as he arrives to retrieve the Frisbee.

"Sorry," he murmurs, not looking at her. He is staring down at the other girl, the beautiful blonde who has apparently not noticed the proceedings. Only when his shadow falls across her face does she open her eyes. She blinks up at him, then reaches for the shiny disc next to her.

"Hello," she drawls. "I believe this is yours."

"Uh, yeah." He reaches down and takes the toy as she smiles up from the towel. "Umm, are you two going to Duffy's Friday night?" He is beginning to tremble.

The blonde smiles. "Probably. Not many choices on this island, are there? Yes, Nancy and I will be there."

"Humph!" Nancy offers to the conversation, still flicking sand from her arms.

"Well, I'll be there, too," the boy stammers. "Maybe I'll see you there."

"It's a small club. I don't see how you could miss us." The

blonde is laughing now, shading her eyes with her hand, watching him.

The other boys arrive behind him.

"Hello, ladies," the smaller white boy calls. "Catching some rays? Don't let that nasty sun burn those gorgeous gams."

The girls giggle.

The boy with the Frisbee is not going to let these oafs ruin his chance.

"So," he says to the blonde, "would you like to go for a swim?"

"I don't think so. Go play with your Frisbee." She and Nancy laugh.

"Oh, go swimming with him," the smaller white boy sneers. "Give the kid a break. Everybody knows he's in love with you."

"Shut up!" The larger boy punches him, hard, on the arm.

Screaming with derisive laughter, the smaller boy grabs the disk and runs off down the beach, followed by the black boy. Deciding that he will not speak to the other boys for at least two days, the larger boy, whose face is now a vibrant red, turns from the giggling girls and walks away, dispirited.

The last thing he hears from behind him is the blonde's clear voice calling after him as he goes.

"Duffy's. Friday."

He turns around and smiles. . . .

Late Friday night, the boy from the beach is climbing the stairs to the tiny club above Creque Alley in town. His passage is blocked by the descent of the two girls from the beach. He looks up into the face of the beautiful blonde above him.

"Hello," she says.

"Hi," he whispers. "Hello, Nancy."

"Humph!" the dark-haired girl replies.

"I see you made it." The blond girl is smiling.

"Uh, yeah. Are you going to dance with me tonight?" Tremble, tremble.

"I can't. My mother said I have to be home at eleven. It's nearly that now. We have to go."

"Oh." He stands aside to let them pass.

"Another time," she says as she and Nancy pass him and continue down the stairs.

He watches them go, mentally kicking himself. Finally, with a sigh, he continues slowly up the stairs into the club, to join his friends. . . .

Two years later, at a party in a beautiful two-story living room, dancers are moving feverishly to deafening rock music. On a balcony above the action, several people chat and drink, surveying the scene below them.

A tall young man, seventeen and nervous, has just spotted a beautiful blond girl on the balcony above him. She is alone, he is happy to see, leaning on the railing in her pretty blue dress. He plants himself directly below her and calls up to her.

"Hi there."

She looks around, puzzled, wondering who has spoken. At last she glances down and sees him. "Hi there, yourself."

"Having a good time?" He grins in what he hopes is a disarming fashion.

"Sure. Are you all right? You look funny."

"Uh, yeah, I'm fine." He wipes the sickly smile from his face. "Would you like to dance?"

"Sorry, I'm with someone."

At this precise moment, another young man joins her on the balcony. He is carrying two drinks, one of which he hands to the girl. The young man on the dance floor below knows him slightly, but can't quite remember his name. Something cute like Binky or Dinky—Bunky; that's it.

"Oh, well." The young man on the dance floor shrugs, resigned.

Before she turns to her escort, the beautiful blonde smiles down at him.

"Did you ever notice," she calls, "that we always seem to be on different levels?"

She laughs and turns away. . . .

Two years after that, on the porch of the Wilder residence on a cliff above the harbor across from town, Linda Wilder sits reading the Virgin Islands Daily News. Her son, Joe, stands at the railing, smoking a cigarette and watching two poodles fight for possession of a rawhide bone.

"Well, how do you like that!" Linda exclaims, looking up from the society page. "Cathy Tremayne's boy, Bruce, is getting married. Isn't he the one you kids call Bunky? I always thought he was so unattractive. . . ."

"He is unattractive," Joe mutters. Then a horrible suspicion arrives in his mind. The breath leaves his body and the blood leaves his face. "Uh, who—whom is he marrying?"

"Let me see," Linda says, perusing the paper. She spots the name and it registers. "Oh, dear." She stares up at her son.

Joe turns away and leans on the railing, gazing out at the harbor. A sailboat is moving slowly by through the water below the house. Three men sit in the stern, drinking beer and laughing. He wishes suddenly, with all his heart, that he could leap from the porch into the bay and swim out to join them, drink beer with them, go wherever it is they're going. He has just returned to St. Thomas from his sophomore year of college, and the long summer stretches emptily ahead.

"Damn it," he whispers as the boat below him catches the wind and glides away toward the horizon. . . .

Several years later—five years before the Brandt's New Year's party—Joe sits in his Greenwich Village apartment, entertaining a vague acquaintance from St. Thomas who is in New York on a business trip. The acquaintance, whose name is Bill something, has been anesthetizing Joe for the past hour with dull St. Thomas gossip.

"Oh!" Bill suddenly says. "Did you hear about Bunky Tremayne? Wasn't that awful?"

Joe sits up, instantly attentive. "What about him?"

"Offed himself!" Bill announces with that curious note of triumph that creeps into the voices of the bearers of shocking news. "Walked into the sea and just kept going. Business problems, apparently. Went broke and was about to go to jail, or something like that. Just about a year ago. His wife found him washed up on the beach the next morning. It must have been terrible for her! She was in the hospital for a while, but she's home now. She's taken up painting, of all things! She does watercolors and stuff, you know, local scenes. Sells them in the shops downtown. They're very good, actually. Do you know her, Joe? Elsa, her name is. Beautiful woman. . . ."

Joe freezes, staring.

When my paralysis passed, I took a deep breath and turned around.

"Hello, Elsa," I said.

I stared. The straight, fine blond hair was shorter now. It fell to her shoulders, then curved slightly inward. She was still tall and slender, still lovely. Even now she gazed at me with the unsettling, frank expression I remembered. She held a wineglass in her right hand, and she was wearing something white and clinging, I think. I didn't much notice: my attention was drawn to her face. Features, expression, and hair were the same, but something about her had altered. I had not seen her since before her marriage, and her husband was now dead. I calculated: it had been twelve years, all in all. I don't know why I wondered what had changed in her. I should, rather, have been surprised that anything about her was the same.

"I didn't know you were on the island," she said.

"I arrived the day before yesterday. News can't travel that fast, even on St. Thomas."

She laughed. "I suppose not. How have you been?"

How had I been. Odd: everyone else had said, "What have you been doing?" or, "What are you up to these days?" Here was someone—someone I barely knew, although I had loved her from afar, as it were—who asked only about my welfare. Or was I reading too much into it? Probably.

"Well enough," I said, smiling for no good reason. "And you?"

"I'm okay."

"I understand you're painting now."

"Yes." She shrugged.

"I'm a writer," I said.

Her light laugh transformed her face. "As well we know! I read *Bridge of Sighs*. Whenever you have a book published or a play produced, it makes the local papers."

"I have a good agent."

"Beautiful."

"What, my agent?"

"No. The book. A young American falling in love and coming of age in Venice. Did that really happen to you?"

"No. I just imagined it one day, while I was having coffee in the Piazza San Marco."

"It seemed so real. That young man, and that Italian girl he idealized. She was so—elusive. I really began to worry that he'd never get up the courage to speak to her—"

"Yes, well . . ."

"—and she wasn't nearly as unattainable as he seemed to think. Just an ordinary, nice young woman—"

"Yes, well . . ."

"It must be wonderful there."

I nodded. "Except for St. Thomas, it's the most wonderful place I've ever seen."

"Are you back for good?"

"No, I don't think so."

"So this is a vacation?"

"Yes. I come here when I can, to visit my sister and my friends."

Her gaze traveled around the room and came to rest on something behind me. The smile left her face.

"Is Frank Jensen one of your friends?" she asked.

"Yes."

She nodded. "Yes, I seem to remember you were always with him and—somebody. The Three Little Pigs, or something."

I laughed, blushing. "Musketeers, if you please!" I turned and pointed across the room at Dennis Grey. "He was the third. I'm glad you almost remember."

She smiled. We stood there for a few moments, just looking at each other in a casual, friendly way. I wondered if I should offer condolences: it had been six years since Bunky Tremayne's death, and I hadn't known him. I barely knew her.

"You don't have to say anything," she whispered.

I blinked.

"It was in your face," she continued. "You were about to say how sorry you were to hear—et cetera. Skip it."

I thought fast. "How's your drink?"

She smiled again. "Fine. Do you plan to go to the Reef while you're here? I'm there most days, on the patio near the pool. The hotel employs me to paint there. The tourists like to watch me work. I've been there a couple of months now. It's doubled my income."

"I see," I murmured. I hadn't seen this woman in years, and I was beginning to tingle again. Just like that. "So I guess you'd be there day-after-tomorrow at about four, if I were to drop in and buy you a drink?"

"I'll be there," she said, and then she glanced over my shoulder. "It's lovely to see you again, but now you must excuse me. I'm here with a friend, and he's looking around for me. I promised him a dance."

Oh. "A particular friend?"

The frank stare bore into me again. "Just a friend. I'm not seeing anybody now. If I were, I wouldn't have accepted your invitation for a drink."

I laughed. "Which you initiated."

She laughed, too. "Yes. I'm very good at that, aren't I?"

The sound of her laughter remained with me as she went back across the room to join a huge, bearded, red-haired man who was apparently waiting for her. I watched her go, smiling to myself.

Then, in a flash, it came back to me: she, too, had received a phone call from Hubert Jensen on the night of his murder.

* * *

It happened then, just after Elsa Tremayne left me alone in a corner of the room. Perhaps it was the crowd, or the noise, or the heat. Or, more likely, the fact that I was at that moment thinking of the judge. I can't even define exactly what "it" was, though I was becoming familiar with the feeling. There was a sudden rush of cold through the stuffy, smoky living room. I closed my eyes, aware of the hairs on my arms and neck, feeling the buzzing weakness spread through my limbs. I gripped my glass in both hands to keep it from falling. A numbing flush spread over my face.

I opened my eyes and scanned the room. There was no music at the moment. Everyone stood chatting in small groups, as they had been doing all evening. But something, somewhere, was different.

Someone was watching me. I could feel the eyes, as I had felt the silent facade of Haven View staring, reaching out; trying, perhaps, to communicate. Only this energy was different. It was less urgent, less pleading, darker, more—

Malevolent. I remember thinking of that very word as I glanced cautiously about the room. My hostess was regaling a group with some amusing anecdote. Her husband was nowhere in sight. Lee and Paul were talking to the hairstylist, Bertram, and his friend. Biff Court and Honey were ordering drinks from the bar. Frank was still on the couch, still talking to the man I'd noticed him with earlier. I now recognized the man as his law partner, whose name I could not recall. Dennis and Jenny were standing near me with another young couple. Elsa was on the far side of the room, her back to me, laughing with the bearded giant. No one appeared to be taking any notice of me.

The coldness dissipated as suddenly as it had materialized. Stupid, I told myself. Nobody's watching me. It's just something walking on my grave, or whatever. A spasm. I looked around again. How many of these people did I really know, anyway?

I shrugged and shook my head. Don't be silly, I thought. What I need is a little fresh air. I turned toward the sliding glass doors that led out to the balcony.

And stopped.

Tangera Jensen stood just inside the glass doors, staring at me.

"I have been looking for you, Joseph," she said, smiling as she came toward me. The tangerine aura preceded her. "I wanted to wish you a happy New Year. Frank and I must get back to the house. It is nearly midnight, and we promised Helen." She took my hand in hers. "Come and say good-bye."

She led me across to the front entrance where Frank was now waiting. As we met him there, we were joined by Dennis and Jenny, who were also leaving. Abby Brandt arrived for farewells.

There was a moment, then, when the Three Musketeers were together. I placed a hand on the shoulder of each of the other two.

"Happy New Year, boys," I said.

Frank and Dennis laughed and I joined them, remembering old times, New Year's Eves long past. Then, with many kisses and hugs from Abby Brandt, the two couples went out into the night.

I danced with Abby, and then with Lee. I thought of asking Elsa to dance, but when I looked for her I was informed that she and her escort—the big, bearded man

I did not know, and to whom she had not introduced me—had already left the party. Finally, about ten minutes before the new year, I at last made my way through the glass doors to the balcony for a long overdue breath of cold midnight air.

I stood leaning against the railing, looking down at the lights of the city. Noises—music, shouts, laughter—floated up the hillside from other celebrants, other gatherings. Somewhere below me a steel band was playing. It was dark on the balcony, dark and chill and refreshing. The sounds of the party behind me were soft, muffled, far away. I must have been there for several minutes when the voice came from the shadows to my left.

"The famous Joseph Wilder in repose."

He had been sitting there all the while, at a small table off to the side of the balcony, watching me. I could barely make him out in the gloom. I heard, rather than saw, as he raised a bottle from the table and filled a glass. Then my host rose and came over to stand next to me at the railing.

"Cigarette?" he slurred, offering me a gold case.

"I have my own, thanks." I pulled one from my jacket.

He lit us both up and inhaled deeply. We studied each other in silence for a moment. Now, in the light, I could see his dark, oddly unfocused eyes.

After a while he said, "Your eyes are blue."

That couldn't be denied. "Yes."

"And you're—what? Six? Six-one?"

Oh, boy. "Umm—"

"You're very good-looking. Sexy."

I turned and started toward the glass doors. His hand on my arm stopped me.

"You needn't be alarmed," he said, chuckling. "I'm not one of those. I'm just sizing up my competition."

I shrugged his hand away. "You're drunk."

"Not really." He shook his glass, tinkling the ice within it. "Soon, perhaps; shortly after the new year. A new year, a new beginning. A clean slate." He leaned over, his elbows on the railing, the glass and cigarette in the same hand dangling over the edge. "Too bad there's no such thing. We don't get clean slates. We pay for our crimes, don't we?"

This was a foreign film, and I couldn't keep up with the subtitles. "Look, Mr. Brandt—"

"Abel. Please."

"Okay, Abel. I'm not your competition, whatever that means."

A slow smile came to his face. "I saw you dancing together."

"Are you talking about Mrs. Brandt?"

He whirled around and waved his glass in the direction of the party. "Look at her."

I followed his gaze. Beyond the glass doors, in the center of the room, Abby was performing what appeared to be a shimmy around Bertram.

I began to laugh. "I don't think you'll find him a threat—"

"No, but there are others, aren't there? At least the last one had the decency to pay me for the honor—or is it dishonor?"

I'd had enough. I was halfway to the door when he spoke again.

"What are you doing here, Joe?"

Champagne corks were popping inside, and glasses were being filled. I turned around.

"Your wife invited me."

"That," he said, "is almost humorous. I mean, what are you doing in St. Thomas?"

"I don't think that's any of your—"

"If he killed him, there's not a lot you can do about it, is there?"

Instinct propelled me closer to him. *"What?"*

"Your friend Frank," he said. "Hubert. That's what everyone's saying, you know. Have you come to see if it's really true? Or do you think you can pull a Sherlock Holmes and clear his name?" His laugh was low and cruel. "Good luck. A crime without a corpse is one thing, but a crime without evidence is something else. And there isn't any evidence. Somebody saw to that."

I looked him straight in the eye. "Anybody we know?"

Whatever reaction I expected, it wasn't the one I got. Abel Brandt burst into wild laughter and slapped me on the shoulder.

"Oh, that's great!" he cried. "Perfect! I like you, Joe, I really do. I hope we can be friends. 'Anybody we know!' " I watched as he slowly regained control. At last he took a deep breath and a long sip. "Everybody we know, actually. There's quite a list of—possibilities."

"Yes," I said, thinking of something he'd said a few moments before. "The last one paid you for the honor—or dishonor. Judge Jensen mentioned you in his will, I believe."

Abel Brandt wasn't laughing now. He was watching his wife simulate lovemaking with a large, dark-haired man to the accompaniment of a screeching, thumping rock tune. He went over to the table, poured another drink, and tossed it back.

"Hubert Jensen was my friend," he said.

He came back to join me at the railing. I put my cigarette out and looked at the view. He stood with his back to it, watching the dancers. He leaned closer: our arms were touching.

"Would you look at them," he whispered. "The elite, the well-to-do, the moneyed classes. St. Thomas's own Four Hundred, having another party. They're very good at partying, aren't they? My wife is one of the best. Everybody's bored, so they find amusements. They go a little crazy. They have parties. They pair up, and then they re-pair. Re-pair, get it? That's just what they *don't* do. They break things, like rules. Next thing you know, certain people's sons marry certain undesirables, if you get my drift. They're all rich and beautiful and bored to tears. And this island doesn't provide them with that many options—unless you just love to snorkel, which who does? So they swill and smoke and snort and screw themselves into a stupor. That's how desperate they are. They don't know what else to do."

He uttered a dry, mirthless laugh. His voice came to me through the darkness, from outer space.

"All this business about mongooses dancing. You want to know why they dance? Because everything shakes. The coconuts fall from the palm trees, the waves come crashing to the shore, and the mongooses dance. It's the vibrations. From all the fucking that goes on around here."

At that moment the sirens began. Everywhere, below us and behind, a thousand voices were raised in happy shouts. A crack, like thunder, rolled up the hill from the Waterfront, and in the next instant the sky exploded in every color of the rainbow. Inside, beyond the glass doors, someone started a lusty chorus of "Auld Lang Syne."

I left him then. I walked away from the railing and entered the room, pushing through the joyous throng to join my sister and her husband. Paul handed me a glass of champagne.

A new year, I thought. A new beginning. A clean slate. Too bad there's no such thing. . . .

"There is," I said aloud. "I *know* there is."

Paul turned to look at me, puzzled. "There is what, Joe?"

I shrugged, laughing. I kissed Lee and shook his hand.

"Happy New Year!" I cried, and then I held my glass aloft and joined the singing.

5

RUMBA

The second day of the new year began with rain. At noon, in the middle of the downpour, Lee and I dashed down Main Street, ducked into the Scandinavian Silver Center, and made our way up the stairs to the restaurant on the second floor.

It was a nice little place for lunch, all lacy white and Wedgwood blue. The clientele on any given afternoon was a Who's Who in St. Thomas business and society. I was not surprised to see Abel and Abby Brandt at a large table across the room with four other people. I recognized several of my mother's friends, and everyone seemed to know Lee. Half of the room smiled and waved as we were shown to our table. The food was excellent.

It was after eggs Benedict, over coffee and cigarettes, that I asked Lee about the Jensens. I told her what Abel had said at his party two nights before and waited for a comment.

She glanced over at the Brandts' table and nodded. Then she lit another cigarette and sat back in her chair, watching me.

"It's true, she said. "Everywhere you go on this island, you hear the same opinion: Frank killed his father. But that's not all. Some theories are more elaborate. There are those who think she must have been involved, too . . . Tangera. What do you know! I remembered her name! She told the police that Frank was home with her. If he wasn't, she probably knew where he was. She could even have been with him, for that matter." She leaned forward. "Think about it, Joe. It's the most logical explanation. They had the most to gain."

I shook my head. "What about Helen? She got Haven View and half the money, right? And Abel let something else slip the other night. He said, or hinted, that Hubert was having an affair with Abby."

Lee giggled. "My God! I wasn't sure he knew. Everyone else did. I first heard about that years ago. But you can't be sure Helen knew about it. You saw her the other day: she's always like that. Amelia Earhart could be living in her guest room, for all she knows. Besides, I don't see her swinging a machete, do you? Poison, maybe . . ."

"Okay," I conceded. "Abel, then." I looked over at his table and lowered my voice. "A fit of jealousy."

Her hand flew to her mouth, stifling a scream of laughter. "If that was Abel's idea of justice, quite a few guys would be walking around without any heads!" Her smile disappeared. "Sorry. That was tacky."

The waiter arrived with a coffeepot and replenished our cups. Lee looked down at the table. As I watched, an expression of confusion crept slowly into her face. She glanced up at me with a furrowed brow.

"Where's the cream?" she asked. "I'm sure it was here a few minutes ago. . . ."

We both looked around the surface of the table for several moments. Then I spotted the tiny pitcher behind the rack of sugar and artificial sweetener packets and handed it to her. She smiled and murmured thanks, then raised the pitcher up over her coffee and poured. A stream of white flowed down into the dark, steaming coffee, clouding it.

Everyone has moments when an idea suddenly begins to form in the mind, and then it just as suddenly disappears. Something about the creamer, and about what Lee had been saying; the juxtaposition of the two. In this case—the murder that had brought me here—there was no evidence, but there was one clue. I almost hit upon it then, at that table in the restaurant. Only several days later would I realize why I automatically asked my next question.

"You just mentioned Helen swinging a machete. Frank said something the other day about a machete disappearing. If it's missing, how do they know it was the murder weapon?"

Lee thought about it, then shook her head. "Speculation, I guess. It was in the papers that way, about the missing machete. The coroner said the weapon was a long, sharp blade, like a sword or—oh, I don't know. It's a pretty fair assumption, wouldn't you say?"

I nodded, after a while.

After lunch Lee drove me to a car rental agency on the Waterfront. She then left for work, and I embarked on my own in a light blue, high-powered, automatic Chevette. Just the kind of car I hate, but renters can't be choosers. For a reasonable weekly rate I had transportation.

With two hours to wait until my date with Elsa, I decided to take a long, updated look around the island. The morning rain was gone; now the sun had broken through the clouds. It would be a clear, warm afternoon.

Down the Waterfront I drove, past the airport and the university to Brewers Bay, Fortuna, and the West End. Slowly around the island's circumference. Up hills on the North Side to all the familiar, elevated places: Dorothea, the Agricultural Station, Crown Mountain Road, Four Corners, Mafolie . . .

Different, yet the same. I said that to myself as each new section of the island arrived to surround me. More houses here, a better road there, a lush green everywhere. Sudden, dazzling views of ocean from various heights. So beautiful, so well remembered, and yet so strange to me, a native son who had become more familiar with an environment of asphalt, concrete, metal, and glass.

I was thinking of that contrast when I arrived at Drake's Seat, the tourist attraction above Magens Bay. It is actually a seat; a large stone bench where it is said Sir Francis himself would perch to take in the view, or watch for his fleet, or something like that. The standing zone in front of the monument was crowded: two open-air, canopied buses were stopped there, and more than twenty tourists milled about, pointing, laughing, and clambering over what was once reserved for the great man alone.

I'd never stopped here in all the years I'd lived on the island because it was for tourists. Oh, what the hell, I thought; I'm a tourist now, too. I pulled over and got out of the car.

It was lovely: the bench, the boisterous visitors, the panoramic stretch of Magens Bay below us. I could feel the sun burning down on my skin, smell the fragrant air. I leaned back against the hood of my rental car and lit a cigarette.

A little blond girl, not impressed by the view or the historical fascination of the seat, arrived before me and held up a grubby, much-fondled doll for my inspection. I smiled and reached down to shake the doll's hand, but the child, immediately suspicious, clutched it to her and beat a hasty retreat. A taxi arrived from the direction of the beach and deposited a fresh-faced young couple—obviously honeymooners—in our midst. A blue Mustang appeared from the opposite road, the one that had brought me here, and pulled up behind a bus. An enormous young blond man emerged and went to the railing, his back to me, to gaze out at the view. Behind me, in front of the sacred bench, three men and a woman who were old enough to know better were attempting a four-part harmonized rendition of a popular Calypso song with more laughter than musical notes. A large group was collected around them, applauding and encouraging them with loud good nature. A sudden, cool breeze through the clear afternoon sunlight brought with it the faint scent of tropical flowers.

Heaven. It even said so on the license plates: America's Paradise. No wonder there were so many vacationers. Where else could you see this? Hubert Jensen's death seemed all the more macabre. How could it have happened here, on this island? Murder had no place here. That kind of anger, that much hatred: why these in a place where everything was acceptable, as long as one was acceptably eccentric? I would have to think about that.

I looked around again. The impromptu concert had come to an uproarious end. The buses were pulling away, bearing their happy, sunburned cargo off to further delights. The honeymooners had produced a camera and were asking the large blond man to take a photo. Without turning, without speaking, he waved them away.

Great, buddy, I thought. You don't look like a tourist: that's a wonderful way for a local to treat the people who are the island's primary source of income. I motioned to the couple. They handed me the Polaroid and stood grinning, arms about each other, with the vista behind them. Snap. When I gave back the camera, I congratulated them on their wedding and welcomed them to the Virgin Islands. With a smile for them and an annoyed glance in the direction of the blond man, I got back in my car.

Time had flown: I now had fifteen minutes to get to the Reef. I made my way as quickly as possible down the hill to town, around the Waterfront, past Haven View and out to the hotel. Luckily for me, there was actually a parking space in the overcrowded lot, not too far from the main entrance.

As I was locking the car door, the sudden, loud honking of a horn caused me to glance back at the entrance to the lot. A car had stopped there, right in the middle of the road, and the taxi behind it was blasting, telling it to get a move on. The first car's engine revved, and it turned quickly around and sped out of the lot and away toward town, but not before I had a good look at it and its driver.

It was the large blond man in the blue Mustang.

*   *   *

The Frenchman's Reef Holiday Inn is an amalgam of the usual and the unexpected. The buildings themselves are the standard, generic piles one finds everywhere in the world. Classification: resort hotel, subsection: tropical. Eight stories high; a study in white symmetry, wrapped rather dramatically around a cliff on a point facing the harbor. A spacious lobby, complete with loud carpet, loud fountain, and loud, exotic birds in loud, exotic cages. Several restaurants, bars, and night clubs; huge blue-green swimming pool; upper and lower concourses of shops; and the inevitable glass elevator descending from the hotel to Morning Star Beach, site of beachfront bungalows, more restaurants, bars and shops, tennis courts, volleyball net, and equipment for all conceivable water sports. Everything and more for the discriminating visitor.

I found Elsa on the patio just off the lower concourse, next to the crowded bar above the crowded pool. The sun poured down on the hotel and everything gleamed, including her golden hair and her lovely, suntanned face. I almost hadn't recognized her with her dark sunglasses and wide-brimmed straw hat, a huge pink hibiscus flower tucked behind her left ear. She was executing a pastel study of a large woman who sat facing the easel, smiling self-consciously. Several tourists in standard-issue uniform—"I slept on a Virgin (Island)" T-shirts, white tennis shorts and sneakers, peeling pink faces accented with streaks of white Noskote—had gathered behind her, marveling at every stroke.

She smiled up at me. "One moment, I'm almost finished." She signed her name with a small flourish, slipped the portrait into a matte frame, and presented it to the delighted tourist. The woman's husband handed her several bills as the crowd dispersed. She pocketed the money, hung a small OUT TO LUNCH sign on the easel, and led me over to a wrought iron table by the bar.

"Another day, another dollar," she sighed as she sank into a chair, removed the hat and glasses, and dropped them on the table. "I realize it's hopelessly *turista*, but I'd love a strawberry daiquiri."

"So would I." I signaled to the waitress. When she had gone, I jerked a thumb in the direction of the abandoned easel and said, "If you don't mind my asking, how much do you get for those pictures?"

"Depends. That one was thirty. Plain charcoal is twenty. Watercolors begin at fifty, growing with the size of the portrait the client requests."

"Wow. Seems like a lot for fifteen minutes of work."

"I don't charge for fifteen minutes of work. I charge for a lifetime of knowledge."

I laughed. "Very clever."

Her eyes crinkled. "I didn't make it up. Picasso beat me to it." She leaned forward, her arms resting on the table, smiling at me as the huge goblets of juice, crushed ice, and rum garnished with bright red fruit were lowered before us. She was wearing a faded denim workshirt, the bottom of which was tied across her midriff, and a white wraparound skirt over a red bikini. The hibiscus glowed pale pink against her pale yellow hair. With an effort, I avoided openly staring at her. I squirmed a little in my seat, trying to accommodate my suddenly crowded jeans.

"So," she said at last, her searchlight gaze unwavering, "how are you enjoying your vacation so far?"

I leaned back against the chair. The cold iron seared my warm skin, and my pants relaxed considerably. Reality came rushing back: Drake's Seat, the parking lot, the shrill blast of the car horn.

"I'm not sure," I replied before I thought better of it. "I was doing fine until a few minutes ago."

"Anything wrong?"

I remembered myself in time and shook my head. "Not really. I'm just not used to all this unfiltered sunlight. It's been a long time since I've felt it—we don't have it in New York, you know."

I decided, instinctively, not to tell her about the car that had been following me all afternoon. And it had been, I was certain. I just hadn't noticed it until the end of my travels. Had the man been in the restaurant, I wondered, watching me eat eggs Benedict with Lee? God. . . .

"Hello," Elsa said.

I looked up. "Sorry." Talk, Joe, I commanded myself. You've always wanted to be sitting at a table with this woman. Do something. "So . . . I, umm, I understand you sell your paintings in the galleries downtown."

"Yes." She played with the straw in her drink. "I always painted, but never seriously. Not until Bruce died. Of course, after that it was a while before I wanted to do anything, but when I did, I decided it was art. I'd certainly had enough courses in school, and I wanted to know if I could do it for real, you know, for a living. So one day I went down to the beach below my house and set up an easel." She laughed, gazing down at the pool on the cliffside patio below us. "The first attempt was not a success. Something abstract—my first and last experiment with that particular style. But then I realized that I'd been standing there for hours, throwing paint at a canvas, and for the first time in years I was completely relaxed. I liked that. So the next day I tried again. A sea-

scape this time, from life: I simply painted the scene before my eyes."

When she paused, I felt an instinctive need to inter-
ject. "How did it turn out?"

She shook her head absently. "It was very strange.
Water is a difficult model: I should have failed miserably.
It didn't seem as if I was trying something new, but as if
I was remembering something I'd done before." She
looked up, into my eyes. "Several hours later I was standing on that beach staring at my first completed painting.
I still don't understand—it's as if I'd gone into some sort
of trance and someone else had come along and done it,
then I'd awakened to find it there."

I knew the feeling. It's come to me when I've written,
but I'd never heard anyone describe it so vividly before.
It happens very rarely.

"I'd like to see that painting," I said.

She smiled. "Oh, I expect you will. It's in my living
room, over the piano."

"You can play the piano, too?"

She shook her head. "Bruce did."

Bruce, not Bunky. Next subject. "Your home is near
Haven View, isn't it?"

"Yes. Just up the road a piece, as they say. It's on the
hill above a tiny private beach, the one I mentioned.
Where I paint."

I nodded. "You must mean Shell Beach. I know it.
The Musketeers used to swim there. All that property
used to belong to the Jensens."

She was fingering the straw again. "It still does, as far
as I know. We bought our house from him—Hubert."

I reached for my cigarettes and slowly, carefully lit
one. I needed time to digest that, and time to stop a flood

of questions from spilling out of me. I'd always fantasized about getting to know Elsa well: I wasn't going to spoil this chance by alienating her. Not even for Frank. Still, I couldn't help wondering. They'd bought the house from Hubert. Bunky—excuse me, *Bruce*—had committed suicide. For several years Elsa had been using that private beach, one to which only the Jensens, beside herself, had access. And Hubert had placed a phone call to her on the last night of his life. . . .

As if I had spoken, she shook her head. "No, Joe. Please. I know Frank Jensen is a friend of yours, but if you don't mind, I'd rather not discuss that family. I guess you've been told that the judge called me the night he was killed, but I had nothing to do with his death. I—I'd been thinking of buying the beach property, and he was just returning my calls. I went over all that with the police."

I stared. "Elsa, why are you telling me this? I didn't say anything."

She shrugged and finished her drink. "Frank is your best friend. You'd naturally be curious. And you'd be too tactful to come right out and ask the girl you were so crazy about when we were kids."

"You knew?" I whispered, feeling the blood rising to my face.

Elsa laughed, and her lovely blond hair glinted in the sunlight. She reached over to touch my hand.

"Oh, Joe, you are so sweet. Of course I knew. You might as well have been wearing a sandwich board."

"You never let on," I said. "In fact, you pretty well ignored me."

She lowered her eyes. "I can only apologize by citing

two reasons. I was young, and I was in love—but not with you."

No, not with me. Bruce, alias Bunky.

"Back to the drawing board," she said, rising. "And you'll probably be going down to the beach to say hello to Frank's wife."

"I didn't know she was there."

"Oh, yes. Playing volleyball, I expect. If you do drop in, say hello to Willie Whitney for me. He's the man I was with at the Brandt's party." She smiled as I stood up. "Next time, we talk about you. I want to hear about your writing."

"Next time?"

"Yes." She indicated the easel across the patio. "You know where to find me."

She was leaving the bar, moving toward the easel, when I said, "Willie Whitney—he was your date the other night?"

She turned around. "That's right."

I will never learn to shut up. Before I could stop myself I had said, "Judge Jensen called him, too."

The warmth drained from her eyes.

"Yes," she said, and then she walked away.

My third meeting with Tangera Jensen began with my falling at her feet.

When I had discarded shirt, sneakers, and socks to join the volleyball game, she was nowhere in sight. Willie said she was around somewhere, and he insisted on my coming to the aid of his bedraggled little team. He, two giggling young women, and an older gentleman with an obvious propensity for liquor were being slaughtered by three boys and two girls on the other side of the net. I had to wait for Tangera to show up anyway, so why not?

Considering that with his towering height, red mane, and powerful limbs he resembled nothing more than an ad for Nautilus, Willie was unbelievably awkward. He couldn't hit the ball to save his life. His ridiculous performance sent the women and the drunk into paroxysms, so they weren't much help, either. Within minutes I was running all over our half of the court, somehow managing to send a surprising number of failed setups and net balls back to the other side. By the time I had singlehandedly raised the score from 14–3 to 19–18, I was all but hyperventilating. The drunk disappeared at one point and returned with a can of beer, which he held while he played, and Willie was beaned when he decided, in midplay, to steal a kiss from one of our female teammates. The other woman, seeing this, giggled herself right down into the sand where she lay, holding her sides and shaking with laughter, as the ball sailed slowly over the net to land, very neatly, some three inches from her. 20–18. The five people facing us were all blond, blue-eyed, and unsmilingly silent. Their resemblance to Nazis was not merely physical: that well-oiled, five-part machine was going to win this one for the Fatherland.

And win they did. It was on the game point that I—the only member of my team who was still standing—took a futile dive to return an unreturnable smash and landed facedown in the sand. The orange toenails on the lovely, cinnamon-colored feet an inch before my eyes informed me, before I looked up, that Tangera had arrived.

"Why, Joseph, how lovely of you to drop in! Now, you will please abandon that ridiculous posture and accompany Mr. Whitney and me to the bar."

* * *

The sun was setting on the ocean in front of us, and most of the beach crowd had left for dinner. I would have to go soon, too.

The three of us were on chaise longues. I had a cigarette, and Willie was smoking a joint. At Tangera's insistence, we were all sipping piña coladas.

"Haven't had one of these in years," Willie said, indicating his drink. "Beer, usually." He produced a vial of cocaine from a pocket, offered it with no takers, shrugged, and sniffed a bit into each nostril from the tiny spoon on a chain around his neck. Perhaps, I thought, this explained his volleyball technique—or lack thereof.

Tangera, in orange bikini, orange-framed shades, and orange lacquered coolie hat, was quite a vision as she reclined between us.

"I wish you would not do that," she drawled to Willie. "I have no desire to spend the night in jail—certainly not in St. Thomas."

"Yes, Your Majesty," he grinned, inserting roach into clip.

She turned to me. "My friends take pleasure in provoking me. This gentleman, Joseph, is a major supplier— and consumer—of what I suppose you could call recreational substances. I find nothing recreational about them. What brings you to Morning Star today?"

I told her of my meeting with Elsa at the hotel.

Willie said, "Great lady, Elsa. Good artist, good dancer. Good people."

Tangera said nothing. She leaned forward, looking out at the ocean. After a moment, she rose and wandered down to the water's edge.

Willie laughed. "I think we may get a forecast."

"Excuse me?" I said.

He pointed. "She does that sometimes. ESP—something like that." He rolled over on his chaise to face me. "So, you had a date with Elsa."

Here we go, I thought. "Listen, I'm not interfering in anything, am I?"

He shook his head. "I'm just a pal. I was a friend of Bunky's. We hang out occasionally, that's all. If you're interested, go for it." He lit another joint.

"What happened to Bunky?" I asked.

Willie was silent for a moment, then he sat up. "He had a lot of problems. Did you know him?"

"Not really. We were in different groups when we were growing up."

"Well," he said, "he was kind of stupid. He took over his family's gift shops when his father died. He'd always been supported by his family, and the shops were his chance to prove he wasn't just another spoiled rich kid. He wanted to be a big shot. Of course, he *was* just another spoiled rich kid. He had no idea about business. He ran the shops into the ground. Borrowed a lot of money to keep them open, then lost them, anyway. Elsa took a job in a restaurant. They almost had to sell their house. He kind of lost touch with reality. He started loafing around, doing drugs."

I stared at the joint in his hand.

"Oh, no," he said. "I didn't give him anything. Never. I knew he was too crazy to deal with—well, anyway, he owed lots of money, and he was about to end up in prison. I offered to lend them some bucks, but Elsa said no. He just kind of hung out; drinking, using, messing with women—Elsa hit the roof when she found out

about that! She threatened to leave him. The whole island was talking about it. Bad scene."

Tangera wandered up and down the beach. The sun
had disappeared. I looked at my watch. Lee would be
wondering where I was, but I couldn't leave. Not yet.

"What about his death?" I asked.

Willie shrugged and lay down again. "Well, things
got worse and worse, you know? Elsa says that in those
last couple of weeks he started threatening to—do it.
Pack it in. He didn't mention it to anyone else, not even
me. Just her. I wasn't on the island when it happened.
According to Elsa, he just disappeared one night. Went
down to the beach below his house, took some downers,
drank a bottle of Tequila, took off all his clothes, and
went for a swim. He washed up on the sand the next
morning. She found him. She kind of lost it for a while,
but not for long. She's a toughie. They never proved suicide, so the insurance came through."

He stared out over the ocean. When he spoke again,
it was in a sad whisper. "I sure wish he'd come to me. He
never said a word about—what Elsa said he was planning.
Don't you think you'd tell your best bud if you were . . ."
He trailed off, shaking his head.

After a moment, I asked, "What about his debts?"

He snapped out of his reverie and returned his attention to me. "They were canceled. Whoever lent Bunky
the money told Elsa she didn't have to pay."

I shook my head. "Banks don't do that."

"It wasn't from a bank," Willie said. "He tried taking
loans from every bank in town, but they turned him
down. Bad risk. He must have gotten it from a private
source."

"And who was that?"

"Don't know."

I took a breath and plunged. "Why did the judge call you the night he died?"

Willie stared at me a moment. I looked away.

"His wife had approached me a few times," he said at last, "asking for stuff. I never gave her anything, but he found out about it. He called to tell me that if I ever helped her out, he'd put me in jail."

I nodded. "Did you tell that to the police?"

"Sure."

"And they didn't do anything?"

He shrugged. "Do what?"

This is St. Thomas, Frank had said. I was beginning to see what he meant.

I tried one more idea. "These islands have always been the major drop for—recreational substances— between South America and the States. You probably know some of the big people in that scene. Would any of them have anything particular to fear from Hubert Jensen?"

"No," Willie said without hesitation. "Nothing particular. Those are pretty bad guys; you know, outlaws. It wouldn't matter to them who was governor here. Jensen was determined to stop them, I guess, but no more determined than Hughes, or the last governor—or the next one, likely as not. They wouldn't endanger their route by bringing that kind of attention to themselves. They didn't have anything to do with offing Jensen."

I nodded. What he said made perfect sense. No, Hubert Jensen's killer was closer to home: I was certain of it.

Tangera rejoined us as we were rising to leave. Her

usual blithe attitude had completely disappeared: she seemed preoccupied.

"You are coming to Haven View for dinner the day after tomorrow," she told me as she collected her things.

"Am I invited?" Willie asked.

She shook her head. "Good-bye, Willie. I will see you here tomorrow."

"Okay." He gave me a military salute, kissed her hand, and loped off down the beach in the direction of the bar.

We walked to her car. She was silent as we got into the convertible and rode up the hill to the hotel parking lot. She pulled up next to my rental car and turned to face me.

"It is not over," she said.

I stared. "What is not over?"

"I am not sure. Something is about to happen. I know this feeling. It came over me while we were all sitting there."

I studied her expression. "Does it have to do with me?"

"I think so." She looked away, in the direction of the hotel entrance. Then, apparently coming to some sort of decision, she turned again and looked at me, into my eyes. "The feeling I had just now on the beach—I have had it before, and recently. At the party the other night, just as I was coming to say good-bye to you. There was a—a presence. That is the only way I can describe it." She took a long breath and slowly let it out. "I think someone is watching you."

"Yes," I said. "I know."

The surprise registered on her face. "Who?"

"I don't know," I told her, "but I intend to find out."

I got out of her car and walked over to my own, aware of her intense gaze as I reached in my pocket for the keys.

"I will see you at Haven View," she called. "Be careful, Joseph."

I stood in the parking lot next to my car, watching the silver Corvette speed away.

6

TARANTELLA

Tangera's prediction came true the very next day.

As I was leaving my sister's house early in the afternoon, her housekeeper handed me a phone message. Dennis Grey wanted me to visit him at his home at five-thirty. I called him at his office and accepted.

I walked down the Ninety-nine Steps into town. My first stop was the stationery store on Garden Street at the foot of Government Hill. I bought two wire-bound notebooks, one for starters and one as a silent promise to myself. I always do that when I am beginning a new writing project. I'd already paid for them, plus two ball-point pens, before I realized what I was doing. This isn't a writing project, I thought: why do I need notebooks? Oh, well . . .

Three parallel roads make up the principal downtown area of Charlotte Amalie. There were five cruise ships in port that day, and the Waterfront and Main Street were packed and busy. I decided my best bet for a quiet lunch would be Back Street. Wandering down that relatively peaceful thoroughfare, I came upon a secluded little shopping center housing, among other things, a shady courtyard with an open-air restaurant of Middle Eastern design called—naturally—Sinbad's. Only three tables were occupied, so I took possession of a fourth, away from the other patrons.

I made short work of something-or-other on pita bread and two glasses of iced cinnamon tea, ordered coffee from the pretty girl in the obligatory pseudo-Arabian Nights garb, and reached for a notebook. The chatter of the tourists and locals at the other tables faded in the cool, shadowy interior of the café as I sorted things out in my mind, preparing to put pen to paper.

I had some notion of re-creating the murder, step by step, to see if any of it indicated a person, or even a type of personality. Could I fit the incidents of that night six months ago to what I knew of Frank? Helen? Anyone? We're always being told that everyone is potentially capable of murder, but very few people ever actually do it. What sort of person is that?

Staring down at the empty, blue-lined white page, I had another thought. Why a machete? Of all things. If, indeed, it had been the Jensens' machete. There's something so dramatic, so vivid about that particular implement. It has a history in this part of the world. Before the advent of Columbus, two tribes of native West Indians were here, one peaceful and one violent. The Arawaks and the Caribs had many crude tools and weapons. Quite a few of them were on display in the museum at Fort Christian, not three blocks from where I sat. Several of these artifacts resembled machetes. The cutting of sugar

cane, the forging of pathways through tropical under-
growth, the harvesting of coconuts and other local foods:
a machete. There was something almost symbolic, ritual-
istic, about it. Mongoose, iguana, hibiscus, frangipani,
palm, coconut, mango, tamarind, rum, rattan, ceiling
fans, voodoo, obeah—machete.

Frank, Helen, Tangera. Tangera's letter had brought
me here. Something is wrong, she had said. There are
secrets. You are Frank's oldest friend. Please come. . . .

Abel and Abby Brandt. His friend and his mistress.
He and Abel were planning a multimillion dollar series
of condos, hotels, shopping centers: a lot of money.
Money is always a motive; just ask Agatha Christie. Wait
a minute—what money? These plans required that Hubert become governor. The new governor, Hughes, had
other policies. . . .

Willie Whitney and Biff Court. No, they were too
removed from the action, somehow. I had spoken to one
and I would speak to the other, but what could they tell
me? I dismissed them.

Hubert Jensen in the leather chair, headless. Bunky
Tremayne on the beach, naked, facedown, the water
washing rhythmically over him. Elsa . . .

Elsa?

I had been followed yesterday. Why?

The notebook was still blank. I would have to begin
somewhere. In my mind I formed a list of names, preparing to write them down:

Frank—Helen—Tangera—Abel.

Below these, I would group the long shots:

Willie Whitney—Biff Court—Governor Hughes—
Abby Brandt.

I hesitated before mentally adding a fifth name:

Elsa.

When I finally picked up the pen and destroyed the pristine surface of the paper, I did not record the list, nor did I jot down any of the thoughts that had run through my mind in the past few minutes. What I wrote was simple, succinct, and completely surprising. Four words, staring up at me:

Why am I here?

A loud laugh made me look up from the notebook. A noisy couple laden with shopping bags entered the restaurant area. Beyond them, the courtyard was busier than when I had arrived. Several couples and groups were milling about, chattering and pointing. Still more were coming in through the archway from the street—

He was standing in the shadows, close against the vaulted wall of the archway at the street entrance to the courtyard, watching me. Our eyes met for a single second. Then a woman with two small children bustled in from the street and across the square, chiding one of her charges to stop fidgeting and stay close. By the time they had passed by, the archway was deserted.

I was on my feet and running through the tables, down the steps from the dining area and across the courtyard, only dimly aware of the surprised faces of people parting before me and the angry cries of the waitress. When I reached the street, I halted and swiftly scanned both directions. Cars passed, tourists wandered to and fro on the tiny sidewalk; otherwise, nothing. There were several doorways along both sides of Back Street, and there was a cross street a few yards away. He could be anywhere, running down an alley or crouched in any one of several cul-de-sacs mere feet from where I stood. And, of course, there was always his car, the blue Mustang. . . .

It never occurred to me that he might still be in the courtyard. That's why I was so surprised when the attack came from behind me. A large hand clamped down on my left shoulder and whirled me violently around. I staggered backward a few steps, away from my assailant, and assumed a defensive position.

"Okay, you son of a bitch," I yelled, planting my feet and raising my fists. "What the hell do you think you're—"

I stopped, and my arms dropped to my sides. The large man facing me was not the blond guy from the Mustang. He wasn't even Caucasian. Arab, most likely.

"Hey, mister," he said, holding up a slip of paper, "you weren't going to leave without paying, were you?"

A few minutes later, having settled the bill and retrieved the plastic bag with the two notebooks, I stood in the courtyard wondering what to do next.

I was angry. Who the hell was that man, and—more important—who employed him? When guys that size are not on professional football fields, they are often what you could call muscle. Someone wanted an account of my every move, but why? Who was I? A writer visiting his sister in his old hometown was hardly a threat to anybody.

Or was I? I had been asked to come here. How many people knew about that? Of course, I could call Tangera. She would know if she'd told anyone about the letter, or—

Or she could have hired the muscle herself. Yesterday she had "seen" me being followed in her visions, or whatever she called them. Maybe she knew it without any help from Beyond. Maybe she knew everything. After all, she was a logical suspect. But, if that were the case, why ask me to come here in the first place? And why me, for that matter? Why not a professional investigator?

God, I thought, you could go crazy from the questions. But I knew one thing for sure: I wasn't going to tell anyone else that I knew I was being followed. I would find the man myself, and there was only one way to do that.

I walked back to Garden Street and turned right into the large square in front of the main post office. Any resident of the island will tell you that Main Street basically extends from the post office to the old Market Square, several blocks west. Beyond these points is the bulk of the stores and shopping centers catering to the tourist industry. I would walk the length of the street to Market Square and back. He had shown himself twice already: maybe three times lucky. Only this time he wouldn't get away. I would lead him into a confrontation from which he couldn't escape, and I knew just how I would do it.

Along the street are several malls; alleyways running from Main Street to the Waterfront, lined on either side with shops. Palm Passage and International Plaza were too wide; large, open-air shopping centers with no place to hide. But there was one place, in the middle of my route, that would serve my purposes perfectly. It used to be called Beretta Center when I was a child, but now it was known as Royal Dane Mall. It was actually several ancient stone warehouses side by side, with narrow cobblestone passageways criss crossing between them. Dark, confusing paths: the old architects of the West Indies had been fond of archways and cul-de-sacs. As children, the Musketeers had chosen it as the ideal setting for endless games of hide-and-seek, to the chagrin of the harried shopkeepers. It was a virtual labyrinth of roundabouts and dead ends. Foliage abounded in the narrow alleyways, and flowerbeds between the shop doorways burst with wall-climbing masses of green, dotted liberally with yellow, white, and red flowers. I would lead him into this maze, wait in some concealing corner, and grab him. That was the plan, anyway.

I remember wondering, as I walked slowly down the street, if I could find some sort of weapon. Many of the shops sold souvenir Swiss Army knives . . . no. If the guy had intended to harm me, he'd already had several opportunities. His business was apparently to watch and report.

Nonchalance. I looked around me at the shops on both sides of the busy street, all the while scanning the crowds for an enormous blond man in a gray suit. As I walked, I became increasingly aware of the many changes. Very few of the stores were familiar. Most were new and along the same lines: they all had Arab and Indian sounding names, and they all prominently displayed tacky T-shirts ("I'm a Virgin," "I Slept on a Virgin," "My Mother Is a Virgin") and discount stereo equipment. What had once been a charming center for native crafts and quality imported goods was now distinctly seedy. There were still the occasional excellent places for duty-free jewelry and liquor; the lovely, well-appointed shops I remembered from my childhood: Cardow, H. Stern, Tropicana, Bolero, A. H. Riise. But these were surrounded by the T-shirt/electronic Middle Eastern places. How did any of them make a profit, I wondered, if they all sold the same merchandise? It was a crime, really. This beautiful place had been deliberately, systematically desecrated. . . .

He was there, on the other side of the street, slightly behind me. He was making an attempt to keep crowds of shoppers between us, and when I turned my head, he ducked into a shop doorway. The meeting ground I had chosen was in the middle of the next block. Fixing my gaze straight ahead of me, I continued on my way. As long as I knew where he was, I was relatively—

A hand shot out in front of my face, clutching something metallic and gleaming. I took an involuntary step backward and raised a protective arm.

"Genuine silver, mister. For your girlfriend. Only—"

I thrust the hand away and moved on. Hawkers. They seemed to be on every corner; just one more way to turn what had once been a quaint West Indian street into a teeming Baghdad bazaar.

I slowed my pace as I neared the entrance to my trap, waiting for a boisterous gaggle walking behind me to catch up. Under cover of the crowd, I slid sideways into the mall and began to run. The cool, dark shadows of the passage swallowed me. With any luck it would take him a few seconds, even minutes, to figure out where I had gone.

I'd forgotten about the odd echo produced here by footsteps and voices. The walls of the buildings were comprised of huge stones held together by a West Indian recipe for mortar, which allegedly included a mixture of sand and sugar cane molasses to supplement the usual limestone and cement, precious commodities hereabouts in the seventeenth and eighteenth centuries when many of the island's warehouses, sugar mills, and plantation houses were built. These walls were thirty feet high and often two feet thick, and the parallel buildings were placed close together. The cobblestone passageways between them were perhaps six feet wide. In this rabbit warren of some twelve long buildings in four rows stretching the hundred yards from the Waterfront to Main Street, the slightest sound caused a reverberation. The flat, electronic-sounding noise would roll up and down the alleys, misleading the hearer. It was difficult to ascertain from which direction the sound was coming. Good, I thought as I ducked down the first of several branches of the puzzle. If I'm confused, then so is he. Soon I will stop and wait. . . .

Apparently, he had not been fooled. Almost immediately I heard the other set of running footsteps behind me, a loud, steady tattoo.

Considering the number of ships in port, the mall was quiet at the moment. It was about three o'clock, and most of the tourists had shopped and dined already. They'd progressed to bus tours and beaches for the final precious hours before sunset, when the boats would sail.

I rounded two corners, ran past several shops, and emerged in the third of the three parallel passageways. I stopped for a moment, listening. No running behind me now, only voices in the distance and the approaching sound of normal footsteps. He had slowed down.

There was nobody in sight in this alley. Good; a private meeting. I planted myself in full view at the crossroads joining two paths and waited. The sound of the footsteps became louder. Here he comes, I thought. . . .

It was not my pursuer. The native man who came around the corner was younger than I, tall and slim, in jeans. I must have been a vision of distress because he halted when he saw me. Then, with a smile, he stepped forward. I had been mistaken for a tourist lost in the maze, and this kid was going to offer me assistance. I began to frame a polite dismissal in my mind as the young man came up to me and stopped. I would have to get rid of him, and quickly.

When his arm came up, flashing silver, my first thought was, oh, great, another peddler. Only he wasn't a peddler, and he wasn't holding a silver-plated copper necklace. The blade of the knife in his hand was at least six inches long.

The wave of shock that hit me shifted everything into slow motion. I raised my left arm in front of me as the knife sliced down. It glanced off just below my elbow. In my right hand I clutched the bag with the notebooks: I brought it up and smashed it into his face. He fell backward against a stone wall of the alley, legs splaying. The knife fell from his hand. The bag fell from mine. I stepped into the space between his spread legs and brought my right knee up, hard, into his groin. He cried out and slid down the wall to a sitting position.

I ran. At the next corner, I shot a glance back over my shoulder. Already he had risen and picked up the knife.

I cut across alleys, down, back, zigzagging wildly and without aim. The echoing sounds of running footsteps seemed to be coming from all directions at once. At one point, I flew around a corner and barreled into a tourist woman. Both of us went down, her shopping bags flying off to spill their contents in the alleyways. I was up immediately, pulling her to her feet and mumbling an apology. She looked down at the front of her yellow dress and screamed. I was already running again before it registered in my mind that the blood on her dress was mine. My left arm was bright red from elbow to wrist, from the long scratch of the knife.

Time receded from my consciousness. I don't know

for how long I dodged back and forth between alleys, through stores, up and down. I remember horrified faces, and shouts from shoppers and salespeople. And I remember the pounding footsteps behind me, before me, everywhere. Frantically I considered the alternatives: double back to Main Street to emerge in protective crowds, or make my way to the wide open space of the Waterfront. The problem was that at this point I'd lost my bearings. I wasn't sure in which direction I was heading, or where my attacker was. If I tried a long run down a main artery, he might catch up with me.

I saw him once, through the doors of a shop, running down the next alley in the opposite of my direction. I made my way across to what I suddenly realized was the mall leading to the main entrance. The restaurant, L'Escargot, was before me, and just up the alley to my left was Main Street. Escape. What could he do to me there, in broad daylight? I turned and headed for the bright, sunlit entrance.

I didn't get two steps. A sea of gray rose up before me and I smashed into the massive chest of the enormous blond man. I'd forgotten all about him. So, there were two of them, I thought as he raised his hands and grasped my shoulders.

Oh, God, this was no way to die; at the hands of strangers in a deserted alley. I looked wildly around me: no one, anywhere. People passed in front of the entrance on Main Street, but they were too far away. I'd have to try anyway, I thought as he pushed me back against a wall. I opened my mouth and filled my lungs.

My shout was cut off by the vicious clamp of his hand.

"Hush!" he hissed. His face was not two inches from mine, his linebacker's bulk pinning me to the wall.

Then he did the most extraordinary thing. Suddenly, he released his hold on me and stepped back. He cocked his head as if listening for something. It was at this moment that I became aware of the echo, the other running footsteps. His accomplice would arrive at any moment, and between them they would dispose of me.

Our eyes met, mine wide with panic and his two angry slits. He reached with his right hand into his gray jacket and pulled out a gun. From his left coat pocket he produced a two-inch cylinder of bluish-black metal that he quickly screwed onto the end of the weapon.

This wasn't happening. It was all so unreal, so cliché, straight out of a television crime show. He wouldn't dare shoot me here.

Shock arrived upon shock. He looked straight into my eyes and raised the gun. Then he brought up his left hand in front of my face. The message was so universally recognizable that he might as well have spoken: stay here. Don't move.

We both turned at the same instant. The young man with the knife came running around the corner in front of the restaurant and halted not ten feet from us. For one insane, frozen second, he and the large man with the gun regarded each other. I looked from one to the other of them. The world stopped and all of us waited.

Then the young man's eyes widened. In a flash, he pivoted and raced off the way he had come. The big man reached out and grabbed my arm, pushing me roughly toward the entrance to the mall.

"Go," he barked. "Get out of here!"

With that, he brought up the gun and took off after the other man.

I don't think now that I stood there for more than a

few seconds, staring out at the cars and passersby, the sanity just yards ahead outside the alley. It would have been so very easy to walk forward into the street, the crowd, the welcoming sunlight. . . .

I turned around and ran back into the darkness. The first main alley was empty, as was the second. I raced on into the third, and, finding it also deserted, flew down the entire length of the center to the Waterfront. I burst out of the shadows into dazzling white sunlight. I stopped, waiting for my eyes to adjust. When I could see again I glanced swiftly to left and right: nothing. Scanning the huge esplanade along the sea wall across Veteran's Drive, I could see only pedestrians, boats, and seagulls going about their usual business. The two men had disappeared.

I stood there for several moments, catching my breath. Then I went back into the alley and retrieved my bag from where it had fallen in the scuffle. As I made my way back to Main Street, I began to tremble. The full effect was finally beginning to register. The weird, dreamlike quality of the incident—well, it was hardly surprising that the men had vanished. I had only my scratched and bleeding arm to prove that the whole thing had actually happened. The knife, the hand over my mouth; but for these, they might well have been phantoms, what people in this part of the world would call jumbies, arriving from nowhere, performing their mischief, and evaporating.

After a while, the trembling gave way to giddiness. I remember my surprise at finding that I was giggling. A bunch of grown men tearing around, playing cops and robbers in a public place. Ridiculous. Something the

Musketeers would do. Well, it was over now. So why couldn't I stop laughing?

Everyone on the street stared at me as I passed. Blood dripped from my saturated sleeve to the sidewalk, a trail of bright red drops all the way down Main Street. I was late. I had to get back to the house. Clean up. Bandage my wound. Meet Dennis. Ha ha. Oh, my ears and whiskers, I'm late, said the White Rabbit. Nonsense, cried Alice, you're nothing but a pack of cards. . . .

"You're looking well," Dennis said.

I stared. Was that a joke? Apparently not. Perhaps I did look okay, at that. A hot shower, a large bandage on my forearm, and fresh clothes had certainly made me feel better. A light jacket concealed the bandage. Had water not been the precious commodity it is in St. Thomas, and long showers an unaffordable luxury, I might have remained under the cleansing, calming spray for hours.

We were in the enormous, magnificently appointed living room of Great House, the Grey's imposing Danish residence on the top of the hill above the center of Charlotte Amalie. Doors and windows stood open to let in the late afternoon breeze, and through them we looked out at the city and the harbor and, beyond them, the wide expanse of the Atlantic Ocean. Frosty, fruity drinks had been served to us, and the local rum therein was further soothing my jagged nerves. I lounged in an overstuffed planter's chair and concentrated on appearing completely at ease. I was not going to relate today's events to anyone outside of my family until I had an opportunity to evaluate everything and decide whether or not I would remain on the island. At that point, I definitely favored leaving.

I regarded my friend closely. The tall, silent, angry

boy I remembered had matured into quite a different person. The frown was gone, and with it the vague feeling I always got from him that at any moment he might burst into a violent rage. As children, Frank and I had grown so used to his sullen, quiet moods that we'd practically forgotten about them. We were always surprised when an outsider pointed them out.

Once, a girl in our high school class who had chased him around for weeks became peeved when she realized that her efforts were in vain. "That's not a chip on Dennis Grey's shoulder," she'd told a girlfriend in my presence. "It's a sequoia!"

Now, the man who stood before me in his living room was the complete antithesis of his former self. This new Dennis was poised, confident, even extroverted. He punctuated his conversation with quick, effortless laughter. He gave the distinct impression that whatever he was doing, he was in charge of it. He seemed to be completely happy now: I wondered, not for the first time, why the little boy had been so angry.

I thought about his job at Conservation and Cultural Affairs, and about the governor's beautiful daughter. I supposed he had a lot to be happy about. Before I knew what I was doing, I'd said it aloud.

Dennis laughed. He dropped into the chair next to mine, nodding. "Yes, you could say that. I've come a long way. And Jenny—well, she'd make anyone happy. I'm the luckiest slob in the world."

"I didn't notice at the party the other night," I said, "but you've changed. I hardly recognize you."

He smiled and leaned forward. "Don't misunderstand me; I haven't really changed that much. I still feel angry and frustrated. But in politics you learn about that.

You learn to sublimate those feelings. If you want to get work done, you can't sit around like Hamlet. You have to act. I care very much about certain things: this island, my family, Jenny. I'd do anything to keep them from harm, anything at all. Only now I'm much more capable of protecting them. No more of the silent act. I'm a politician!"

We laughed. I settled farther back into my chair, enjoying this new yet familiar man. He redirected the conversation to the subject of me. He asked after every member of my family. He wanted to know about New York, my novels and plays, my Greenwich Village apartment; everything. We talked for a long while as the shadows lengthened across the polished wood floor. I was at ease, relaxed, happy to be there.

At last, Dennis raised his planter's punch in a toast. "Wedding bells."

"Yes." I replied. "Its—what?—a month away now. May you both be very happy."

"Oh, I'll see to that," he said. "Do you know how long you're staying yet? I—*we* want you at the wedding. Can you possibly arrange it?"

I almost agreed then, that afternoon in that lovely house with the delicious drink in my hand, sharing warm feelings with one of my oldest friends. Almost. Then the unreality returned. The strange, dark feelings of Haven View and the unhappy family who lived there. The quiet air of sorrow and barely restrained violence. Two men: one with a knife, the other with a gun. That desperate, headlong chase through the shadowy, nearly deserted shopping center. It struck me then that this afternoon—in the Royal Dane Mall, of all places—I had come as close as I ever want to be. I had very nearly been killed.

"We'll see," I said. I forced a smile, dismissing the

panic, willing it not to return. A telephone on the other side of the room began to ring. Dennis ignored it. After a moment the ringing stopped.

"Okay," he conceded. "But at least you can come for dinner tomorrow night. Clay—Governor Hughes and his wife will be here. And Jenny, of course. I realize it's short notice—"

"Too short," I said. "Tomorrow night I'm going to dinner at the Jensens'."

His smile faded, and he muttered, "Better you than me."

I recalled the party, when he'd said something similar. Why?

"I'm sorry you can't make it," he went on before I could ask. "I was hoping you'd help my father entertain the ladies after dinner. The governor and I will be playing chess. It's become a tradition with us, every Friday night for the past two years. We always used to play at his house, but now they're in the middle of moving to Government House. They haven't settled in yet, so tomorrow night the game will be here. He doesn't like anyone watching him play, so we lock ourselves in a room together, just the two of us. Well, I guess the others can amuse themselves."

"Who wins?" I asked.

He laughed. "The governor, of course. *Always.* I don't want to lose my job—and now he's gonna be my father-in-law!"

We were laughing together when a houseman in a white steward's jacket arrived in the doorway. "Mistuh Grey, telephone. Dey say it's impahtant."

Dennis rose. "Thank you, Eldin. That's probably the Zoning Board. I hope they've made a decision. I'm fighting *more* condos, would you believe it? Our host from the other night. Pig. I should only be a few minutes."

"I have to be going," I said. "Lee will be wanting to see about dinner. Thanks for the drink."

"Sure." He grinned, shaking my hand and moving away toward the phone. "Give me a call sometime. Will you be at the party?"

"What party?"

"The Inaugural Ball. January twentieth. Bluebeard's Castle. Lee and Paul are invited, and so are you."

"Sounds great," I said. "Maybe I'll see you there."

He waved and picked up the receiver. I followed the houseman from the room. I'd barely begun to cross the foyer to the front door when the shouting began. Dennis was furious.

"*What?* Goddamn it, I told them *no!* That beach is world-famous. Now we're supposed to have those ghastly cement-block units all over the hill above it? It's obscene! I won't have it. Stop them!"

My friend, the politician. I smiled as the houseman opened the door for me. I thanked him and went out.

"I don't care *what* Abel Brandt promised them. That son of a bitch would sell his *wife* for cold, hard cash! As a matter of fact—"

The door closed.

7

MOONDANCE

On the evening of Friday, the fourth of January, there was a thunderstorm. The rain began shortly before sunset and continued throughout the night.

This time I was ready for Haven View. Even before I drove the rental car through the huge gates and around the curved driveway, I had braced myself for the strange, inexorable pull. I didn't resist it: I got out of the car and ran through the heavy, pounding rain across the flooded patio, up the steps, and straight into the house.

As Lucien, the gardener who doubled as waiter, lowered a large slice of German chocolate cake in front of me, I surveyed the table.

Helen was doing better this evening. She looked lovely, as ever, and she seemed to be more in touch with her surroundings than she'd been on my previous visit.

She and her daughter-in-law even spoke to each other from time to time.

Tangera was on my right at the round dinner table on the veranda. She wore—inevitably—a creamy orange cocktail dress, and she was making a particular effort to be charming to everyone.

Next to Tangera sat Dr. Deveaux, whom I had not seen since my last visit to his office some twelve years previously. He was that rare, enviable type of man who ages gracefully, growing ever more handsome and distinguished. The silver in his hair only added to the general impressiveness of his tall, lanky presence. The intense dark eyes and even white teeth were rendered all the more romantic by his deep, French-accented voice. Watching him, I silently cursed God for not having made me lanky. Well, at least I was tall. . . .

Frank, on the other side of the table, said little and ate less. He had barely touched his chicken divan, and now he was eyeing the cake with a decided lack of appetite. However, he had managed to consume at least two glasses of wine to supplement the two large drinks he'd had before dinner.

The rain continued to fall around us, making our cluster at the table seem that much more intimate. The lights of town in the distance could barely be seen through the downpour.

Throughout the meal I had been aware of Deveaux's exclusive concentration on Helen. He was a serious man, not given to light conversation or careless gestures. As a child I had been afraid of him. When I grew old enough to consider him as a person, not merely as the sinister, white-jacketed authoritarian who hurt me with shots and embarrassed me by touching my private parts, I was still aware of the cold detachment. I mentioned this to my parents once, and my mother had attempted to explain to her thirteen-year-old son the particulars of being a widower. Now, of course, his quiet behavior made more sense to me, but it was no longer in evidence. In fact, I would notice during that evening that his preoccupation with Helen bordered on obsession.

When dessert was finished, Helen announced that coffee would be served in the library, where a surprise awaited us. When we rose, I smiled as Deveaux fairly ran around the table to take Helen's arm and escort her into the house. Tangera attached herself to me, and Frank, who did not seem to be enthusiastic, slouched behind us, another full glass of wine in his hand.

The library was a beautiful room. The mahogany floor and furniture gleamed, as did the floor-to-ceiling bookshelves that covered the two longer walls. The end of the room that opened onto the veranda was dominated by a gorgeous Steinway grand piano. In the center of the floor was an enormous, deep blue and red Oriental rug. Looking back, I'd say this was the only downstairs room in the house I would describe as being cozy.

We settled on couches; Frank and I on one, Helen and Deveaux on the other. Tangera chose the leather-upholstered mahogany chaise longue in one corner, reclining in a pose that reminded me of paintings of Mme. Recamier. Helen served coffee from the silver service on the low table in front of her.

Eunice arrived in the room, followed by George. The child was dressed in a short-sleeved white shirt and black shorts, and he was carrying sheet music. So this was the surprise. George walked somewhat hesitantly to the piano and sat. Helen waved Eunice into a chair. Tangera clapped her hands in anticipation, everyone else smiled politely, and I grimly prepared myself for the inevitable, fumbling rendition of "Für Elise."

What followed could not have been more of a surprise. I will never forget that next hour. My initial shock was succeeded by delight. I've attended my share of piano concerts, but not one where the star was a ten-year-old boy. He began with a dramatic performance of "Solfegietto," his fingers flying expertly over the keyboard. This was followed by Beethoven's "Pathetique." After that, Bartok.

He paused after this, turning to look a question at Tangera. She nodded and rose from the chaise to join him. The two of them executed a wonderful, four-handed "Marche Militaire." Tangera returned to her seat, and George ended the recital with Rachmaninoff.

The others had heard him before, so I was the only one in the room who hadn't expected it. I applauded louder than they, and as George rose to leave, I shook his hand. He smiled shyly up at me, and then his mother ushered him from the room.

Lucien brought in a drinks tray. I stayed with coffee, as did Tangera and Deveaux, but I noticed that Frank and his mother switched to brandy. During the next hour, the rain outside was not the only thing steadily pouring.

The more Helen drank, the less she and Tangera had to do with each other. I noticed, near the end of the gathering, that the younger woman regarded the older with impatience, even distaste. Helen, for her part, seemed to be peculiarly aware of this.

Her condition, I noticed, produced a fascinating variety of reactions. Tangera was annoyed, Frank withdrew even further into himself, and Deveaux became positively solicitous. It was touching, really, the way the unhappy, lonely doctor seemed to be reaching out to a woman who, as far as I could see, treated his presence with a polite indifference.

I thought about that. I knew from my own experience that we are forever concentrating on the people who couldn't care less about us, whereas the ones who are, in their turn, attempting to engage our attention are the very people who so often go unnoticed. I watched Helen and Dr. Deveaux that night; chatting, parrying, missing glances and failing to recognize hidden meanings as the endless rain continued outside the room. I wondered, once again, why it is that we always seem to love the wrong people.

At last the gathering came to an end. Helen, who had barely spoken for the last fifteen minutes, was becoming visibly restless. Deveaux took this as his cue to rise and announce that he must be getting home. He kissed Helen on the cheek, shook hands with the rest of us, and departed.

As soon as he was gone, Helen excused herself and bade us all good night. Frank picked this moment to ask me to stay the night at Haven View. We could talk late into the night, he said, and I wouldn't have to worry about driving home through the rain at all hours. I accepted.

Saying that he would call and inform Lee of this change of plans, Frank escorted his mother from the room, leaving his wife and me alone.

Tangera rose from the chaise, poured two brandies, and handed one to me. She sat beside me on the couch.

"Mud in your eye," she said, clinking my glass with hers. We laughed and sipped. After a moment she said,

"Thank you for keeping my secret about my letter to you. You know Frank better than anyone, and you must remember how he resists any attempts at assistance. I am glad you will be staying, Joseph. I think Frank will talk to you, especially if I disappear. That is exactly what I plan to do. I am tired. Trying to be sociable with Helen just drains me. I feel as if I have been running a race."

I wasn't going to get into that.

"George is quite a prodigy," I said. Remembering the duet, I added, "And you're not bad, yourself."

She stared at me a moment, then looked away. "My aunt's piano lessons are practically the only happy memories I have of my childhood." She indicated the Steinway with a wave of her hand. "Of course, we had no such instrument in my house in Martinique. There were my mother and six children in three rooms. My aunt and I would walk to the parish hall of the church in town three miles away. Twice a week. The priest let us use the piano there; a very old, battered spinet, horribly out of tune. It got me out of doing chores at home, and I really did enjoy it. It was the only privilege that distinguished me from the other children."

I'd never thought about where this woman had begun. I suppose I would have imagined a pleasant, middle-class existence on that island, if I'd wondered at all. This revelation came as a surprise.

"How did you get from there to the university in St. Thomas?" I asked.

She leaned back against the cushions, contemplating her brandy. "My other natural talent: languages. The nuns in the school there noticed my facility with Latin and English. One in particular, Sister Marie Claire, took a special interest. It was she who helped me to obtain the scholarship and the student visa."

I regarded her closely. I took a good, long look at the beautiful young woman next to me; the stylish hair, the expert makeup, the lovely clothes and jewelry. I found myself staring at her perfectly manicured nails. The taste, the poise, the charm and grace that defined her every action: these had not been acquired on a dirt farm in Martinique. No, something was missing. . . .

"Even with the scholarship," I said, "you must have needed money to come here. How on earth did you manage?"

She smiled then, and she tilted her head slightly to one side, watching me.

"I managed," she said. "But enough about all that. There is something I want you to do for me."

She rose and went over to one of the bookshelves along the opposite wall. She searched for a moment and pulled out a volume. From the writing desk in the corner she produced a pen. Then she rejoined me on the couch.

"Here," she announced, extending the book to me. "I want you to sign this."

I looked down. It was *Bridge of Sighs*, and it was not the autographed copy I had sent Frank upon its publication. I smiled as I took the pen from her and opened it to the beige endpaper. I wrote, *For Tangera, who has made this trip to St. Thomas so memorable. Love, Joe.*

"I read it twice," she said as I returned the book to her. "I will never forget that young man, John Challenger. He was obviously you: I thought he must be. And that old Venetian gentleman, stage-managing John's affair with the girl. Lovely. I wept when the old man died."

"I'm flattered," I murmured.

"I developed such a picture of John—of you—in my mind. Young, romantic, lonely; just waiting for some wonderful woman to come along and bring meaning to your life. And, sure enough, that is who you are." She smiled. "You even look like John—as I imagined him when I was reading. Thank you."

She put down the book and reached for her brandy. She drank and placed the empty snifter on the table before us.

It happened at that moment, as she leaned forward with the glass. The citrus scent wafted toward me and her arm brushed my thigh. I realized, with a guilty surge of surprise, that I was acutely aware of her breasts, her naked arms, her long, slender neck. It wasn't the earring that attracted my attention: I was staring at her earlobe.

She turned her head very slowly and looked directly into my eyes. The surprise on her face was, I thought, every bit as great as mine. We sat there, staring.

The door opened and Frank came back into the room. He was carrying another bottle.

"I figured we'd be out of brandy by now," he said. True: the bottle on the tray was empty.

Tangera stood up.

"I'm for bed, darling," she told her husband. "You two can have all the brandy you want. Has the guest room been prepared?"

Frank nodded. He took his wife in his arms and kissed her.

"Thank you for tonight," he said.

She understood whatever he meant. I could guess, myself.

Tangera then approached me. I don't know if my involuntary cringe was noticed. She leaned over and kissed my cheek. Her scent overwhelmed me. I tried to smile.

"Good night, Joseph," she said. "I will see you in the morning."

As she was leaving, Frank stopped her for a moment. "I thought I'd sleep in my old room tonight, okay? We may stay up late, and I don't want to disturb you."

She nodded. "Fine. Good night." With a final, meaningful glance at me that I tried not to notice, she left the room. For the first time since my arrival in St. Thomas, I was alone with Frank.

After a moment's companionable silence, he said, "She's very beautiful, isn't she?"

Oh, boy.

"Yes," I replied, not meeting his gaze. "She's lovely."

He sat on the couch next to me and reached for the bottle. "Sometimes I wonder why she stays. This can't be what she was expecting."

He filled both our glasses. We toasted and drank. I reached for a cigarette, forming a delicate question in my mind.

"Frank," I finally said, "have you ever thought about leaving here? I don't just mean this house; I mean St. Thomas. Take Tangera and go to New York, or Florida, or another island. Anywhere . . ."

He leaned back against the couch, slowly nodding. "Kiddo, I think about it all the time. Remember that Sunfish we used to have? Every now and then I dream about sailing. I'm out there all alone, just me and the water and the sky. I wouldn't have any particular destination; I'd go to many places. Other islands—South America, maybe. Just go, you know? See the world . . .

yes, I think about that." He was staring off into space, drifting on some vessel to parts unknown.

"What about Tangera?" I asked.

The boat crashed abruptly on shore. He looked over at me.

"She doesn't like sailing," he said. "Look, I know what you mean, Joe, about getting away. But I can't. Mother is—well, she'd never leave Haven View, and we can't just . . ." He trailed off, shaking his head. Downing his drink in one gulp, he reached again for the brandy.

"So," I said quietly, "what are you going to do?"

He jumped up and turned to face me. "I know what you're trying to say, and I appreciate it. I really do. I have Tangera, and my own life, and I can't just build my world around Mother, right? Well, I have to—at least for a while. Until she's better. You've certainly noticed what he did to her!"

He began to wander around the room as he spoke. I leaned back and listened.

"God, I hated him! I wasn't good enough to be his son. He never loved us. We were just—possessions. Like Haven View. He was the great lawyer, the great judge! He was going to be the great governor. I wasn't smart enough, or motivated enough. I didn't have any balls! That's what he always told me. And I stayed here under his roof and took that crap. Because of her. She was getting worse all the time. She was already a drunk when I left for Harvard. By the time I got back—I couldn't just leave her alone with him.

"And you know what? What's so awful about the whole thing? She *loved* him! She was crazy about him. She still is. Nothing mattered to her: his abuse, his neglect, his mistresses—God knows he had plenty of those!

And she just sat there, *loving* him! Finally, I couldn't take it anymore. I couldn't stand him, and I couldn't stand her *allowing* him to—"

He was at the piano now. He turned around and came over to me.

"I'll never forget the night I met Tangera. She was so exciting, so warm—so *normal*. I knew in a matter of minutes that I was going to ask her to marry me. If she'd have me, I'd get the hell out of here and try some—some relatively sane existence."

He was standing over me now, glaring down. He didn't look as if he was going to burst out laughing. I was surprised when he did just that.

"Oh, God, Joe, listen to me!" he cried, throwing himself down on the couch. He doubled over, shaking with mirth.

I smiled. "What's so funny?"

"Me! Carrying on like that. I'm sorry. This is the first time I've ever said all this to somebody."

"Hey," I said as lightly as I could, "all for one and one for all."

He recovered from the laughing fit and poured another drink. "Yeah. I've missed you, Joe. I don't have a lot of friends on this island." He began to giggle again. "Certainly not now. They all think I'm a murderer!"

I watched him as he laughed, waiting for him to recover and go on. At last he took a deep breath.

"Do you know what that son of a bitch put in his will?"

Hubert hadn't changed his will to disinherit Frank. There hadn't been time, but I would not learn that until later. I didn't know what he was talking about.

"What did he put in his will?" I asked.

Frank leaned forward, smiling. "He wanted to destroy Haven View! He wanted it to be demolished—pulled to the ground. Then we were supposed to sprinkle his ashes around the rubble. Can you believe that?"

"No," I said, looking around the library. It really was a lovely room. Now it was my turn to pour brandy.

"Yep!" He giggled, obviously appreciating my reaction. "He split everything between Mother and me—everything but the house. He didn't want anyone living in it after he was gone. His dogs and his palace. I've heard of destroying pets, but a *house?!*"

I nodded, remembering a long-ago image; the poem we'd had to learn in high school. I closed my eyes and rattled it off:

> " '*In Xanadu did Kublai Khan*
> *A stately pleasure dome decree.* . . .' "

"Exactly!" Frank cried. "The *arrogance* of the man!"

We laughed and drank.

"Well," I said, chuckling, "you obviously didn't obey his wish."

This sent Frank into another paroxysm of laughter. He jumped to his feet. "I did better than disobey. Come with me, my friend."

I rose and followed him out of the room and down the hall to the door of Hubert's office. Next to the door was a small table bearing a potted plant. He reached into the pot, pulled out a key, and unlocked the door. It swung slowly open, yawning pitch-black before us.

"I know you don't like this room," he said as he switched on the light and the blackness disappeared. "You can just stand there in the doorway. Look."

He was pointing over at the shelves behind the judge's desk. Careful not to enter, I leaned forward and peered across the room. There, on the shelf at eye level, inches from the actual site of the murder, stood a large silver urn.

Frank's laughter followed me as I turned and made my way quickly back to the library. I was draining my snifter when he joined me again.

"You should have seen your face!" he cried.

I shook my head in disbelief. "How did you ever get Helen to agree to *that?*"

He shrugged and picked up his glass. "She didn't have a say in the matter. She left it all up to me. I simply informed her that we would not destroy the house. She would stay here, and Tangera and I would live here with her—for a while, at least. And I told her that we'd put him in his office because, despite what happened there, it was one of his two favorite places in the world. And I didn't want to scatter his ashes on that beach."

"What are you talking about?" I asked.

"His other favorite place. Shell Beach. Don't you remember, Joe? That night the three of us sneaked down there to drink beer and smoke cigarettes. How old were we, thirteen? We'd been there for an hour before we realized he was there, too. Sitting at the end, on that damned rock of his. He used to sit there for hours, staring out at the ocean. He must have known we were there that night, but he never let on. Two, three nights a week, right up until he died. If he wasn't in his office, he'd be sitting on that rock. He said it was his escape from the world."

I remembered the night, but I hadn't known the judge's visits there were habitual. I shuddered.

"Elsa lives above that beach," I said.

Frank smiled. "You still like her, don't you?"

"Yes."

He picked up the brandy bottle and the two snifters.

"I used to date her," he tossed off, ever so casually. "Before I met Tangera."

"You *what?*"

He laughed at my expression. "Come on upstairs. I'll give you all the gory details."

He went out of the room, up the stairs, and down the hall to his bedroom. I followed close behind him. At one point on the stairs I stumbled and reached out to grip the banister. He whirled around and grabbed my arm.

"Not used to all this brandy," I mumbled as we proceeded.

The room was exactly as I remembered it. The blue chenille bedspread, the gauzy blue curtains, the deep blue carpet complementing eggshell blue walls. The bookshelves were still crowded with everything from Mother Goose right through the maturing process to Melville and Dostoyevsky. Everywhere between the books were his famous Aurora models of sports cars, one of his two great passions from childhood. The five or six now-tarnished gold trophies on the top shelf bore witness to his driving prowess and to his other love, swimming. Above the bed was a large, terrible paint-by-number of a clown that had always reminded me of Red Skelton.

I turned and looked down at his desk next to the door. There it was, our pride and joy, in its place of honor. A large, rather intricate three-masted square-rigger of balsa that had taken the three of us the better part of a week to assemble. It stood there, still glorious in its bottle. The bottle, of course, was plastic: two halves glued together.

Getting the ship into the bottle was not quite the challenge it should have been, but try telling that to three very proud twelve-year-olds.

And there, next to the model, was the Secret Place, an enormous white and pink conch shell. Automatically, I picked it up and reached inside.

"It's empty," Frank said as he placed the glasses on the night table and filled them. "I didn't know you were coming."

We laughed together, remembering. The shell, with its capacious interior, had been Frank's secret until I stumbled upon it. One day, while playing, I had stuck my hand in the opening and discovered treasure. Three wrinkled cigarettes, several dollar bills, some loose change, a Playboy centerfold, and a Ramses condom. This last item had been purloined from the mens' locker room at the yacht club, he told me. He was saving it for the Big Day. We were twelve: we didn't know these things had time limits.

From that day on, the shell had been our covert means of communication. Even Dennis had never known about it. We wrote stupid notes: dirty jokes; treasure maps; graphic physical descriptions of Miss Grotowski, our music teacher, who resembled Raquel Welch. As we grew older, of course, it had fallen out of use. I'd forgotten all about it until this moment.

I looked around the room. I'd forgotten so much. . . .

He came over and handed me a glass.

"So," I said, turning to face him, "what's all this about you and Elsa?"

He laughed. "Don't get all bent out of shape; there really isn't much to tell. About two years ago I ran into her at the Reef. She was painting some tourist, and I watched for a while. We got to talking, and next thing I knew we were having dinner. I had a nice time, so I asked her out again. We sort-of-kind-of unofficially dated for a few months. I liked her. Hell, even Father liked her. Anyway, I got the feeling that she didn't really like me as much as I liked her. Then I met Tangera."

"And?" I said, watching his face.

"And nothing. End of story."

I stared. He flushed and looked away.

"Okay," he went on. "*Almost* end of story. A few months ago—I don't know, April—we were all at a party. Tangera was dancing with someone, and Elsa came over to say hello to me. We were just, you know, chatting. But Tangera went nuts. She said something catty to Elsa and dragged my ass out of there. 'That woman was making a pass at you,' she said. I said no, that it was all over between us. And Tangera screams, 'Well, *she* doesn't think so!' And that was that. Until—"

He stopped and reached for his brandy.

"Until?" I wasn't letting him off the hook.

"Damn it, Joe! Okay. *Until* that morning, after the night he was killed. I went to my office. It was a Saturday, and I had a terrible hangover, but I had a lot of work to do. Anyway, there was a message on my answering machine. It was Elsa, asking me to have lunch with her sometime as soon as possible. She said she wanted to talk to me about something. I was about to call her when the phone rang. It was Tangera, with the news about Father. Lucien had just called her.

"I remember getting sick, throwing up in the office bathroom. It was such a shock, and I had been queasy even before I heard. I don't know where that hangover

came from: I don't usually get them. As soon as I could,
I came here. I forgot all about Elsa's call.

"The next time I saw her, months later, I asked her
what she'd called about, and she said it was nothing. It
didn't matter anymore. She certainly hasn't been flirting
with me lately. Like I said, it's over. It was over when I
met Tangera."

I picked up my snifter and stared at its contents for a
moment, then put it down.

"I can't drink this," I said.

"Look, Joe, I would never have told you this if I
thought it would upset you."

"I'm not upset," I lied.

"Well, I know you like her, but be careful. The more
I think about it, the more it seems that maybe she *was*
coming on to me. After I'd married Tangera. Besides,
there was something going on between her and Father. I
never understood that phone call he made to her the
night he died."

I watched him carefully. "She told me she was talking
to him about buying Shell Beach."

Frank stared, then shook his head. "Father would
never have even considered selling it."

"I don't think," I replied, "that she ever considered
buying it."

Frank looked at me and smiled.

"Yeah," he said, nodding slowly. "She's mysterious.
Remote, you know what I mean? I noticed that, even
when we were seeing each other. Sometimes she'd sort
of go off into her own private world. I used to think
maybe she spent a lot of time remembering her husband."

"I think so, too," I said. "I'm feeling a little dizzy, Frank. Would you mind if I called it a day?"

He opened the door for me. "Sure, I'm kind of tired myself. Good night. And, Joe—"

I turned in the doorway.

"Thank you," he said. "For remaining a Musketeer."

I laughed, patted him on the shoulder, and fairly staggered away down the hall.

I lay in the darkened guest room, listening to the storm outside. The rain was crashing on the tin roof above me, and the wind whistled in the shutters at the window. The bed, the room, the house itself fairly vibrated with the force.

I checked the luminous dial of my watch. Nearly four-thirty. It had been two hours since I'd left Frank's room and come here, prepared to sleep. With all the brandy, not to mention the overload of information to which I was growing accustomed on this visit, I didn't anticipate that sleep would be a problem. I was wrong. Twice I had risen and gone into the bathroom to splash water on my face and rinse my parched mouth. Too much alcohol: dehydration. That, and a troubled mind. This house made me uneasy, from outside and within. *Hubert*, I thought for the hundredth time in two hours, *doth murder sleep.*

Murder.

I sat up, switched on a lamp, and lit a cigarette. The ashtray on the bedside table was a white porcelain rectangle. In the center of it was a painting, a whimsical representation of a native steel band. Under it, the legend: St. Thomas, U.S. Virgin Islands. How picturesque, I thought. So far from my own actuality.

Tangera was asleep in this house, just across the hall, and she was alone. Her scent was almost in this room with me. That neck; the lovely, curved line up to the small, delicate ear. Tiny waist and hips, the breasts generous but not too large. . . .

Stop it. I was sitting in my friend's house, coveting his wife.

Elsa. She was not off limits: she had even expressed a definite interest in me.

As she had in Frank.

I lay back on the pillows, feeling my excitement wane, the heat leaving my body. This island. This goddamned—

I don't remember now just how I was able to hear it above the wind and rain outside. It was coming from so far away that at first I assumed it was subliminal. I had been fantasizing: steel bands and beautiful women. It could have merely crept into my unconscious. Theme music, if you will. I sat up, holding my breath. I closed my eyes and listened.

It was real, all right. It emanated from some point downstairs. It was familiar: I had heard it a thousand times before. An old, probably classic recording. A soft, insinuating instrumental arrangement. "The Girl from Ipanema."

I rose and went over to the door. Opening it a crack, I strained to listen. Yes, there was music, and there was movement, as well. Someone was downstairs.

Insomnia loves company. I was only wearing my underpants, so I slipped on my trousers and shirt and moved silently out of the room, closing the door softly as I left. All the bedroom doors were closed. I tiptoed to the staircase and descended. I stood at the bottom of the stairs, orienting myself, determining the direction of the music. It seemed to be coming from outside now, directly in front of me. The huge front doors of the house stood open.

Then I saw her.

She was standing on the veranda, her back to me. As I approached the front door, I noticed that she was clad in a filmy white dressing gown. She seemed to be looking out at the lights across the harbor as she swayed in time to the music. There was a large portable player on a table near her. She was humming. The rain beyond her poured down on the patio as she stared at the distant lights, barely visible in the storm.

I stood in the doorway, watching her. I had opened my mouth, preparing to make my presence known, when something stopped me.

Still with her back to me, she reached up and pulled the flimsy material from her shoulders. The robe wafted to the ground. She was naked.

The swaying and humming became more pronounced. I stepped backward into the darkness of the front hall, staring. The rain and the music continued, mingling hypnotically.

Then, slowly and gracefully, Helen Jensen began to dance. She raised her arms, holding an imaginary partner as she moved in a smooth, gliding motion around the veranda. Her eyes were open, her gaze fixed on the air in front of her. She smiled dreamily as she whirled.

I remember thinking that she must be asleep. I searched my mind for what little I knew of somnambulism. Don't disturb her, I thought. That's not good. I wasn't sure why, but I'd been told that often enough. I'd never seen anyone sleepwalking before.

My initial surprise had subsided, and now I became aware that something else was wrong. What was it? I had come down the stairs, listening to the music. I had looked about me in the front hall. . . .

It hit me then. I froze, and a cold band of fear tightened around my chest. The paralysis spread instantly through my body, and for a moment I was incapable of movement. When the shock passed, I took a deep breath and turned around to confront what I had already seen and not noticed.

The door to Hubert Jensen's office was wide open.

I turned again to look at Helen. She danced, unaware of my presence. My eyes traveled from her to the source of the music. On the table next to it was a silver tray. On the tray stood an open bottle of wine.

And two full glasses.

I took a step back and turned around, preparing to escape up the stairs to the relative sanity of the guest room. I was stopped by the sound of a door closing somewhere above.

I took cover in the shadows under the staircase. Someone was moving upstairs, and I didn't want to be discovered. Everyone would end up being embarrassed, and it was none of my business in the first place. I listened as the footsteps above me descended the stairs.

Whoever it was stopped, as I had done, at the bottom of the staircase. I heard the soft breathing and imagined that Helen was once again being watched. I stuck my head cautiously out of the shadows and peered around the stairs.

It was Frank. He was wearing a dark blue bathrobe, and his tousled hair was outlined in the light from the front doorway. Beyond him, through the door, Helen danced on. The music stopped for a moment, then began again. "The Girl from Ipanema." It was obviously a compact disc player, programmed to repeat that one song over and over.

I watched from my hiding place as Frank walked through the hall and out to his mother on the veranda. Good, I thought. It must be cold out there, with the rain. I was shivering, myself.

Frank picked up the white gown and wrapped it around his mother. He reached down and turned off the music, then he took his mother gently by the arm and led her back into the house and up the stairs.

I watched it all, the whole sad performance, knowing as I watched that this had happened before, probably many times. Then I waited several minutes under the staircase, until I heard the doors opening and closing and I was certain that Helen and Frank were back in their rooms. As I strained my ears, waiting for silence, I raised a hand to my mouth to stifle the sudden coughing. My throat was scratchy, and my fingers were cold against the hot skin of my face. When I finally came out of the darkness and headed up the stairs, I became aware of the aching in my shoulders and chest.

It was pitch black in the upstairs hallway. My shivering hand fumbled for the doorknob, and a sharp pain shot up my arm as I turned it. I made my unsteady way over to the bed and fell across it. Too much to drink, I thought. Too much cold, damp air; too many secrets; too much madness.

This time I had no trouble falling asleep: in seconds, I was unconscious.

*   *   *

I was traveling downhill, and the sunlight was blurring my vision. I could taste the bile in the back of my throat. If I didn't concentrate, I would lose control of the car.

When I'd made my shaky way down the stairs, Tangera was alone at the table on the veranda. She had just finished breakfast, and she smiled brightly as I joined her. My stomach was churning as I fell into a chair next to her, refused food, and asked Lucien for coffee and aspirin.

This was apparently the right house for such a request. Lucien returned to the table with bicarbonate. Eunice had also sent herbal tea—not coffee—and dry toast, along with her orders to consume both. I tried, but the sight of the bread brought on a wave of nausea. Tangera made small talk as I pushed the toast around on my plate, waiting for the medicine to have some effect on my queasy stomach and throbbing temples. No reference was made to last night. That moment between us in the library might never have happened. I couldn't think about that now.

I was running a fever. I could feel it growing, and my voice was hoarse from the increasing scratchiness in my throat. My three or four hours of fitful sleep seemed to have done nothing to stem the tide of illness.

Tangera continued to smile at me. She asked me how I had slept, and I searched her face for any knowledge of what had taken place after she had retired. Did she know about Helen's dancing? Apparently not: I could see nothing in her eyes but a polite interest.

As my fever increased, so did my confusion. I remember thinking that I had to get out, away from Haven View, away from my sad friend and his pitiful mother and his beautiful, seductive wife. I mumbled replies to

Tangera's comments at the table, trying to keep up my end of the conversation. I don't remember a word of it now.

I do remember the last thing she said as I finally broke free and made my way to the parking lot. I must have made some apology for leaving so abruptly, without seeing Frank or Helen. She walked me to my car.

"Good-bye for now, Joseph," she said, reaching up to kiss my cheek. "We must do this again soon."

I stumbled into the car and pulled away, glancing briefly in the rearview mirror at the lovely woman in the orange dress grinning and waving from the patio. Then everything blurred. By the time I drove through the gates, I could barely see.

The car was moving much too fast down the winding mountain road. The dizziness and fever were impairing my judgment. Stop it, I thought in panic as another wave of nausea hit me. Just stop the car before you kill someone. Like Hubert Jensen. No, he was dead. That had been Frank, or Helen, or Tangera, or—

I slammed on the brakes and pulled over to the side of the road, just in the nick of time. I flung open the door, leaned out over the gravel, and vomited.

8

LIMBO

I have decided that the following forty-eight hours, though uncomfortable, were necessary in the long run. It was during this respite that several things became clear in my mind, and several courses of action presented themselves to me. If anything in that storm in St. Thomas can be said to have been resolved, the resolution had its beginnings in those two days of calm—the eye of the hurricane—that preceded the devastation.

When I staggered from the car into the house on Blackbeard's Hill, Lee immediately put me to bed. I slept, woke, drank tea and soup, took the aspirins Lee brought, and slept again. At one point, in the middle of the night, I had a temperature of one hundred four. Lee piled on blankets and left me alone.

I regained full consciousness in the middle of the following afternoon. When I rose and opened the shutters at the window, the bright sunlight poured into the room.

The fever had broken and I was ravenously hungry. The image that stared back from the bathroom mirror was a shock: I must have lost five pounds in as many hours, and I was haggard and pale. A shave, a hot shower, clean clothes; sometimes the most ordinary acts can be exquisitely pleasurable. A fresh razor, soap, and shampoo had washed the sickness from me. Riding the wave of my self-restoration, I phoned Snips and made an appointment with Bertram for four o'clock, two days hence. That was his earliest opening: he was obviously popular.

Though the illness had passed, I still felt drained of all energy. Lee, who had forsaken work on my account, sat me in the living room with a blanket over my knees and headed for the kitchen. She reappeared with my request—steak, salad, and a baked potato—and watched, astonished, as I wolfed it down and asked for dessert.

We spent a quiet evening together, and I finally began to think rationally. After Lee won her third game of Yahtzee in a row, she reached for her current mystery novel and I got a notebook from my room and sat on the couch across from her.

I glanced at the cover of Lee's mystery and smiled: P. D. James. Good Lord, I thought, we should only send P. D. James a plane ticket. Who else could make sense of all this? Lee loves mysteries, and for a moment I seriously considered interrupting her reading and telling her everything. I hadn't shown her Tangera's letter. She knew nothing of the huge blond man in the blue Mustang, the chase in the mall, Helen Jensen's naked dancing. My other sister, Marla, is witty and fun, but she's terrible at games and figures. I'm moody and emotional and romantic. It is Lee, of the three of us, who possesses that practical, methodical mind most useful in these situations. Her husband, of course, has a computer for a brain. If I had felt able to talk to Lee and Paul then, at that point in the situation, I really wonder what the three of us might have—

No. I knew I wouldn't tell them. They didn't give a damn about Haven View and its inhabitants. Their first concern would be for me. They'd scream and yell, maybe even call the police, and they'd slap me on the next plane to New York. And I did not want to leave St. Thomas. Not yet.

I got up and went out onto the porch. I stood there, staring across the harbor at the lights of Haven View. The now-familiar feeling washed over me. *Come here. Please. Something must be done.*

I didn't think then, and I don't think now, that Hubert Jensen was speaking directly to me. In life, he had barely been aware of my existence. Besides, I didn't accept such things: ghosts and voices and messages from Beyond. Nonetheless, some sort of signal seemed to be emanating from Haven View, and I was the one who seemed to be receiving it.

The lights winked. I nodded. I turned around and went back into the house, knowing what I would do. I would stay here in St. Thomas until something was done. Until Frank and his family were at peace. Until that house no longer beckoned.

When I woke on the following morning, my new and glorious resolve was shaken to its core. I woke feeling better that day, the lingering illness having vanished in the night. I wasn't sure what the day would bring, but I was beginning to form some positive ideas. The shadows of the past few days seemed far away, incongruous, in this sunny house. Through the window I could see the kind of late morning you can only find in the West Indies. Feeling better than I had since I got off the plane, I fairly floated out of the guest room.

Lee was at the dining table in one corner of the enormous living room. She had apparently heard me stirring: at the place next to hers were coffee and cinnamon toast. Judging from my sister's face as she read, I concluded that P. D. James was moments away from identifying the murderer. Not wishing to prolong the agony by interrupting her, I reached for the *Virgin Islands Daily News* on the table in front of me.

If it hadn't been for the bold headline, I probably would never have noticed the photograph. That's what I believe now, at any rate. After all, I had only seen his face for a moment.

The words screaming up from page one read: "Governor Vetoes Proposed Condo Complex." Accompanying the article was a large photo of Clayton Hughes at his desk, signing some document. Standing next to him, peering over his shoulder, was Dennis. I smiled as I noted the look of triumph on my friend's face. I scanned the article briefly. Dennis was quoted several times, and Abel Brandt was mentioned as the losing party. His construction company was behind the proposal, along with a developer from the mainland. It had actually made it through the Planning Board and the zoning people before the governor had stopped the whole thing.

Blah blah blah, said the article. We must keep the 'virgin' in Virgin Islands. We must preserve the pristine beauty and unspoiled, uncluttered serenity of et cetera. My eyes traveled down the page.

And stopped.

I stared at the photograph in the bottom right-hand

corner. Could it be? I wasn't really sure. I read the tiny headline: "Dead Man Found." His name meant nothing to me, nor the fact that he was an illegal alien from Trinidad. He had been twenty-six years old, and he had a long, detailed police record. Breaking and entering, felonious assault, attempted rape, unregistered weapons. A juvenile detention home in Trinidad; later, prison. Nice guy.

At my only meeting with him, he'd been carrying an unregistered weapon. A long, ugly knife.

He had been found in an alley above Back Street, right next to Biff's Bar. The Danish name for the place was spelled out in the paper, but we locals had always referred to it, for reasons I won't repeat, as Pee Pee Alley. He had been lying there among trash cans for two days before anyone bothered to notice that he was dead. He had been struck on the head by what the paper inevitably described as a "blunt instrument." I, of course, could have told them what the blunt instrument was: a large, nasty looking handgun with a silencer attached.

Two days ago I would have freaked. Blubber to Lee, call the cops, run to the airport. Back to New York, to Hudson Street. Another bad play. Another verbose, impenetrable novel. Two days ago, not today.

Today I wanted answers. I wanted to piece together, to finally *know* what had happened to Hubert Jensen. I had people to see, questions to ask. I even had a protector of sorts, however murderous. I was going to get to the bottom of this if it—

Killed me? Watch the phrasing, Joe.

Today, I threw down the paper and reached for the cinnamon toast.

* * *

They were six big, unattractively modern two-story buildings, placed pretty much in a straight line on the ridge above one side of Magens Bay. Eight units to a building, with huge plate-glass windows and sharply geometrical metal balconies facing out. If you placed several white tissue boxes end to end, you would approximate the aesthetic effect. Standing on the beach near the waterline, I would have been looking up at them.

I regarded the large model with distaste. I had been waiting for nearly fifteen minutes in Abel Brandt's outer office, and there was little else in the room to engage my attention. Certainly not the mousy, unfriendly secretary who watched me with surreptitious suspicion from her desk. She had announced my presence on the intercom, told me in a flat, Midwestern drawl to wait, and returned to her typing. From the clacking sounds that intermittently filled the office, I clocked her at about ten words a minute.

The model was a representation of the project that had made the news this morning. Brandt's Folly. This grotesque of chrome and alabaster would never leave the table before me.

Good.

"Joe Wilder. A happy meeting on a dark day."

Abel was standing beside me, hand extended. We shook. He wore a loud shirt with a tropical print, white linen jacket and slacks, and Top-Siders. His attire belied him: if this vision of a perfect West Indian gentleman had his way, they'd pave paradise and put up a parking lot.

He didn't seem to be taking the news badly. He grinned at me. "You aren't here to spy for your friend, Mr. Grey, are you?"

I smiled and shook my head.

"Good," he boomed. "In that case, I can invite you to lunch. You don't have any other plans, do you?"

Smile. Shake.

"Fine. I'm meeting a friend at Papagayo's. You like Mexican food, don't you?" He was already leading me toward the door. "Hold my calls, Jane."

The mousy woman nodded and resumed her hunting and pecking.

I told him I'd take my own car and we traveled separately from town, over Raphune Hill, and out toward the Fort Mylner section of the countryside. Having grown up in a house with more than twenty animals, I knew the way to this particular restaurant with my eyes closed. It was next door to the veterinary clinic, on the edge of the housing project called Tutu. This lower-middle-class enclave was a large configuration of cottages nestled in the valley and on the hills across the highway from the clinic. It was actually rather charming, in a ghastly sort of way.

That is what I remembered of the land around the restaurant. It is not what I discovered now.

I parked next to Abel's car. He was waiting for me at the entrance to the restaurant. As I got out of my car, I turned to look at the little village of Tutu.

It was there, all right, but it had multiplied. I stared in horror at the sight.

Shock number one lay before me, directly across the road. A huge yellow shopping center dominated the foreground, surrounded by cars. I could see a supermarket, a deli, a multiplex cinema, and Heaven only knew what else. The cottages I remembered were crowded on the hills behind it. My eyes traveled up to the mountains above the project. Huge, long buildings like the ones in the model lined hill and dale. Condominiums, co-ops, apartment houses; all the way up, up to Donoe Road, where there were even more. Little boxes on the hillside. Everywhere.

In all of this panoramic vista, there was barely a patch of green. I might as well not have been on a tropical island at all. From this vantage place, I could have been in Pittsburgh.

Paradise, paved.

One of the people responsible for this outrage was standing behind me, waiting. Summoning a huge smile from nowhere I can think of, I joined him and entered the restaurant.

The quesadillas were delicious. I had plenty of time to enjoy my meal: I certainly had precious little to add to the conversation.

Abel's lunch date was a small, rotund, balding gentleman from New York whose name I forget. I remember a permanent smile and dark eyes that glittered more than the gold on his fingers and wrists and around his neck. He had only been on the island a few days, and he had not tanned properly. His face was a bright, almost neon pink. I've heard this unnatural color described as a honeymoon tan in honor of the couples who spend two solid days in the sun, trying to get a tan much too quickly, and the rest of their vacations—well, elsewhere. Mr. Whoever had an unusually loud, high-pitched whine of a voice, and he punctuated every word with his hands. He and Abel leaned toward each other and barked their rapid-fire dialogue with much laughter and gesticulating. They barely paused long enough to shovel incredible amounts of food into their mouths.

I gathered, between the guacamole and the espresso, that Mr. Whoever was the famous partner in the now-derailed condo scheme. I also learned that he had no table manners whatsoever, and that the young woman back at his hotel, with whom he was acquiring a honeymoon tan, answered to the name of Misty and was definitely *not* Mrs. Whoever. Nudge, nudge, giggle, giggle.

I ate in silence, watching Abel Brandt and wondering why he had so readily invited me along. He had not so much as inquired as to my reason for arriving at his office. He seemed abrupt and businesslike, yet oddly friendly.

It was as the coffee was served that Abel leaned even closer to his business partner and stated, clearly and firmly, that the condominiums above Magens Bay were far from dead. He lowered his voice and mumbled something about extra funding so that "hinges" could be "oiled." At least, that's what I think he said. The other man nodded vigorously, apparently agreeing to the proposition. When he tried to pursue the matter further, Abel raised a finger to his lips and turned his attention, at last, to me.

Perhaps he'd had too much sangria, or he may have been waiting until he had his friend as a witness. He could have been biding his time until he had me at a disadvantage, until he'd fed me an excellent lunch on his expense account. Most likely, it was a combination of all three. At any rate, when Abel finally focused on me, he launched without preamble into a monologue.

"Okay, Joe, let's see. You came to my office today because you're working your way down a list of suspects. Did I kill Hubert Jensen? I've already told you that I did not. Of course, if I had, I'd probably say that, anyway.

But I didn't, and neither did my wife. He was a very dear friend.

"Was he having an affair with Abby? Yes, he was. My firm keeps a hotel room on permanent rental for Stateside guests." He waved a hand to indicate his friend. "Abby took Hubert there occasionally. She's taken other people there, as well, and she's mentioned recently that she wouldn't at all mind having you as a guest. If you want to pay her a visit, you have my blessing. Abby is— high-spirited. She likes excitement and fun. I, on the other hand, have only one serious passion in my life, and that is my company. I love my wife and she loves me, and we get along well together. How she chooses to amuse herself is entirely her business.

"I miss Hubert, and I will miss him every day of my life. We did great business together, and we made a lot of money. If he'd lived, we would have made a lot more. But that is not going to happen, because one Friday night last July his son—yes, Joe, his son!—Franklin Bennett Jensen, went to Haven View and murdered him." He took a deep breath. "Is there anything else you'd like to know?"

I stared at him for a long moment.

"No," I said. "I think you've covered just about everything."

"Good. Would you like some more espresso?"

"No, thank you. I should be going."

He smiled. "The next name on your list?"

I smiled right back. "Something like that."

Abel shook his head and chuckled. "I'll say one thing for you, Joe. You're loyal to your friends."

I rose to leave, nodding to Mr. Whoever, who nodded back. "Thank you for lunch, Mr. Brandt."

"Abel," he said. "And, Joe, you won't repeat anything you heard here to any friends in the government, will you?"

I smiled.

"Of course not," I said, and I left.

It is amazing how easy it is to lie to people you dislike.

As I came out of the restaurant, I looked again at the overcrowded view across the street. My gaze traveled down from the hills to the shopping center. To the parking lot in front of the shopping center.

To the blue Mustang in the parking lot.

I didn't even think about what I did next. I turned around and reentered Papagayo's. Unseen by Abel and his companion, I crossed the restaurant and went out a different way. I circled behind the veterinary clinic next door and emerged across the street from the other end of the shopping center. I crossed the street and went into the parking lot. Bending low so he would not see me approach, I made my way through the rows of cars until I stood behind the Mustang.

He was sitting in the car, watching the entrance to the restaurant across the street.

I held my breath. Slowly, carefully, I edged forward until I was next to the car, just behind the driver's door. I leaned down until my mouth was inches from his ear.

"Don't turn around," I said.

He stiffened, and his right hand rose instinctively toward the holster under his jacket. Then, realizing that a gun might be pointed at him, he stopped.

"I just want you to listen," I said. "Then you can go. When I leave here, I'm going to Frenchman's Reef, and I don't want you following me anymore today. I don't know whom you're working for, but I want you to take them a message. Tell them to come to me, talk to me, let me know what they know. If they can. Please tell them that for me." I took a deep breath. "And thank you. Whoever you are."

Still looking straight ahead, he spoke. "Be careful. Don't trust anyone."

Frustration made me shout my next words. "Help me out here! Do I know your employer?"

He almost turned then. He cocked his blond head toward me, and for a moment I had the impression that he was going to say more.

The car's engine came to life. He pulled back, gliding past me and out of the parking space, and drove away.

I watched him go. I stood in the lot for several minutes, waiting for my racing heartbeat to return to normal. When it did, I went over to the shopping center, found a pay phone, and called Dennis's office. He wasn't in, and I left no message. I hung up, making a vague mental note to talk to him as soon as possible.

Then I made a big mistake: I forgot all about Abel Brandt and his business partner from New York. I would not remember lunch at Papagayo's again until several days later, and even then I did not do what I should have done about it. It was only much later that I realized my stupidity.

I walked back across the street to my car.

"Hello, Elsa, it's Joe. Joe Wilder."

"Hi, Joe."

"I'm at the Reef. They tell me you didn't come to work today. Is everything all right?"

Pause.

"I guess. I just don't feel like—"

"You're not ill, are you?"

"Oh, no, Joe. Nothing like that. I'm just a little . . ."

Pause.

"Well, I won't bother you. I was just—"

"Wait, Joe."

"Yes?"

"I just made some iced tea. Why don't you come over here?"

"Are you sure you—"

"Yes. It's such a lousy day. Perhaps you can cheer me up. Do you know the way here?"

"Sure."

"Okay. I'll see you in a while."

Click.

It was a small, pretty house situated on the hill just above Shell Beach. There was a living room/dining area opening onto a suspended sundeck. A tiny kitchen and a fair-sized bedroom completed the layout. My impression was one of light and airiness, with many windows and doors open to the sunshine. Furniture, carpets, bedspread, and utensils were all in shades of beige, pale blue, mint green, and chocolate brown. Bookshelves, colorful island paintings (by Elsa), and large bowls and vases of tropical flowers added touches of graceful hominess.

The most dramatic corner of the house held the baby grand piano, on one side of the living room. What was eye-catching was not the instrument itself, but the large, beautiful seascape that dominated the wall above it. I stared.

She placed a tall glass before me and sat in the armchair across from my couch.

"I see you're inspecting my first major work," she said.

"I'll say. It's really amazing, Elsa. If I had created that, I'd do nothing but paint for the rest of my life."

She smiled and raised her glass in a toast. "Mutual admiration society."

Despite the smile, I could see that there was definitely something troubling her today. She looked pale and drawn, as if she had not had enough sleep lately.

This woman always made me feel self-conscious. To cover my awkwardness, I stood up and went over to the piano.

"Cheering up music," I said as I sat and uncovered the keyboard. I struck a few chords to get the feel of it. It was badly in need of tuning. After a moment, I launched into a rusty, discordant, but lively rendition of Joplin's "The Entertainer."

She watched me play. At one point, I glanced over at her and our eyes met. She was staring, and on her face was an expression of great sadness. After a moment, she rose and wandered out onto the sundeck. When I finished the piece, I closed the lid and went out to join her.

She leaned on the wooden railing, gazing out at the wild thicket of trees stretching down from the house to the beach below us. The gentle afternoon breeze played in her hair, sending sparkling gold strands wafting in all directions. A single tear moved slowly down her distinctly unrosy cheek.

"I'm sorry about the piano," she said. "The last time it was tuned was six years ago today."

I placed my hand on her arm, trying to smile. "Six years ago today? You certainly have a memory for dates."

She turned to face me. "Yes. Today. It was exactly six

years. You see, the tuner was here that day. Except for
me, he was the last person to see Bruce—" She broke off
and stared once more down at the trees, then out at the
water.

So. That explained it. I didn't even bother trying to
think of something to say. I leaned closer and put my
arm across her shoulders. We stood there for a long time,
watching as the shadows lengthened and the sun descended over the western mountains. I thought about my
reason for coming to see her today: questions. Callous,
nosy, prying questions. I would not ask any of them now.
Not today, at any rate.

I left her in the early evening. There was really nothing I could do here. I didn't know her well enough. Not
yet. Even so, I made one more attempt as she walked me
to my car.

"You shouldn't be alone this evening," I told her.
"Can I take you to dinner?"

She shook her head. "I'm already spoken for. Dinner
and a movie with Willie."

"Oh. Well, don't let him drive."

She almost smiled. "I never do."

The green-eyed monster prompted my next comment. "For people not dating, you two seem to spend a
lot of time together."

For the first time that afternoon, Elsa laughed. "Oh,
Joe, get real. Willie Whitney is a pothead and a beach-
comber. He drinks, he deals, and he plays more pool than
Minnesota Fats. He's a terrible liar and a terrible run-
around. He will sleep with virtually anything that can't
outrun him, regardless of race, creed, color, gender, or
marital status. Despite all that, he is one of the most

charming people I know. He was Bruce's best friend, and now he's my best friend."

I got into the car, looked up at her, and smiled. "Can you outrun him?"

She laughed again: she looked good when she laughed. "Constantly."

I laughed, too. "Can you outrun me?"

She leaned down and kissed my cheek.

"I don't know yet," she said. "Thanks for coming over. I feel much better. Good night, Joe."

It wasn't until I was driving away, down the hill past the entrance to Haven View, that a small, nagging doubt crept into my mind. It wasn't about Willie. It didn't even have anything to do with what Frank had told me about her. Something else . . .

It hit me all in a rush. I pulled over to the side of the road and sat staring at the lights in the harbor before me. Something she'd said. Something that didn't make any sense, not after what Willie had told me on the beach the other day. No, it definitely did not make any sense. Unless . . .

Oh, God, I thought as I finally drove back out onto the road. More questions . . .

Later that night I stood alone on my sister's balcony, looking out once again at the harbor lights. I was thinking about all the events since that moment nine days ago when I'd sat in my mom's apartment in New York, talking to the reservations clerk.

Suddenly, for no reason that registered at the time, I found myself thinking back on an incident from my childhood.

The grounds of Haven View. Afternoon. Summer. The three boys, age twelve, are playing a game. Dennis has just found Frank's hiding place, in the branches of a tree, and climbed up to tag him. Joe has emerged from a nearby bush to scream, "You're it! You're it! Frank is it!" Frank presses his face against the trunk of a tree and begins the slow—and slowly quickening—count to one hundred. Joe grabs Dennis's hand and drags him off around the side of the house.

"Where are you taking me?"

"Hush! Just come on!"

They circle the building until they arrive at the steps to the kitchen. Indicating that Dennis must help him, Joe pulls aside the branches of the shrubbery that runs the entire length of the back of the house and scurries through to disappear. There is a space under the kitchen, behind the bushes, about four feet high and ten feet deep, just large enough for the two of them to conceal themselves. Dennis follows.

"Wow!"

"Neat, huh?"

"I'll say! I never knew this place was here."

"Frank showed it to me a couple of weeks ago."

"Totally boss!"

"Shhh!"

The two boys push aside watering cans, rakes, hoes, and other implements and sit, breathless and giggling in the darkness, waiting.

Hours seem to pass before the inevitable running footsteps are heard on the flagstones beyond the hedge that conceals their hiding place. The two of them hold their breath as Frank pokes around. They listen as he checks under the kitchen stairs, over by the servants' quarters, even in the doghouse. Queen is there, very pregnant, and she does not appreciate the intrusion. Joe and Dennis try to stifle their laughter as she barks her outrage at the obviously startled Frank, who emits a loud scream.

It is the laughter, unable to be checked, that exposes them. With a cry of triumph, Frank dives through the shrubbery and into the crawl space.

"Okay, you turkeys!" he shrieks. "Now you're gonna get it!"

Dennis scrambles back behind a pile of paint cans to escape the touch of death. Joe, helpless with laughter, grabs a machete and brandishes it before him in mock self-defense.

"Tag me and you die, sucker!" he cries as Frank reaches out toward Dennis and slaps his ankle.

"You're it!" Frank announces.

With a groan, Dennis covers his eyes and begins loudly counting to one hundred.

Joe drops his makeshift sword and slithers past Dennis, out into the light. Frank has already disappeared, so he is on his own. He flies from the kitchen courtyard and around to the other side of the house. He jumps up onto the veranda and dashes in through the nearest open door. The house has been designated off limits in the game, but nobody said anything about using it for shortcuts to other places of concealment.

As he leaps into the room, he collides with the piano and stands, panting, getting his bearings. This is the library, he thinks. Through that door and down the hall is—

He freezes, the realization slowly dawning on him that he is not alone in the room. There, seated on a couch half in shadow, reading, is Judge Jensen.

The man reaches up and pulls the reading glasses from his face. He sits there, silently inspecting the boy next to the piano.

"Ah," he says at last. "Master Wilder. And where are you off to in such a hurry?"

When he finds his voice, Joe stammers, "Excuse me, sir.

We're playing hide-and-seek, and I was just . . ." He trails off lamely, knowing how ridiculous it sounds. He waits by the piano, staring.

The judge studies him some more. "Hide-and-seek? I see." His voice is low, but not unfriendly. "And who is winning this game of hide-and-seek?"

Joe takes a few more steps into the room.

"Well," he mumbles, "I've only been 'it' once all afternoon, so I guess I am."

The man on the couch slowly nods his head.

"Yes," he drawls. "You seem like a very capable young man. I read in the paper recently that you won a contest."

Though nervous, Joe can't help but smile. "Yes, sir. The Interscholastic Short Story Contest. First prize."

"Interscholastic? There must have been quite a few entries."

"About two hundred, sir."

"Two hundred! That's quite an achievement. And do you intend to become a professional writer?"

"No, sir. I want to be an actor."

Judge Jensen raises his eyebrows. "Ah, yes, the family tradition. Will you be as good as your mother, do you think?"

"I'll certainly try, sir."

Joe is startled when the judge laughs.

"An excellent answer. No false modesty, but no fear, either. My son should have your wits." He shakes his head then, looking away. Finally, he gives the boy one last, penetrating appraisal. "Yes. A very capable young man . . ."

There is a great commotion from the yard outside as Frank and Dennis search the grounds, calling Joe's name. Joe backs toward the door to the veranda.

"Excuse me, sir," he says. "I'd better get back out there before they have a fit."

The man watches, smiling, as the boy turns and runs from the room.

I stared out at the view from Lee's porch, remembering. Three facts were clear in my mind:

Strangers weren't the only victims of the judge's Dobermans. They had always barked at Frank.

I had briefly been holding in my hand what was very likely to have been the murder weapon.

The incident in the library was the only time I had ever been alone with Hubert Jensen.

9

$\diamond$

TANGO

I spent the next day lying on the beach. Magens Bay was still one of the most gorgeous places I've ever seen, with its endless stretches of fine, too-white sand, its warm, too-blue water, and the towering rows of palms stretching back to the hills behind. God at His best: even Hollywood could not have invented it. Of course, Abel Brandt's housing scheme didn't mar the perfect view. Not yet, anyway . . .

My mind was on hold. I swam, ran up and down the shoreline, ate junk food from the concession stand; all the activities of an unconcerned, untroubled tourist. I'd even borrowed Lee's P. D. James novel, but the moment the inevitable group of suspects arrived, I cast it aside. No murders, please. No puzzles. Just sand and surf and magical, penetrating warmth. I slathered my naked self with oil and lay back on the most garish beach towel I could find—a brightly colored, anatomically correct, nude young woman stretched out on her back above the legend "Lay Me on a Virgin Island." I couldn't even be bothered to sit up long enough to look around for my guardian. If he was here, fine. We could both take the day off.

I must have dozed at some point. One minute it was about two o'clock, and the next thing I knew it was three-thirty. I ran to the men's showers, donned my recently acquired hot pink "I'm a Virgin (Islander)" T-shirt and white jeans, and headed for the parking lot. I'd waited two days for Bertram's haircut: I wasn't about to miss it.

Bertram surveyed me from my straw hat and reflective Foster Grants to my white espadrilles.

"Either you have a lovely sense of humor or you've lost your mind," he remarked as I entered Snips, his high-tech symphony of pale gray, pale yellow, and mirrors on the Waterfront in the center of town. He waved me into a chair.

"Now, before I forget," he went on as I settled in, "here are Lee's tickets for the Arts Council gala. And she told me to ask if you wanted any." He handed me a small envelope.

"When is it?" I asked.

"Day after tomorrow. Alvin Ailey Dance Company. *Everybody* will be there. Then there's a party at Letitia Stewart's house. Do come, Joe. It'll be fun. The tickets are mindlessly expensive, but it's all in a good cause."

I had an idea. "May I use your phone?"

I called the Reef and asked for Elsa. She seemed pleased by the invitation, and I finally had a real date with her.

"Put me down for two," I told Bertram as I hung up.

There was a middle-aged woman in the other chair being tended to by an efficient-looking young girl. Bertram introduced the girl, who smiled at me and returned to her task. After that, she and her client paid no attention to our conversation, which, as it turned out, was probably a good thing.

"So, you grew up with Frank Jensen," Bertram said as he lowered my head into the sink. "I never really knew him until Tangera entered our lives. She was a student at UVI when she first came in here. I took one look at her and—well, instant crazy. Add water and stir."

"I heard her use that expression," I said.

"She got it from *me*," he snapped as he towel-dried my hair. He inspected me in the mirror before us, nodded to himself, and reached for the scissors. I knew better than to insult him with the usual trim-the-sides-and-take-a-little-off-the-top nonsense. I lit a cigarette, closed my eyes, and thought of England.

At the Brandts' house, when we had first met, he had reacted peculiarly to my announcement that Frank and I were old friends. It had seemed to me that he was not particularly happy about it.

"I'd never met Tangera before I got here last week," I said. "I guess you've known her longer than she's known her husband."

"My dear," he replied, "it was I who introduced them."

Pay dirt. "I didn't know that."

"Oh, yes," he went on. "She came here to have her hair done and we became pals. We used to get all dressed up and go out dancing. One night we were—I don't know, someplace—very late. We were on the dance floor when she saw him and pointed him out to me. There he

was, in a dinner jacket, leaning against the bar, with that
black hair and those dark eyes. He was staring at us—
well, at *her*, to be precise—and he just seemed so *intense*.
'That's Frank Jensen,' I told her, 'the richest bachelor on
the island.'

"And, you know, she did the most extraordinary
thing. She stopped dancing and stood there in the middle
of the floor, staring right back at him. I mean, Donna
Summer or somebody was positively decimating the
sound system, but I could have sworn I heard Andy Wil-
liams singing 'Lara's Theme.' Well, I knew what to do. I
led her over to the bar right next to where he was standing, and I made like it was this big accident. 'Oh, hi,
Frank,' I said, and he said hello, and I went, 'By the way,
do you know Tangera?' And they stared some more. I,
with my usual tact and diplomacy, took off, but I kept an
eye on them. They talked for a while, and then they
danced. Then more talk. Like that, you know? And all
the way home in the car she kept going on and on about
him. I'd never seen her so excited.

"As I dropped her off, she turned to me and said, 'I'm
going to marry him, Bert.' Just like that. I guess I
laughed, but she was serious. She just knew, somehow.
Two months later they were married—by a justice of the
peace in Puerto Rico, of all things. That was my first
experience of her gift, or whatever you want to call it.
She's psychic, you know."

He put down the scissors and reached for an electric
razor.

"I probably shouldn't say this to a friend of his," he
whispered, "and you must *never* repeat it to Tangera, but
I don't like Frank Jensen. I'm sorry, but he gives me the
absolute creeps. He's so completely humorless. I mean,

that was awful about his father, but Frank was unhappy long before that." He paused, then added, "You know, I've always questioned his motive in marrying Tangera."

Our eyes met in the mirror.

"That's funny," I said. "Given the circumstances, most people would question her motives."

He regarded me for a long moment.

"A girl does what she can," he said. "Don't get me wrong: Miss Helen Keller could see they're crazy about each other. It's part of what I dislike about him—he's so jealousy protective of her. He resents her friends, and that includes me. But that's not what I'm getting at. I'm just wondering how quickly he would have married her if it hadn't been for Hubert. It was no secret that Frank hated him—the whole island knew that. I only met the man a couple of times, and 'ill-of-the-dead' and all that, but he *was* a bit of a horror movie, wasn't he? And Tangera was so conveniently inconvenient. A black lady from Absolutely Nowhere, Martinique, third shack on the right." He shook his head and reached for the blow-dryer. "I don't know, I just can't get rid of the feeling that Frank was *using* her, somehow. As some sort of—of weapon."

Better that than a machete, I thought. I glanced over at the two women: they were deep in some conversation of their own. Even so, I lowered my voice.

"Who," I asked Bertram, "do you think killed Hubert?"

He turned off the blow-dryer and came around the chair to face me. He, too, was aware of the others in the room.

"We're done here," he said, "and you're my last client today. It's nearly five—cocktail hour. May I buy you a drink?"

My hair was beautiful. He'd parted it on the other side from my usual separation, and he'd managed to get it up and back, out of my face. I stood before the mirror, smiling. From the neck down I was Harry Tourist, with the pink Virgin shirt and white pants and shoes. But from the eyebrows up I could pass for the cover of *Esquire*.

"Hell," I said, handing him a credit card, "I'll buy *you* one."

Biff was standing behind the bar of her club when we arrived.

"Howdy!" she called to Bertram as we came from the sunshine into cool darkness. She waved us onto bar stools.

"Hello, darling," Bertram said, leaning across to kiss her cheek. "I've brought a friend today."

She smiled and extended a hand. "Hi, I'm Biff. Welcome to St. Thomas."

Bertram roared with laughter. I removed the sunglasses and watched as her face registered surprise.

"Joe Wilder!" she screamed. "I didn't recognize you in that getup. Bertram, you should have told me. I thought you were cheating on Carlos."

"Perish the thought!" he rejoined, and they were off on a familiar routine of daily gossip as Biff placed drinks before us and I looked around.

The club was an attractive, well-appointed place. The bar ran the length of the room, and there were leather-lined booths along the wall behind us. To my right, up three steps, was an open-air terrace with wrought iron tables and chairs surrounding a small dance floor. In one corner, a small native man sat playing a piano. A medley of Rodgers and Hammerstein. Stairs led down from the bar to what was presumably a lower level of rooms that would be open later in the evening. Candles provided most of the light in the bar, and the terrace above was bathed in the last afternoon sunlight.

Two men sat at the other end of the bar, and a few tables and booths were occupied. A waiter moved from group to group with a constantly laden tray. A lone couple—a man and a woman—danced on the terrace. Farther off, at one of the tables, a young man who wanted desperately to be Judy Garland was singing "Do I Love You Because You're Beautiful?" along with the piano. During the next hour, as twilight descended, the place filled considerably as shops and businesses closed and their tired proprietors made their way to the many watering holes around the island. The end of another day . . .

"Now," Bertram said, turning to me as Biff went off to serve other patrons. "As we were saying. I didn't want to get into it at the shop, walls having ears and all that. You asked me who killed Hubert. I don't know, of course. I guess it could have been anybody. But I will tell you this: if it was a member of the family, it was probably Frank."

I nodded. "That's a popular theory."

"Think about it, Joe. Helen Jensen is not really a consideration. She's just out there where the trains don't run, as they say. And Tangera didn't do it."

"You seem very sure of that," I said. "Do you think Tangera's capable of violence?"

He nodded vigorously. "*Capable*, yes: she could kill someone as soon as look at them. I mean, we're friends and all that, but she *does* have a temper. She's fun and exciting most of the time, but I would never want her as an enemy. That would be scary. Getting in her way is not something I'd recommend. But I don't think she'd walk up to anybody—even Hubert—and cut their head off. Frank . . . I don't know. Of course, any number of people wanted him dead."

Biff had arrived in time to hear the last part of his speech.

"Gee," she said, "I wonder what you're talking about."

Bertram grinned. "The prime suspect, herself!"

She cackled and slapped the surface of the bar. "Isn't that the damnedest thing? I was one of the last people to talk to the old coot. God, I hope I *never* see the inside of that police station again. They kept me there for hours!"

"Were you really a suspect?" I asked as innocently as possible.

"Hell, yes!" she bellowed. "He threatened me! Can you imagine? That police lieutenant must have asked me a hundred times if I knew anything. And poor Honey, sitting there in that place with all those big, burly men around her, explaining as delicately as possible that I'd been home in bed with her at the time. You should have seen their faces!"

"Hubert threatened you?" I was beginning to sound like the village idiot.

"He sure as hell did!" She beckoned to us, and we three bent our heads together. "He calls me, see, and tells me that the Health Department has some problems about my place, and that several neighbors have complained about the noise late at night. And there's this rumor I've been serving minors! Now, I know my neighbors, and I have friends in the Health Department, if you know what I mean. I know every kid on this island, and they're *not* coming in here! So the judge is talking total horse puckey. I wait to hear what he's really up to. Well, he says, maybe he can do something to help me—if I can help him."

She lowered her voice further. "There's this local senator, see. A Democrat; one of Hubert's biggest opponents. Well, everybody's been speculating for years about which side his bread is buttered on, dig? Not that anyone cares; it's just your usual idle chat. So Hubert—this big, pompous, soon-to-be governor—asks me if I can confirm any rumors. That's what he said, 'confirm.' He, like, has *files* on all these people! So I'm supposed to say, 'Yeah, Hubert, I saw this Democrat and Bertram in the middle of my dance floor, doin' the deed!'"

"Oh, please," Bertram intoned. "He's not my type."

Biff shook her head, remembering. "God, what a creep he was! Anyway, I said, in my refined, ladylike way, 'I resent your implications, sir!' Actually, I told him to do to himself what the bishop did to the chorus girl."

"Chorus *boy*," Bertram corrected.

She smiled, regarding her friend fondly. "Yeah, chorus *boy*."

"So," I said, "who killed Hubert?"

Biff laughed and rolled her eyes.

"Somebody wonderful," she said, moving away down the bar.

Bertram had turned to look over my shoulder at the entrance to the club.

"Speaking of which!" he cried.

I knew before I turned around. The pianist, quick on the uptake, had segued suddenly from "Love, Look

Away" to a slow, insinuating tango version of "Tangerine."

There she was in the doorway, grinning. She was wearing white slacks and a rather scanty halter of her signature color. Surrounding her, framing her, were six or seven members of the beach crowd, Willie Whitney tallest among them. As her courtiers ascended to the terrace and filled the largest table, she extended her arms. In a flash, Bertram was in them.

"Tangie, darling! She's here, and the world is once again remarkable. Innkeeper, ale for all! Ale for the horses! Oh, what fun!"

"Hello, Bert," she said. She looked past him to me. "Who is your friend? Let me guess: he is a certified public accountant from Akron, Ohio. Am I close?"

Bertram howled. "No, dear. Despite the tourist drag, it's our very own Mr. Wilder."

She feigned surprise. "Well, so it is. Hello, Joseph. Your hair looks marvelous. Another masterpiece, Bert. Come, join the club." She led us up to the terrace. More chairs were added to the table and we all squeezed in.

Willie was holding hands with his pretty partner from the volleyball game, so I restrained myself from asking if he'd enjoyed the movie with Elsa last night. There were several other boisterous men and women, laughing and chattering and calling for drinks. I looked around at them all: failed artists, failed writers, and bored alcoholics from some of the island's richest families. The beach crowd, down to the last dreary, distasteful, obnoxious detail. In all my life I had never seen such a group of losers collected in one place.

After a while, Tangera turned to me. "Dance with me, Joseph."

She took my hand and led me away from the table. The pianist was playing an extended, jazzy version of her theme song. The next thing I knew, I was standing there swaying in Tangera Jensen's arms. Her hands were behind my neck, her body pressed against me.

We danced. Several minutes passed before I became aware that the others from the table had joined us on the dance floor. Everyone had partners except Bertram, who solved that problem by grabbing the waiter and dancing with him. There was much laughter and shouting all around us.

I was uneasy with her today. My first reaction when she had arrived was a guilty flush, which I had attempted to conceal. I didn't like this, being in such close proximity to her. I didn't like my own response to the feel of her cool, soft hands on my skin. I suddenly realized that I was annoyed: with her, with myself. That is my only justification, my only real excuse, for what happened next.

She smiled up at me. "You are awfully stiff today, Joseph. Has it been a while since you held a woman?"

"I'm not—in the best of spirits," I replied.

"Frank was asking about you. He was sorry to miss you the other morning. Have you spoken to him since then?"

"No," I said.

"When are you planning to see him again?"

"I don't know, Tangera. Will you be at the Arts Council thing?"

"Oh, yes," she said, moving even closer to me. "He will see you then—and so will I. Perhaps we will dance together again. If you do not have a date, we could—"

"I'm going with Elsa Tremayne," I said.

She glanced sharply at me. "Oh. Well . . ."

She looked away, but her voice had revealed it. I drew back and made eye contact with her.

"What's the matter with that?" I asked.

"Oh, nothing . . ."

"Yes, there is. You don't seem to approve."

"I did not say—"

"You don't like Elsa, do you?"

We had stopped on the dance floor. She started us again, dismissing my comment with a light laugh. "Oh, Joseph, do not be ridic—"

I pulled sharply away from her.

"You don't like her," I repeated.

She regarded me for a moment. "As a matter of fact, no. There are very few people on this island I can truly say I dislike, and that woman is one of them." She smiled as she said it.

My annoyance had ripened into anger. At that moment I didn't find her remotely charming. "What's the matter, Tangera? Are you afraid of a little competition?"

She laughed. Her eyelids lowered dreamily, coquettishly, as she gazed at me.

"You are being very rude, Joseph," she cooed. "I'm not afraid of anything. You should know that by now."

The song was nearing its conclusion. She pressed her cheek against my shoulder, and we were dancing again.

"Besides," she breathed, "I seem to be winning this particular round."

I pushed her from me and held her at arms' length, gripping her elbows. "What's that supposed to mean?"

She must have known that I was angry, yet she persisted in laughing. "Oh, Joseph! Have you forgotten the library the other night? The way you look at me every time we are in the same room together? Compete, indeed. I should say I have already made quite a bit of headway."

"She used to date your husband," I said. Where the hell had that come from?

Now, at last, her eyes flashed.

"He did not marry her," she said. "He married me."

I stood there, my fingers digging into her bare arms, as the pianist drowned us out.

There was a scattering of applause. I looked around at the others on the dance floor and dropped my arms to my sides, preparing to go back to the table.

He could have gone on to play anything else in the world. He didn't. He launched into a lively version of what was obviously a very popular local song.

The Girl from Ipanema.

We both turned our heads to stare at him. When she looked back at me, I could see the surprise in her eyes. She quickly composed herself, covering for her slip in the only way she could, on the spur of the moment. A slow smile crossed her face and she resumed her languid air.

"Elsa Tremayne," she said sweetly. "Please! The day I compete with such a person as that, the devil will be handing out parkas."

That, coming on the heels of that song, was her fatal error. I grabbed her hand, nearly crushing it with the force of my grip. She emitted a squeal of pain as I fairly dragged her from the dance floor and down the steps. I strode across the bar toward the farthest, most isolated booth.

"You are hurting me," she whispered as she stumbled along behind me.

When we arrived at my destination, I flung her down onto a banquette and slid into the booth across from her. Only then did I release her hand.

She was furious. Her eyes bored into me as she rubbed her wounded wrist. "How dare you? Have you gone mad?"

I leaned across the table, thrusting my face close to hers. I pressed my hands down against the surface of the polished wood to keep them from shaking. I have rarely felt such rage.

"Hello," I croaked, unable to control my voice. "Perhaps you don't realize who I am. My name is Joe Wilder. Frank Jensen is my best friend. You sent me a letter asking me to come here for his sake, or so you claimed. You're my best friend's wife, and I am sick and tired of you and your games. Your orange clothes—"

"Joseph—"

"—and your orange perfume—"

"Joseph!"

"—and your whole goddamned orange bag of femme fatale bullshit!"

"*Joseph!*"

I leaned back against the leather seat, breathing heavily. She was staring at me, almost through me. The lovely, exotic creature I knew had completely disappeared. The woman who faced me now was someone I had never seen before. When she spoke again, her voice had the same tone as mine.

"Forgive me if I was flirting," she hissed, "but it is the only way I know to treat men. Because it is the only way they have ever treated me."

She paused, breathing deeply, waiting for her words to sink in. Then she continued.

"I discovered my power when I was twelve years old. That was when my father—the man my mother *claimed* to be my father—started in on me. Do you understand that? My second lover was my older brother. It was no use trying to fight them, and I could not tell anyone.

"You asked me the other day how I got to St. Thomas. Well, figure it out. I grew up with filth and poverty and ignorance all around me. It was all I knew. But I also knew that other people were better off than we were. I longed for the day when I could get away from that place.

"I had only two weapons at my disposal: I was very smart and I was very pretty. One day when I was fifteen, I washed my face and put on my only good dress—which happened to be orange—and I walked into town. There were hotels there, with bars in the lobbies. I sat in a bar in my orange dress, and it all began. For three years, once a week, I walked into town. So different from the trips with my aunt, for the piano lessons! Rich tourists, rich natives—it really didn't matter.

"One local businessman took a great liking to me. It was he who taught me about the finer things: clothes, jewels, etiquette. I learned all I could from him. He once told me something I shall never forget. One evening—I was in his bed at the time—he looked at me and said, 'Tangera, you are the only girl I ever met who could probably get whatever she wanted. From anyone.' That was when I got out of his bed. I sold his gifts and saved the money.

"Then I walked smiling back to the convent school. Back to Sister Marie Claire, who in addition to being a nun was also a lesbian. She was only too happy to help me get away—to remove temptation from herself, I suppose. I smiled so innocently as she prayed over me and fondled me and arranged for my visa.

"Let me have a cigarette."

I lit us both up and sat there, waiting. I could think of absolutely nothing to say. Finally, she continued.

"Frank once asked me how I obtained money in Martinique. I told him that a group of parapsychologists paid me to test my extrasensory perception." She laughed, low and bitterly, and shook her head. "No one has ever tested me. I suppose you could call it my third weapon, those feelings. I knew I was coming here long before I actually came. After that, it was merely a question of making my vision a reality."

She took a long drag on her cigarette and slowly exhaled.

"And what did I find in St. Thomas? Another man attempting to buy me. It was not until after Frank and I were married that I finally met the Jensens. We had a disastrous dinner together at Haven View. Helen said nothing, but Hubert and Frank ended the evening in an enormous argument. Hubert was discussing me, and the 'repercussions' of marrying me, as if I was not sitting right there! I did not say anything; I got up and went outside and sat in the car, waiting for Frank.

"I would like to be able to tell you that was my only meeting with the judge, but it would not be true. One day, about a month before his murder, he arrived at our apartment. Frank was at his office, and I was alone. He appealed to my 'better judgment,' as he called it. His son had been impetuous, he said, but I looked like a reasonable young woman. It was up to me to bring Frank to his senses.

"I asked him to leave. That was when he delivered his coup de grâce: five hundred thousand dollars. For me to disappear. Permanently. I picked up the telephone. I told him I was calling my husband and telling him to come and get his insane father out of our house. So, he left. I told Frank about it, and I presume they had another fight. Then, on the night he was killed, he called Frank and told him he was being disinherited. The next thing I knew, I was a murder suspect."

She shook her head in disbelief. "Perhaps I should have stayed in Martinique, after all. Now I live in that awful house with that strange woman and a husband who is losing his mind. Why do you think I wrote to you?"

She crushed out her cigarette, rose, and stood looking down at me. Her voice was as cold as ice.

"I created myself," she said. "I invented Tangera because I *had* to invent her. Walk a mile, Joseph. In my *orange* shoes. I regret that letter. I regret ever having met you. You cannot do anything for my husband. You cannot do anything, period. Go back to New York." She leaned down until her face was inches from mine. "And if you breathe one word of this to Frank, you will be sorry. I shall see to that."

She started to walk away. I stood up and grabbed her arm from behind. She stopped, but she did not turn around.

"I saw your face," I breathed into her hair. "When we were dancing. When he started to play 'The Girl From Ipanema.' You know about that. We both know about that. You're never going to get Frank away from that house."

She stood quite still for a moment. Then she walked,

moving swiftly across the bar and up the steps, back to Bertram and Willie and the others.

I had no choice but to follow.

I left the bar soon after that. I smiled at the beach crowd, shook Willie's hand, and thanked Bertram for everything. None of them seemed to have noticed what had occurred. Tangera and I had both remained relatively silent since our return from the other side of the room. When I rose to leave, she didn't even glance at me. I waved to Biff as I descended from the terrace and went out of the club.

The sound of thunder reached me as I made my way west on Back Street and climbed Government Hill toward my sister's home. I had just reached the bottom of the Ninety-nine Steps and paused, preparing myself mentally for the steep ascent, when the sky opened.

I looked around for temporary shelter. I was debating whether to go into Hotel 1829, at the base of the steps, to wait out the downpour when, glancing in the opposite direction, I saw a woman I recognized and a man I did not know standing on the porch of Government House. I ran down the street to the governor's mansion and up the front steps to join them.

"Hello, Ms. Hughes," I said, removing my straw hat.

She regarded me, her large, serious eyes taking in my tourist uniform. When she spoke, it was in a low, quiet voice.

"Hello, Joe. I thought I told you to call me Jenny."

I laughed. She did not.

"You did—Jenny. But there's something a little intimidating about the governor's daughter. I'll get used to it, I expect. Do you live here with your parents?"

"No. Just visiting."

The native man next to her was a tall, broad-shouldered football-player type in a blue suit. She turned to him and spoke. "Let's wait until the rain stops, Milton."

He nodded and moved away down the porch. He stood at a distance from us, watching but not listening. I thought briefly of my own professional shadow and wondered if he was somewhere nearby, watching us on the porch.

Here, I thought, muscle makes sense. Important officials and their families are the people we expect to have bodyguards. Corporate executives. Movie stars. Sheikhs. Disaffected writers from Greenwich Village . . .

"I'd almost forgotten," I said, "how the weather can be in this part of the world."

She leaned on the porch railing, staring out at the wet street.

"Yes," she replied after a moment. "It can be deceptive. Sometimes the rain will come out of nowhere. When you least expect it."

I studied her as she watched the shower. Today she was dressed tastefully and sensibly in a dark blue suit and white blouse. She was holding an umbrella: despite her words, she had anticipated this particular patch of bad weather, and she was prepared for it.

That's when it struck me, what had eluded me at the Brandts' party when I had first seen her. It was this very quality—level-headedness, or common sense, or whatever—that matched her so ideally to Dennis. He could be willful and volatile: moody, some would call it. Despite his recent claim of new maturity, I knew that the old Dennis was just under the surface. Perhaps Jenny Hughes was what he needed to keep things in perspective.

"What do you do, Jenny?"

"I'm a teacher. Fourth grade. And I work with special children. I'm aiming for a doctorate in special education. My ultimate goal is to do that full time, working with kids who are challenged."

"Do you want kids of your own?"

She turned from the railing to face me.

"Yes," she whispered, almost inaudible through the sound of the rain. "I want that very much."

I grinned and reached over to take her small hand in mine.

"Well," I said, "you've already solved the husband part. I'd say you're well on your way. But now you've got the wedding to occupy you. And I want you both to know that I'll make every effort to be there."

Carefully, without wanting to be awkward, she removed her hand. "Oh, really, Joe, you mustn't go to any trouble. You must have things to do back in New York. I mean, if you can't make it, I'm sure Dennis will—"

"I'd like to be there, Jenny. The Musketeers, you know."

She studied my face, slowly nodding to herself. "You're a nice man. I'm glad Dennis has a friend like you."

"Actually," I said, "he has two of us. Whatever problems Frank has been having, I'm sure . . ." I trailed off. Jenny had turned and motioned to the other man.

"Milton, the rain seems to be letting up. We'd best

be going." She turned back to me. "I beg your pardon, Joe, but I really am late now. I'm meeting people for dinner, and—well, it's been lovely seeing you again."

"Yes," I said. "Perhaps we can all get together soon."

It was she who reached out this time to give my hand a brief squeeze.

"Perhaps," she said. "Good-bye, Joe."

She turned and followed Milton down the steps to a limousine. He held her door, then closed it behind her. He produced a cellular phone and spoke briefly into it before getting in the car and driving away.

The torrent had diminished into a light drizzle. I left the porch of Government House and made my way up the Ninety-nine Steps. Just before entering the gate into my sister's yard, I glanced back down the way I had come.

He was standing at the bottom of the steps, looking up at me. I smiled and waved. He did not seem to be amused by the friendliness of the gesture. I pointed at Lee's gate, put my hands together on one side of my face in a pantomime of sleep, and made an okay sign with my fingers. He nodded once. Then he walked away.

Lee and Paul had guests for dinner, and I was late. Everyone turned as I entered the living room. I stood there, smiling at them all, aware of the damp Day-Glo T-shirt clinging to my body. A small puddle formed at my feet from the dripping straw hat and sunglasses I clutched in my hands. The white espadrilles made squishing sounds when I moved.

Lee stared a moment, then burst into giggles. "Excuse me, sir. This is a private residence. If you're looking for Blackbeard's Hotel, it's across the street."

The room resounded with laughter.

"My God, Joe! If you're going to mug the day trippers, you're supposed to steal their wallets. Not their *clothes!*"

10

TWIST

I could feel the tension from the moment I arrived, and it grew steadily as the evening progressed. In view of that, what happened at the Arts Council reception isn't really so surprising.

"Welcome, welcome!" Letitia Stewart called as she approached us across her living room. "Hello, Joe. So nice to have you back on the island. How's Linda?"

"Mom's fine, Mrs. Stewart," I said. "She sends her love."

The handsome elderly woman smiled graciously as she turned to Elsa and took her arm. "Mrs. Tremayne, how are you? You've never been to my house, but there's something here you may recognize."

I followed the two women through the crowd of guests to the other side of the room. Our hostess waved her arm, indicating the large island scene in oil that dominated the far wall.

"Oh, for Heaven's sake!" Elsa cried.

"Beautiful," I said.

The older woman nodded. "Quite beautiful. I fell in love with it the moment I saw it in the Riise Gallery. May I call you Elsa? Joe, you're not a little boy any longer. You may both call me Letitia. I like it when young people address me by my first name. When you're my age, you'll understand why."

She led us through a partition to the dining room. A makeshift bar had been set up next to the long table set for the buffet. Hams, turkeys, roasts, salads: there was enough food for an army. Letitia saw me staring at the enormous feast and smiled.

"The dancers will be joining us shortly," she said. "Have you ever tried to feed artists after a performance? Rather like that scene in *The Good Earth*, with the locusts. Joe, your sister's here already, and I think you both know everybody. We'll have supper as soon as the guests of honor arrive—and weren't they marvelous?"

We agreed. The performance had been superb; various dances from the company's repertoire.

I looked around as the bartender handed us drinks. Lee and Paul waved from across the living room. I saw Abel and Abby Brandt, Biff and Honey, Bertram and Carlos. Frank and Tangera were standing near the doors to the garden with Dr. Deveaux and—surprise!—Helen. I had seen her in the auditorium during intermission, but I somehow hadn't expected her to make the trip up the hill. Certainly not to this particular party. Yet here she was.

Biff's pianist had been engaged to entertain. Tonight's medley of Broadway's best was courtesy of Lerner and Loewe. Melodies from *My Fair Lady* trickled through the rooms as I checked off all the familiar faces. The Brandts and Letitia Stewart had similar guest lists. Different house, different function: same crowd.

Two large native men, one of whom I recognized, came in through the main entrance and did a quick, thorough survey of the terrain. Then they turned toward the front door and nodded. Everyone watched, fascinated, as Governor Hughes and his wife entered. There was a smattering of applause as the pianist—always on cue—abandoned "The Rain in Spain" for a brief, rather humorous rendition of "Hail to the Chief."

The man called Milton and his fellow attendant converged on the governor as he smiled and acknowledged the greeting with a wave. He was a tall, imposing, slightly overweight gentleman in a light gray suit, the color of which perfectly matched his hair. Iris Hughes, like her daughter, was small and lovely, almost regal, with that ageless beauty possessed by certain women. She wore a brightly printed gown of African design. The First Couple was followed into the room by Jenny and Dennis and a handsome, elderly man and woman I recognized as Dennis's parents, John and Caroline Grey.

With everyone focused on the governor, I took the opportunity to look around and note various reactions to his appearance. Biff and Bertram were smiling brightly, obviously impressed. Frank stared coldly at the man while, at his side, Tangera, in her fiery red and orange beaded dress, was apparently inspecting the tiles at her feet. Helen Jensen frowned as she raised a cocktail to her lips. Beyond her I noticed Abel Brandt, the only person in the room who had his back to the governor. Mouth pursed, arms rigid at his sides, he peered intently out at the view.

Letitia led the brigade to surround the newcomers, and the entertainer returned to his contemplation of the Iberian precipitation. I giggled.

"What's so funny?" Elsa asked.

I shook my head. Even I wasn't sure why the evening was beginning to amuse me. I wasn't intoxicated, or particularly tired, or anything like that. It was the tension, I suppose. All these people in the same room. For whatever reason, from that moment on, nearly everything I saw and heard seemed to strike me as being hilarious. As things became worse, I became worse.

When I went over to say hello to the Jensens, only Frank seemed pleased to see me. Helen barely acknowledged me, being more interested in the contents of the glass in her hand. Deveaux watched her nervously. Tangera gave me a silent, frosty once-over and turned away. I beat a hasty retreat.

At one point, Dennis beckoned to me from his side of the room. I excused myself from Elsa and went to join his group.

Mr. Grey shook my hand, and his wife reached up to kiss my cheek. I was a college student when we had last met, so they made much of my physical and professional evolution. They—like everyone else on the island, apparently—had read my novels. How was Linda? My sister in New York? Was I coming to the wedding? Weren't the Ailey dancers wonderful? Fine, fine, I'd try, and yes, they were really super. I stifled the laugh that welled up in me as Dennis presented me to the governor and Mrs. Hughes. They, too, were old friends of my mother, but I'd never met them before.

"So," Clayton Hughes beamed, nearly crushing my

hand in his hearty clasp, "I finally meet our young man of letters. Are you enjoying your visit?"

"Oh, yes," I replied. "I haven't seen my sister in quite a while—not to mention the Musketeers."

Smooth, Joe. I watched the governor's face, waiting to see if he'd rise to the bait.

He did. "Musketeers? What do you mean?"

"Oh, Dennis, of course. And Frank—Frank Jensen."

I turned and pointed across the room to where Frank stood with what remained of his family.

"I see," Clayton Hughes said slowly.

"We were all kids together," I went on. "I thought maybe I could come down here and cheer Frank up a little. Ever since—well, you know. . . ."

"Joe," Dennis cautioned. He stood slightly behind the governor, fixing me with a sharp glance over the man's shoulder. The sight of his grave face threatened to set me off. I pretended not to notice him.

"Yes," Hughes said, nodding. "That was a terrible thing. Really terrible. Of course, I can't say that I saw eye to eye with Hubert Jensen—or even liked him, particularly—but it was terrible, nonetheless."

He'd said 'terrible' three times. I quelled a rising sob.

"Terrible," I echoed. "It must have been terrible for you, too, Your Excellency. I mean, you were one of the last people to speak with him."

"Joe," Dennis warned for a second time. I, for a second time, ignored him. The governor didn't seem to notice anything unusual about the direction in which our conversation was going.

"Yes, I suppose," he said. "I never much enjoyed receiving calls from Hubert. He was always rather bombastic. A bore, really. He seemed to take pleasure in vexing people. And that night he called me at my home, which I must say I did not appreciate. He started in on me, telling me about all the changes he would make when he was elected. Very sure of himself. According to him, I didn't stand a chance. But we must work together, he said, regardless of the outcome. I must support his plans, he said. Get the Virgin Islands out of the Dark Ages. More hotels, a new jetport—*gambling!*" He shook his head dismissively. "I wasn't going to listen to that. I just handed the phone to somebody and went on to my next move. And then, of course, we all heard the news. The very next day. *Terrible!*"

He'd said 'terrible' again. Oh, God, I was going to lose it, right in the face of the governor of the Virgin Islands.

Letitia Stewart, bless her heart, chose that very moment to arrive before His Excellency with several dancers eager to meet him.

"A pleasure, Mr. Wilder," he said as he shifted focus. "Ah! *Les artistes sont arrivee. Bienvenu aux Iles Vierges!*"

Oh, dear. I scurried away before I could hear more of his attempt at French, and before Dennis could scold me.

Some while later, after we had all snacked on ham and turkey and such, I was leaning against the piano, Elsa at my side, giggling to myself as our musician worked his way through *Brigadoon*. Island society was networking at gale force, and here and there I could see dancers leaping about and laughing, illustrating amusing backstage stories for their delighted listeners. Lee wandered over to join us.

"Hi, you two," she said. "Enjoying yourselves?"

"Apparently," Elsa sighed, jerking a thumb at me and

rolling her eyes. "Your brother can't seem to stop laughing."

Lee nodded. "Yes, he can be weird. Don't let it frighten you, Elsa. But, hey, Joe, if you *really* want a good one, check out Helen Jensen over there."

We looked through the crowd toward the other side of the room. Tangera was seated in an enormous rattan fan chair in one corner, holding court with six or seven men. Frank and Deveaux had disappeared somewhere. And there stood Helen, temporarily alone, in her long black dress. She held a glass and surveyed the scene.

As we watched, a woman I vaguely remembered as an old friend of my parents went over to join Helen. The woman smiled and said something. Helen glanced at her briefly and replied. With a shocked expression, the woman moved quickly away. Helen smiled and drank. The woman went to join a small group nearby. She said something and pointed toward Helen. They all looked over at Helen and shook their heads sadly.

"Oh, wow!" Elsa whispered.

"Paul was the one who noticed it," Lee said. "She's been over there doing that for quite a while now."

"Excuse me," I said, already crossing the room.

As I arrived before her, Helen was examining her drink. She looked up and gave me a lopsided smile.

"Hello, Joe. You're just in time to help a lady. I seem to be all out. Would you be a love and freshen this for me?"

"Helen, do you really think you should?"

"I really think I'd *better*—oh, God!"

This last was muttered under her breath as a heavy-set, pleasant-looking gentleman came up to her and took her hand in his.

"Helen, darling," he said. "So good to see you out and about again. Did you get our flowers? We were so sorry about Hubert. He was such a dear friend."

She pulled her hand away from him. When she spoke, her voice was low and surprisingly articulate. "My husband was never your friend. Get away from me, you tired old phony."

The man stared at her, mouth agape. He shook his head, as if to clear it, and hurried off. She turned back to me and smiled.

"Oh, I am enjoying myself immensely!" she said. "This is the first time I've been at a party alone with these creatures. I don't have to be the judge's wife, the diplomatic consort. At last I can tell them *exactly* how I feel about them. Now, how about getting me that drink?"

"No, Helen."

Her eyes widened, then closed contemptuously. "Fine. I'll get it myself. Musketeers, indeed!"

I watched as she teetered off toward the bar, and I was smiling again. Get it together, Joe, I thought. That's not funny; it's sad. But I was still chuckling to myself as I made my way over to the corner, through Tangera's group of courtiers, and leaned down to whisper in her ear.

"I think you and Frank had better get Helen out of here. She's had enough."

Tangera raised her head and stared directly into my eyes. If looks could kill . . .

"I am not interested in what you think, Mr. Wilder," she announced. "I am not interested in *you*. Please go away. *Now.*"

Ouch. She and her courtiers watched as I straightened up and grinned down at her. Two could play this game.

"I beg your pardon," I announced. "I mistook you for someone else. A girl I met once in a bar in Martinique. She was wearing something orange. Have a nice day."

I laughed aloud as I strode across the room to join Elsa. I felt the eyes burning into my back every step of the way.

Back at the piano, I was smiling around at the crowd, half-singing "How to Handle a Woman" with Wally, the pianist. Everyone seemed to be having a good time. Elsa had gone off somewhere with Lee. Tangera continued to electrify her suitors from her throne. Frank was elsewhere in the room, talking to Deveaux. Dennis was at the center of a small clutch, holding forth on some political issue. The governor worked the room, accompanied by Dennis's parents. Our hostess and the First Lady were gossiping with a group of women in one corner. Bertram and Carlos were talking to the dancers.

Abel Brandt, in mid-network, suddenly found himself standing next to Dennis. The two men stared at each other for a moment. Then Abel turned away, only to come face to face with Frank. He took a step backward, eyeing Frank with obvious distaste. Caught between the rock and the hard place that were my two friends, Abel drained his glass in one gulp and took off to the bar. I stopped desecrating "Take Me to the Fair" long enough to slap my knee.

It occurred to me, fleetingly, that there was something I wanted to tell Dennis about Abel Brandt. . . .

Wally had just abandoned the medieval England of

Camelot for the turn-of-the-century Paris of *Gigi* when Letitia arrived next to me at the piano. To the tune of "The Night They Invented Champagne," she and I watched Helen sailing slowly toward the bar.

"That woman is punishing me," Letitia said. "I only invited her tonight because I feel so sorry for her. I didn't really expect her to come. The last time she was in this house, I had to ask Hubert to leave. Oh, well. Do you need anything, Joe?"

"No, thanks, I'm fine."

She smiled and went off to attend to her other guests. Helen Jensen ordered a double. I started to laugh again.

Abby Brandt, in a blue sheath slit to the hip, was wiggling around the floor to the accompaniment of "Thank Heaven for Little Girls." Our eyes met. She extended her arm and crooked a finger, inviting me to join her. I smiled—well, giggled—and shook my head. She shrugged and returned to her one-woman show.

Dr. Deveaux went over to Helen and said something to her. Frowning, she turned away from him. He reached out and grabbed her arm. She yanked herself from his grasp, spilling her drink in the process, and stalked off.

One of the Ailey dancers came over to request some music that everyone could dance to, and Wally dropped *Gigi* like a hot potato. He launched into "Twist and Shout," and the whole room came to jumping, spinning, twisting life. Letitia clapped her hands with delight as nearly everyone, including the First Couple, joined in the fun.

Elsa materialized and dragged me out to the middle of the room. Lee and Paul gyrated nearby. Faces flashed around me: Bertram, Biff, Honey, Jenny Hughes. Abby Brandt seemed to be dancing with three men simultaneously. Abel, unsmiling, watched silently from the side-lines.

I looked around as I danced. Near Abel stood Helen, who stared at the revelry as she slowly drained another glass. Beyond her, in the corner, Tangera surveyed the scene from her fan chair. As I watched, Dennis walked over to Tangera and leaned down to speak to her. He raised an arm, indicating the makeshift dance floor. Tangera never looked directly at him. With a polite smile she shook her head, rose from the chair and walked away from him. Moments later, I noticed her dancing with one of her courtiers.

At one point everyone seemed to change partners, and I found myself dancing with Jenny. She smiled shyly as I twisted in a full circle around her. My sides were beginning to ache. This fact struck me as funny—what else was new?—and, between the movement and my uncontrollable laughter, I was soon forced to leave the floor. Elsa took my hand and led me to a couch. By then, even she was giggling.

I fell back against the cushions and gasped for air as Elsa stood looking down at me. Before I could prepare myself for it, she leaned forward. Her golden hair enveloped my face as she kissed me.

She pulled back a little. Smiling, her face inches from mine, she whispered, "No, I can't outrun you. Consider me caught."

The good time, when it ended, died a quick and horrible death.

The dancing phase of the evening soon burned itself out. Only the professionals among us could have gone on much longer. Elsa had wandered off in search of refreshments. I was alone on the couch when Frank arrived and sat next to me.

I smiled perfunctorily. After saying hello when we'd arrived, I had been giving him a wide berth all evening. I didn't realize until he was sitting there just how uncomfortable I was with him. The last time I'd seen him had been at Haven View, when he'd collected his mother from the rainy veranda and taken her back to her room. To compound my discomfort, I had since alienated his wife, who had told me things Frank did not know, did not suspect, about her. And now I was supposed to act as if nothing had happened.

"Hey, Joe. *Qué pasa?*"

I shook my head. "*Nada.*"

"Having fun?"

"I guess. . . ."

He studied me for a moment. "What's wrong, Joe?"

I looked away. "Nothing."

He leaned forward. "Don't give me that. You were there the other night. I saw you duck under the stairs before I came down. You—saw her. Like that."

I was on my feet before I realized I had moved. "That's really none of my business. I need some fresh air. Excuse me, Frank."

As I walked away from him, it occurred to me that I had no definite goal. I saw the open doors to the garden and immediately aimed for them.

I suppose Letitia's yard was beautiful. There was a patio with wrought iron furniture surrounded by tropical flora. There were hibiscus and bougainvillea and enormous century plants. Blue floodlights shone up from the bases of tall palms, casting the place in dramatic lights and shadows. The breeze was cool and lightly scented by flowers and sea. The West Indian garden of your dreams: under other circumstances, I would have enjoyed it. But Frank was upsetting me. Not only had I witnessed the pathetic scene on the veranda, but he was aware of it. I now had another secret from him, thanks to Tangera. And there was something else. . . .

"Joe."

He had followed me, of course. It was probably too much to hope that he would not. I stood looking out at Letitia's lawn, unable to turn around and face him.

"Your mother is drunk, Frank," I said. "Why don't you take her home?"

"She didn't come with us. She came with Deveaux."

I couldn't stop the laugh, or the sarcasm in my voice. "Well, you seem to be so dedicated to her welfare—"

"Stop it, Joe." He stood beside me now. I could tell without looking that he was watching my face.

"You killed your father, didn't you?"

He was silent. Still, I didn't look at him. I'd finally said it, what I believed from the start. Maybe that was why I hadn't dropped everything and come down here last July. How could I explain that to him? I'd been in New York, preparing a play for production. He'd been here practicing law, married to a woman I'd never met, full of loves and hatreds and resentments of which I knew nothing.

And that, I realized at that moment in Letitia's garden, was the real problem. Not that I suspected he'd murdered Hubert, but that we were no longer friends. How do you tell someone you've known forever that you're not close anymore? That you've both gone your own ways? I didn't know him as I once had—or thought I had. For all I knew, he really *had* murdered Hubert.

And what if he had? What was I supposed to do? Keep silent? Go to the police? I'd never considered that: I'd never considered anything. *Go back to New York*, Tangera had said, *you can't do anything.* She was probably right.

Still he was silent. He stood there watching me, neither confirming nor denying. What was he thinking?

This was it, the reason for my earlier euphoria. The mounting tension I'd sensed all evening. I would go back inside. I would find Lee and Paul, people I loved and understood, people for whom I could do something. I would get Elsa and take her away from here, to somewhere quiet where we could be alone. Here I was useless, and I was beginning not to care.

"I don't know, Frank," I said, finally turning to confront him. "I just don't understand how your life could turn out to be so shabby."

At last he began to respond. He opened his mouth, forming words.

"There you are, Joe."

The voice came not from Frank but from behind him. We both turned to see Dennis coming toward us from the house. Beyond him, Jenny Hughes stood in the doorway watching us.

When we were children, Dennis had been the one who could most easily take charge. Perhaps that was why, of the three of us, his life seemed to be the most successful. There was something unmistakably authoritative about him, when he wanted to create that effect. He did so now.

"Frank," he said, fixing him with the steady gaze of a fearsome school principal, "you'd better go do something about your mother. She's making a spectacle of herself."

The one-two punch. I had set it up, and Dennis delivered the final blow. Without a word, Frank left us and walked past Jenny into the house.

"Sorry, Joe," Dennis said as we watched Frank go. "The governor asked me to do something before Helen ruins the party."

"Yes, of course," I said. "I just wish we could do something to help Frank. I didn't know how bad things were. I came down here because I didn't really believe—"

"Oh, Joe, for God's sake, stop it!"

The explosion of his voice arrested me. I stared. He was watching me now, our faces mere inches apart. I had never seen him this angry before, not in all those years.

"Just stop it!" he repeated. "You came running down here. You didn't believe. Let's help Frank. What the hell can *we* do about it?"

I couldn't think of anything to say to that. After a moment, Dennis reached out and put his hand on my shoulder. The passion was gone; now his voice was sincerely, almost unbearably reasonable. I listened as his words echoed what I had been thinking only moments before.

"Things change, Joe. We're not the same people anymore. Each of us has a life the others don't really know anything about. The Musketeers—well, that was a long time ago. You and I aren't responsible for Frank. He's a grown man. He has to take care of himself. Just let it go."

"I can't," I said. "I keep thinking, what if I were in his position?" I looked up. "Or you? I've always thought of the two of you as my closest friends. What if it were you?"

"You'd go to the police," Dennis said. "No matter who it was. We all know that much about you. Your sense of right and wrong is pretty overwhelming. It always has been."

He was right, of course. Then: at that time, the new Joe Wilder had not yet made his debut appearance. The man I was then agreed with his assessment. All that would change, though, sooner than we knew.

"Look, Joe," Dennis said, "maybe you should just go home. Frank will be all right. The case is closed: there's nobody around to press charges, or anything. Get away from it."

"But, your wedding—"

"That's not for another month. You can come back for it."

Yes. I'd wanted to solve the mystery; now I'd changed my mind. I could live with suspicions, it seemed, but not with facts. What could I accomplish by remaining? I was just about to throw in the towel and take Dennis's—and Tangera's—suggestion when another thought occurred to me.

Dennis.

I studied his face, trying to form words. He noticed my expression and leaned forward. Our words did not even reach Jenny, who watched us from a few yards away.

"What is it, Joe?"

"You," I said. "You knew. All of this. That man—he's yours!"

Dennis stared. "What man?"

"My bodyguard," I whispered. "In the blue Mustang. He killed the creep with the knife. The one who tried to rob me, or—"

I stopped. Everything else was falling into place, and I didn't want to think about it.

The creep with the knife.

Frank.

He wasn't sent to kill me, but to scare me away. To stop me from asking questions and send me back to New York. That's what I thought then, and I still believe it.

At least part of my guess, however, was obviously incorrect. Dennis didn't know what I was talking about. He watched me, his face a study in genuine amazement.

"Bodyguard?" he said at last. "What bodyguard?"

It was at that moment that the shouting began.

I was the first to move. I ran across the patio and into the living room. I stopped short, frozen by the sight. Dennis and Jenny halted in the doorway behind me, staring.

Helen Jensen stood just inside the main entrance to the house, facing the room. Deveaux was next to her, watching helplessly. Frank and Tangera were before her, apparently unable to move. Everyone else stood in a semicircle, gazing on in horror and embarrassment.

"That's right!" Helen cried. "Everybody stare at the freak! You've been doing it all night. Everybody laugh at the crazy lady!" She threw her glass to the floor. It shattered in front of her.

"Helen," Tangera said. At the same moment, Deveaux reached out to take Helen's arm. She slapped his hand away.

"Stop that! Stop grabbing at me. I can walk out of here unassisted, thank you very much! I'm not *that* drunk!"

She looked slowly around at the sea of astonished faces, her lips curling in an awful parody of a smile.

"So nice to see you all again," she announced, her voice dripping with poisoned sugar. "Letitia, darling, you must come to Haven View sometime. It's only fair that I get a chance to throw *you* out of *my* house!" She glared at her hostess. "That's what she did! She threw Hubert out of here. She's been dining out on that story ever since, the wrinkled old prune!"

Tangera turned to her husband, who was staring at the floor. In desperation, she took a step toward her mother-in-law. "Helen, *please!*"

" 'Helen, *please!*' " Helen mimicked. "Spare me your false concern, you sleazy little harlot! As if I didn't know about *you!*" She surveyed the crowd. "As if I didn't know what you all think of me!"

Until now, her performance had merely been outrageous. Now she did something downright peculiar. She looked slowly around at every face in the room. Her last words were barely a whisper, but everyone heard them.

"As if I didn't know who killed my husband!"

She laughed. It began softly, a low gurgle of unamused contempt, and rose in volume to a wild, uncontrollable shriek. It grew within her, filling the room, echoing around us all.

At the height of her hyperventilated abandon, she slowly toppled over backward. She never hit the ground. Deveaux was there to grab her in mid-fall. He picked the unconscious woman up in his arms and rushed from the house. After a moment, Frank and Tangera followed him. Everyone else stood frozen, staring at the door.

Wally saved the day. No Lerner and Loewe this time: with a bang and a flourish, he filled the ominous void with a loud, lively rendition—God bless him!—of "So Long, Dearie." The room burst into laughter and applause. Everyone moved, everyone talked at once. Letitia ran over to kiss the pianist's cheek, and the party resumed.

But not for me. Elsa was suddenly at my side, taking my hand in hers.

"That woman is insane," she said. "Let's get out of here."

We quickly circled the room, exchanging farewells with the governor, Dennis and Jenny, Biff, Bertram, Abel and Abby. I made it clear to Lee and Paul that they were not to wait up for me, thanked Letitia for—much embarrassed laughter—a lovely time, and led Elsa out to my car.

The beach was my idea.

It was very late when we pulled up in front of her house. As I turned off the engine, she leaned over and kissed my cheek.

"Come inside," she said.

They were the last words either of us would utter that evening. Well, almost, but the others don't bear repeating.

We went into the house. She fixed drinks for us and put some soft music on the stereo. Jacket, tie, shoes, and socks ended up on a couch, to be found the following morning. She disappeared briefly and returned, her dress replaced by shorts and T-shirt. Drinks in hand, we moved into each other's arms and danced in the living room.

The warmth of her body; the scent of her hair; the frank expression in her eyes dispelled all memories of that disastrous party. I felt myself relaxing in her company, her house, her world. The breeze through the open doors and the sound of the surf below us put the obvious thought into my head. I placed my arm around her shoulders. Entwined, heads bent together, we made our way out of the house and down the dark, tree-lined path to the bay.

The sand was cool under our bare feet. We embraced in the darkness, swaying slowly to the rhythms of the breakers, the rustling of the trees, the hundred sounds of the nighttime beach. We whispered to each other then, not that it mattered. There was no one nearby to hear us, not for a million miles.

I woke just before dawn. The sound of the surf penetrated my sleep, and a chill breeze washed over my naked skin. I sat up on the sand, my arms automatically clasping my shoulders.

The sky above the horizon to my left was already beginning to lighten. I must have slept soundly, as I had not been disturbed when she pulled away, extricating herself. Yet this had obviously happened at some point: I was alone on the beach.

I had just begun to look around for her, to wonder if I should go up to the house, when I heard the sound of her footsteps crunching across the sand. In a moment she was standing above me, clothed, a large, folded blanket in her hands. We laughed together as we spread the blanket under us. She removed her clothes and lay down, reaching for me.

Afterward, just as the sun arrived, I drifted once more into sleep.

Fool's paradise: such an appropriate phrase. I spent the night and the morning on the beach, making love for the first time since I couldn't remember when. And never once during the interlude—for that is what it was, I see now, a passage between movements—a single thought of all that had come before. This was not the beach where her husband had been washed ashore, nor had it been the property of another corpse. None of that had happened. No troubled friends or haunted houses, ruthless barons or exotic whores. That was some other island.

And then, of course, it all came crashing back. We smiled and kissed and wandered up the hill to the house. To the real world, and the telephone's insistent ringing.

It was Lee. She had been trying to reach us all morning, ever since the first news reports had interrupted her breakfast.

By the time I arrived at Haven View the police and the ambulance had come and gone, and Helen Jensen's body was already on its way to the morgue.

11

DANCE OF DEATH

There were, at that time, two newspapers, two major radio stations and one television network in St. Thomas. In order to drive through the gates of Haven View that day, I had to make my way past cars and equipment. Lucien and a large native man I'd never seen before were keeping the various news teams at bay. It took some maneuvering and much honking and gesticulating to get the car into the driveway. I managed, finally, and the huge iron gates clanged shut behind me.

I found them all in the living room, that odd, silent group that had gathered in the wake of this latest tragedy. They stood or sat about the place, still as statues, as if they had been posed there in tableau by some stark, eccentric filmmaker. Ingmar Bergman: that was my first, inconsequential thought as I wandered in to join them. They all should have been wearing white. Someone, a woman, should have gazed intently out of a window, murmuring some abstract, mournful monologue about the loss of the sunlight on the glistening wheatfields. God is dead and the darkness is upon us. Slow fade. Roll credits.

Tangera was hardly dressed for Bergman. An airy silk kimono, boldly printed in black, white, and burnt orange, had been thrown over a creamy peach nightgown. She sat at one end of a couch, her bare feet curled under her, clutching her upper arms as if the room was too cold for her.

Next to her on the couch was Frank's law partner, whose name, I finally remembered, was Hammond. He was a small, rotund gentleman with a kindly face, a well-kept head of white hair, and a well-cut tropical suit. I looked at him and thought of Claude Rains. He cradled a coffee cup in his hands, peering down into it as if the dark liquid held some vital secret.

Dennis was sprawled in a large chair across from them. I'd called him as soon as I'd gotten off the phone with Lee, and he'd arrived before me. He was visibly uncomfortable: he looked silently from one face to another, almost appearing to size up everyone else in the room as potential antagonists.

Frank and Deveaux were the only two standing. The doctor was at the French doors looking out over the veranda, lost in thought. Frank, clad in striped pajamas under his blue bathrobe, stood directly behind his wife, gazing down at her. He seemed to be making a thorough inspection of her hair.

All things considered, I suppose I could have done or said any one of a hundred things when I walked into that room. But I was like a child who has been given too many birthday gifts. He dives into them, tearing open package after package, delighting in each new surprise. Eventually, worn down by the enormity of it, by the surfeit of sensations, he invariably falls asleep. Already weary, with most of my surprises yet to come, I crossed the room and fell into an armchair next to Dennis.

He was the only one to acknowledge my arrival. He reached over and squeezed my arm lightly with his fingers. We exchanged a look. He shook his head and shrugged.

I looked down at the forearm that Dennis had touched. My jacket had been left in the car, and I had rolled my sleeves up to the elbows. The long scratch was nearly gone now, barely visible under my new tan. I looked up at Frank, who had probably caused the wound. Then I closed my eyes and settled back to wait.

We sat in silence for a long time. A servant—Lucien's wife, presumably—arrived with more coffee and a cup for me. I had finished one coffee and was reaching to pour another when Tangera stood up. She looked around at everyone, her gaze resting at last on her husband. For a moment the two of them regarded each other, then Tangera turned away.

"I cannot stand this," she whispered. With that, she walked past Deveaux and out of the house. The rest of us watched her as she wandered across the patio toward the trees, her brilliant kimono fluttering gently behind her.

Her exit triggered some sort of release in Frank. Fairly sighing with relief, he came around the couch and sat where she had been, next to his partner. There was a brief whispered consultation, and Hammond glanced over at me. Then he turned back to Frank and nodded. Frank leaned forward, confronting Dennis and me.

"It was a heart attack," he said, watching our faces.

There was an earnestness in his manner, and his tone of voice was practically an entreaty: *Please believe me.*

Dennis and I exchanged another quick glance.

"You mean at the party?" I asked. I saw her again in my mind; falling backward, being scooped up by Deveaux and carried away.

The doctor, who had been standing quite still in the doorway all the while, turned to us.

"No," he said, his French-accented voice flat and emotionless. "Later in the night. She was awake in the car. I put her to bed. She was all right when I left the house." He looked at Frank. Was there a challenge, some hint of recrimination in his words? I wasn't sure.

Dennis cleared his throat. "Um, didn't she have some sort of history, or something . . . ?"

"Yes!" Frank cried, unable to conceal the eagerness in his voice. "Yes, she did. High blood pressure, same as me. She had to take pills for it."

He sat there nodding vigorously at us, as a dog will do when attempting to distract its master from the puddle on the floor. His performance suddenly annoyed me, absurd as it was. It was important to me that he should know I was not beguiled.

"Oh, Frank," I muttered. "Helen had to take a pill to butter her toast."

Deveaux strode across the room and stood glaring down at me.

"Don't say that!" he cried. "Don't you dare speak that way!"

Stupid, Joe. The arrow had missed its mark and struck another. I blushed, as well I should. When we lose our patience, my sixth grade teacher had advised, we lose our dignity.

Then, as if to prolong my embarrassment, Pierre Deveaux began to weep.

"She was not strong," he said, turning away from us. "She was kind and gentle. Her heart—she had a heart attack. The paramedics examined her. I examined her. Even the police could see it was her heart. She was—she was lying on the floor next to the bed. She looked so helpless, curled up on her side, with that picture in her arms. . . ." He trailed off, sobbing quietly, his arms hanging heavily at his sides. His final word was a long, low moan of anguish: "Helen!"

He stood there for a moment, his back to us, shaking his head. Then he walked out of the house and across the patio. After a moment, we heard his car start and pull away down the drive.

It occurred to me as the sound of his car faded that these were his first words to which I'd paid the slightest attention. I don't mean as a child: "Breathe in," or, "Say 'ah,'" or, "Drink plenty of fluids." But during this visit to the island, I'd seen him twice. He'd spoken all through the dinner party in this house, not to mention Letitia's reception. Yet this is the first time I've actually recorded anything he uttered. He'd struck me as insignificant, almost comical, and that was my mistake. He was a man, with feelings. He experienced love and loss and pain. And all the while I had ignored him, as Helen had ignored him. We shall not pass this way again, I thought, and any small thing I could have done for him remained undone. I never saw Dr. Deveaux again. I knew then—and I know now—that there are victims beyond dead bodies.

"Forgive me, Frank," I offered into the silence. "I'm sorry about your mother."

He rose from the couch. "Forget it. Austin, could you

stay a while longer? There's something I want to discuss with you."

His partner nodded.

"Good," Frank continued. "You two come with me. I want to show you something."

Dennis and I got up and followed him across the hall to the judge's office. We watched as he produced the key from the flowerpot on the table and unlocked the door. Only Dennis went with him into the room: I remained in the doorway, watching. Frank walked over to the shelves near the desk. Next to the urn containing the judge's ashes was a large, silver-framed photograph. He took it from the shelf and held it up for our inspection.

It was an old picture, fading and slightly blurred. Hubert must have been about twenty-five and Helen was several years younger. They sat, cheeks pressed together, grinning into the camera. I studied their faces: they were young and beautiful and obviously in love.

He never loved Helen, my mother had said. She'd never seen this photograph; it would change her mind. Once, long ago, he had.

"There was a duplicate on her bedside table," Frank told us. "That's what she was holding when Eunice found her."

Eunice. First Hubert, headless, in this very room. Now Helen, sprawled on the floor of her bedroom, clutching the picture. If that woman has any sense, I thought, she's in her cottage right now, packing.

Dennis consulted his watch.

"I have to get to work," he said as he came out of the office. "If there's anything . . ."

"No," Frank replied, following him out to the veranda. "We'll be okay. Thanks for coming."

We stood outside in the midday sunshine, the three of us. So much of our lives, I thought, together. And then apart. We were all thinking the same thing, evidently. We looked at each other in silence for a long moment, feeling mutually the unspoken, unutterable sadness. Then, with a nod to Frank and me, Dennis turned to leave.

The sudden invasion was a complete surprise. We had not seen or heard anyone approaching us, and Lucien's angry cry was a moment too late. The three of us whirled around to confront the tall, thin young native man with the camera who had materialized in the driveway not thirty feet away. He grinned at us and rapidly clicked off several shots. He was in the act of turning to take aim at Tangera, who stared from the far end of the patio, when Lucien came charging up the drive from the direction of the gates. The impish smile widened as he dashed off through the trees and over the wall of the estate. We all stood there, watching him go.

Lucien, furious and mortified, launched into a loud, animated apology. Frank raised a hand to stop him.

"It's all right," he said. "I guess we had to expect that. Just try to keep the rest of them out, okay?"

With a nod, the gardener turned around and marched determinedly back to his post.

Nobody said anything. Dennis shook his head and strode off to his car; Frank turned around and entered the house to meet with Austin Hammond; and I, after a moment's hesitation, walked across the patio to join Tangera.

She watched my approach. As I came up to her, she turned away, leaned her shoulder against a tree, and looked out beyond the boundaries of Haven View toward the harbor. In Yacht Haven, far below us, a hundred boats floated gently on the water. A flock of gulls skimmed the surface among them, scavenging. She seemed to be studying this remote activity.

We'd stood together in this very spot not long ago, on the day of my arrival. I knew her slightly better now in some respects, but, overall, I was certain that I didn't really know her at all.

"You've been out here quite a while," I said. "Calculating your next move?"

There was a time—only days ago—when she might have turned around and slapped me. Or laughed. Or at least said something devastating. Now she just watched the distant birds and slowly shook her head. When she spoke, there was no life in her voice.

"How strange it is, Joseph," she murmured. "As if I had some awful guardian angel. My own personal mongoose." After a moment she said, "Never wish for things."

She'd had no time to apply perfume this morning, not with the uproar, yet even now I was aware of the citrus scent. It must have permeated her skin. The kimono flapped in a sudden breeze.

I walked around her and planted myself squarely between her and the view she was contemplating so raptly. At last she raised her eyes and looked at me. When I was absolutely sure that she would listen, I began.

"I will probably never understand you," I said, watching her face. "You certainly don't owe me any favors. Even so, I want you to do something. Not for me. Not even for yourself. For him. As soon as you possibly can, I want you to take him and get the hell away from this island. His parents are gone now. He has all their money, more than you could possibly ever want. If you sell this house, you'll have even more. You're both unhappy here, and it's only going to get worse. If you think you're outcasts *now*—well, just wait. Scandals don't go away, Tangera. Not ever. Helen's death was apparently perfectly natural, but that didn't stop the police from arriving. The police! They wanted to be sure. Right now, every reporter on the island is outside those gates. Do you want to live like that?"

Now she lowered her gaze to the ground at her feet.

"No," she said. "I do not."

"He's going crazy, Tangera. He's losing it. His father. His mother. This house. Dancing in the middle of the night. God only knows! And all the while his wife is running around all over the place, coming on to every other rich man in sight. Including me. That's why you wrote me that letter. I was some sort of—of *alternative.*"

"That is not true—"

"What *is* true, Tangera? Do you *know* anymore?" I waited a moment, then I let her have it. "He killed Hubert, didn't he?"

Her eyes flashed. "No!"

"He found out that you'd asked me here to investigate everything, and he decided he had to do something. So he sent that thug to scare me away."

"What? What are you—"

"And *you* hired someone to protect me. I was supposed to find out that he'd killed Hubert and go to the police. You'd vamp me with the perfume and the clothes and the fabulous woman routine. The lonely, *rich* writer whose book you so admired. With all the friends in show business and publishing."

"*You* are the one who is crazy!" she cried. She whirled around and took off toward the house.

I was right behind her. "Frank goes to jail; you get his money and run off to New York. No more Helen. No more Haven View. No more hanging out on the beach with a bunch of lowlifes. And no more strange husband who loved his *mother* more than he loved you! Is that what your vision showed you? Your *oeil extraordinaire?* My God!"

I stopped. She was nearly to the veranda now: I wasn't going to follow her into the house. I stood in the middle of the patio watching her go, the vivid kimono billowing. Pretty girl, running.

Then she stopped and turned around. She glanced back toward the doors to the living room where Frank was presumably still in conference. She walked up to me. I looked into her eyes: anger, outrage—and something else.

Fear.

So. Some of my accusations had hit home, but which?

She came very close and spoke in an intense whisper. "I have never met anyone like you, Joseph. No man, certainly. I will make a deal with you. I know nothing about any thug or any protector, and I know for a fact that Frank did not kill his father. He was home all night—I do not even care whether or not you believe that.

"Here is the deal. You go away. Now. Back to New York, or back to your sister and your precious Elsa Tremayne. Wherever. If you do that, I promise I will do as you have suggested. I will get Frank away from here. We can start again somewhere else. I will take care of him. I can do that—I *want* to do that. You are right: I have more money than I could ever need." She paused, searching my face. "He loves me. No one has ever loved me like that before. And now that Helen—well, now that I have his complete attention, perhaps we can make a go of it."

Her sudden, brilliant grin was the last thing I was expecting. For a moment, the vibrant young woman returned, the incredible creature who had leaped from the silver convertible and danced across the patio, bringing all that orange energy into my life. She reached up and brushed her lips lightly against my cheek. My nostrils filled with the scent of her. Tangerine, I thought. She is all they claim . . .

She pulled back, laughing. *"Vous-êtes très, très formidable, monsieur."*

I stared. *"Et vous aussi, madame."*

Then she was gone. She turned and ran lightly across the veranda and in through the front doors. She flew into the hall and up the staircase, the sight of her bright robe fading, fading, until at last it was obliterated by the shadows at the top. Beautiful woman, running.

When my vision cleared, when the breath returned to my body, I went back into the living room.

Austin Hammond was just leaving as I came in. I paused in the doorway, watching the two men shake hands in the center of the room. Then Hammond came toward me, nodding as he passed and went out. I was once again alone with Frank.

We regarded each other across the room. After a moment, he said, "Well . . ."

I walked over to join him. "Sit down, Frank."

He studied me a moment, shrugged, and lowered himself onto a couch. I remained standing before him, looking down.

"I'm leaving in a few minutes," I began. "You probably want to be alone for a while. But before I go, I want to clear up some things. Then I'll go, and we'll never mention them again, okay?"

He nodded, never taking his eyes from me.

I took a deep breath. "All right. First of all, I want to tell you about something Dennis said at the party last night. He said that if I found out who killed your father, I'd go to the police. No matter who it was. Well, I've been thinking about that today, and it isn't true. It might have been once, but not now. I don't want to know anymore. Do you understand that?"

He leaned back, expelling a sigh. "Yes."

"Good. I'm going back to New York. Back to my life. I'm not going to do or say anything about any of this. I'm not a threat to you, or to anyone else. *Anyone.* It's over, at least for me. But before I leave here, there's something I have to know. Please, please tell me the truth. Then I'll go."

He stood up then and came over to stand before me. I looked directly into his eyes as I spoke.

"Did you ever try to kill me?"

He took an involuntary step backward, his dark eyes slowly widening. We stared.

"No," he whispered. "Oh, God, no!"

I leaned forward. I had to finish it. Now. "Did— anyone you know—ever try to kill me?"

Two men in a room, staring. I heard his breathing, imagined I heard the pounding of his heart. When he recovered, he began to shake his head slowly from side to side. I'd seen shock before, but never in this close a proximity.

"No," he said again. "Joe, what are you—"

I held up my hand. To my own surprise, I reached out and touched my fingers to his lips. "Don't. Not another word. Ever."

Then he was in my arms. He fell against me, grabbing at my shoulders, nearly knocking me over backward. I held him, felt the shaking and the pounding in his slender frame. Slowly the tremor subsided and his body relaxed. When I sensed that he was once again in control, I pulled myself gently away. Now there were tears in his eyes. As I watched, one heavy drop broke away and slid down his face. With all the effort I could muster, aware of every muscle involved, I grinned.

"I'll tell you what I told her," I said. "Get out of here. As soon as you can, just take her and go. Anywhere. Away from St. Thomas. I think you'll both be okay now."

I began to laugh, the waves of relief finally crashing through me. He hadn't tried to kill me: whatever else had happened, there was that. He and Dennis had once been my closest friends, and no one in my adult life had ever replaced them. Tangera was his responsibility, not mine. He would have to handle her. If he loved her—and he did love her—he would find a way. I was no longer a part of it.

A slow smile came to his face.

"Yes," he said. "Everything will be okay."

"I'll see you later," I said as I went over to the door. "I won't be leaving for a few days. Let me know about the service for your mother, or whatever."

He followed me across the room. Once more, briefly, I was embraced.

"Sure," he said, standing back to take a long look at me. "I'll be in touch."

I nodded and turned to go.

"If not," he continued with a little laugh, "there's always the Secret Place."

I laughed too, remembering.

"Yeah," I said as I walked out onto the veranda. With a last wave, Frank turned and went back into the living room.

I was just opening my car door when Eunice arrived from the direction of her cottage. She was wearing what must have been her best Sunday dress, and a flowered picture hat was clamped firmly to the top of her head. She carried two large suitcases.

"Joe, can you give me a lift down by Geahge's school? He be gettin' out soon, an' Ah don' wan' him comin' back heah. Ah wan' take him down by my sistuh's house in town."

I took the bags from her and placed them on the backseat. I opened the passenger door for her and she climbed in, settling her enormous bulk and fiddling with the pin of her hat. When she was satisfied that her headgear was secure, she fastened her seat belt and sat rigid, her gloved hands in her lap, staring straight ahead of her.

I got in and drove down the road, past the shouted questions and popping flashbulbs at the crowded gates, and away from the estate.

She never looked back, and she didn't say another word to me except to thank me at her journey's end. Before that, she broke her silence only once. As we descended the hill to the Waterfront, putting distance between ourselves and Haven View, its last rational resident closed her eyes tightly and bowed her head.

"Deah Lahd," she whispered, "in Dy infinite muhcy, please fuhgive de people in dat house."

* * *

I would recall her words the next afternoon, when Elsa gave me the news.

After dropping off Eunice, I went in search of Lee. I hung around the radio station at Mountaintop, watching my sister and the ship-to-shore operators at work. As soon as Lee and Paul could get away, they took me out to dinner. We met up with some friends of theirs in the restaurant and went out dancing. I arrived home very late and fell into bed.

I slept for nearly twelve hours, the quiet sleep of relief. When I woke, it was almost two o'clock in the afternoon. I took a shower and ran out of the house before Lee's housekeeper could deliver the message from Dennis. I jumped into the rented Chevette and drove out to Frenchman's Reef Holiday Inn.

The easel stood alone in its place on the Lower Concourse, the sign hung carelessly from a corner: Out to Lunch. She was sitting at a table nearby, a Bloody Mary and an open newspaper in front of her, gazing down at the guests in the swimming pool below the terrace. As I approached her from behind, she picked up the glass and nearly drained it.

I glanced down at the paper. There was a photograph of Helen, an old studio portrait. Next to it the Three Musketeers stared up from the page, our faces blank with shock at finding the audacious photographer in the driveway.

"Hello there," I said, dropping my hand casually onto her shoulder.

She leaped up from the chair and whirled around. The expression of anxiety on her face was a complete surprise to me. She lowered her head and leaned against my chest.

"Oh, Joe," she whispered, "I'm so sorry."

I placed my hands on her shoulders and studied her face. "What is it, Elsa? What's wrong?"

She looked up, startled, realizing. "You don't know?"

Then she told me.

It had happened while I slept that morning, on a remote stretch of road out past Brewers Bay, beyond the airport. The silver Corvette convertible, top down and obviously traveling very fast, had broken through a guardrail and plunged down a rocky incline into the sea. It had smashed into a large rock in shallow water and stopped, submerged up to the top of the tires. Tangera had been found, still strapped into the passenger seat. She had been rushed to St. Thomas Hospital. She was unconscious, and the prognosis was not good.

Frank—or, at least, Frank's body—had disappeared.

12

CONGA

The following twenty-four hours were mostly a blur. I remember specific things that happened, but not very clearly. My next completely lucid moment would be in the courtyard of the public library the following afternoon. But here's what I recall of the time immediately after Elsa's news.

I sat at the table above the pool with her for a long time, and I think she gave me something to drink. We did not speak. Finally she went back to her easel and I left the hotel. I got in my car and drove out past the airport and Brewers Bay.

In the small crowd around the damaged guardrail I recognized only Jenny Hughes. I left my car by the side of the road and went to join her. We stood together in silence, watching the activity below us. Several policemen were down by the water near the car, pointing and shouting instructions. A group of men was busy connecting cables from the large truck beside us to the rear end of the wreck, preparing to haul it backward up the incline. Two photographers were knee-deep in surf, snapping away. The boats were farther out, bobbing at anchor as Coast Guard divers and local volunteers in scuba gear searched the surrounding area. Now and then they surfaced and called to each other. The sound of their voices reached us, but I couldn't make out the words.

"Dennis was here until a little while ago," Jenny told me. "He had to go, but he asked me to come here. He left a message for you at Lee's house."

I nodded, staring down at the battered Corvette as it broke loose from the water and began its slow ascent.

We remained there for about an hour, waiting. The progress of the search was slow, as each general area of the bay near the rocks was checked and rechecked by the divers. Jenny spoke several times, but I only caught the ends of her sentences.

"—farther out to sea," she said, pointing.

And later: "—must have been going awfully fast."

Her man, Milton, hovered nearby. Twice she sent him to call the hospital on her car phone. He returned to us, shook his head, and shrugged. No change.

At one point there was a flurry of excitement in the water and all the divers converged on one spot. As several of them disappeared under the surface, Jenny reached over and took my hand firmly in hers. We stood there pressing our fingers tightly together until it was clear that whatever had drawn their attention was of no consequence.

Finally, everyone in the water swam back to their respective boats and climbed aboard, pointing out toward the open sea. The engines roared to life and the various craft moved farther away from shore. Then they all stopped again and cast their anchors, and the divers reentered the water.

"—take a long time, Joe. Perhaps we'd better—"

I missed the beginning and the end, but Jenny's message was clear. I nodded, and we walked to her car.

"Thank you for being here," I said as Milton handed her in to the backseat.

"Of course," she replied. "Go home, Joe. It's going to be a long night, I think."

I watched the limousine pull away, then returned to my car.

I know that I drove back to Lee's and left the car. Then I must have gotten it into my head to go down the Ninety-nine Steps into town. I remember walking the entire length of Main Street more than once that day, and at one point I sat on a bench smoking cigarettes on the esplanade at the Waterfront. I watched cruise ships setting sail in the late afternoon, the music of their bands rolling across the harbor. From that distance I could just make out the tiny figures on the decks dancing jubilantly as they were carted off to another port of call, another carefree tropical adventure. Have fun, I thought. *Bon voyage*. Come back soon to our lovely island. America's Paradise . . .

I wanted to think about Frank and Tangera, and about all the events that must have led them to this. One in the hospital, probably dying, and the other . . . wherever. I tried to imagine them getting into the car together. She hadn't known, of course, or even suspected. There had been no visions; not this time. Otherwise, she would never have . . .

It was all too jumbled in my mind. As darkness fell on

the city, I left the Waterfront and made my way back up
the hill to Lee's to wait for news.

On the night of Friday, July twenty of last year, a person
or persons unknown entered the home of Judge Hubert
William Jensen and severed his head from his body. The
weapon involved was a sharp, heavy blade exceeding the
diameter of the victim's neck in length, and, according to
experts, probably substantially longer. The perpetrator
would have to be at least average, probably above average, in physical strength. The height of the perpetrator
was uncertain, as it was not possible from examining
available evidence to determine whether the victim had
been standing or sitting when the blow was struck. Rigor
and coagulation, combined with near-equatorial temperature and excessive humidity, had placed the time of
death in question, but it was somewhat after ten-fourteen
P.M., when the last telephone call from the decedent had
been completed, and well before approximately eight
o'clock the next morning, when the housekeeper, Eunice
Powell of the same address as the decedent, had happened upon the scene. . . .

   Happened upon the scene. I stared at the copy on the
screen before me. What a polite phrase, I thought. Positively mellifluous. Such a civilized way of describing the
entering of a blood-soaked room to confront a decapitated corpse. *Happened upon the scene:* there was no indication in those four elegantly juxtaposed combinations of
sounds of the horror, the actuality of the moment for a
decent, gentle woman of firm religious belief who stood
there, facing a sight of evil she could never until that instant have imagined. The fact that Eunice Powell of the
same address had remained at the same address, tending

to the decedent's survivors, said more about the resilience of the human spirit than any newspaper—with all its lovely euphemisms—would ever record.

I scrolled back a couple of paragraphs. *Available evidence:* there was another one. Available evidence would be the trajectory of the blade as it sliced through living flesh. The heights and angles at which blood had spattered walls and bookshelves. The awful geometry of the violent last moment of a human life.

I shook my head and continued to read. The library was crowded, and a young woman nearby was patiently waiting to use my machine. I had begun that morning of the day after the crash by checking on Tangera's condition and the progress of the search for Frank. No news at either front. Then I had come here, to the second floor of the public library on Main Street. I had asked for the pertinent back issues of the newspapers. A friendly attendant had given me a quick lesson in the use of the microfilm projector, or whatever they called the contraption.

The wife of the deceased, Helen Bennett Jensen—yes, I knew all that. The servants had been asleep . . . the dog . . . ah, here it was: *Others Questioned.* Victim's son, attorney Franklin Bennett Jensen and wife, Tangera. He said he was home that night; she vouched for him. He had received a call from the decedent at about eight o'clock. He had spoken with his father briefly and hung up. The subject of the call, Frank said, was personal and private, and had no bearing on the investigation. Yes, he admitted, it was well-known that he and his father were estranged. No, he had not left his apartment at any time that night. He'd had a great deal to drink, retired at about twelve-thirty, risen at seven the next morning, and gone to his office in International Plaza on Main Street. It was there that he had received the news. . . .

His office.

What was it? Something about his office. A message from Elsa and—being sick. Vomiting in the bathroom. We'd been in his bedroom at Haven View on the night of the dinner party. He'd said something about being sick, about . . .

"I don't know where that hangover came from: I don't usually get them."

Oh.

Oh, God, how incredibly stupid I'd been.

The young woman sitting near me cleared her throat rather loudly and pointed a finger at her watch. I nodded, removed the newspaper file, and relinquished the machine.

He must have figured it out, about the hangover. He never got hangovers, and suddenly—on *that* particular morning—he had a hangover.

I returned the materials to the librarian and prepared to leave. It was nearly one o'clock, I noticed, and I was meeting Lee and Dennis for lunch at L'Escargot, the restaurant in the Royal Dane Mall.

Where I had been attacked.

I paused on the outdoor stairway leading from the second floor of the library. I stared down at the lovely old courtyard below me. Palm, hibiscus, frangipani . . .

Tangera. He'd been home that night, angry after his father's phone call, and he'd had entirely too much to drink. Tangera was with him. He'd gone to bed at about twelve-thirty. About twelve-thirty. And the next morning . . .

I descended the stairs and went over to sit on a bench

in the tiny, cloistered garden behind the library building. The high stone walls concealed the courtyard from the traffic, the bustling sidewalks, the world. I leaned back in the cool shade of the trees, all alone. Completely alone.

The next morning he woke up with a hangover.

Tangera. She would live or she would die. Frank would be found or he would not be found. He was dead. Or . . .

"Every now and then I dream about sailing. I'm out there all alone, just me and the water and the sky. I wouldn't have any particular destination. I'd go to many places. Other islands—South America, maybe."

"What about Tangera?"

"She doesn't like sailing. . . ."

I gazed around at the shadowy green garden as it all began to fall into place.

"Didn't she have some sort of history, or something?"

"Yes! Yes, she did. High blood pressure, same as me. She had to take pills for it."

Helen had thrown her glass to the floor, and it had shattered in front of her. She had looked slowly around at everyone.

"As if I didn't know who killed my husband!"

Frank had fallen asleep that Friday night in July at about twelve-thirty. The next morning he woke up with a hangover, and his father was dead. Three nights ago, Helen had announced to a crowded room that she knew the identity of her husband's killer. The next morning she was dead. Yesterday, Frank's car had crashed through a guardrail and slid down a forty-foot incline into the sea. Frank, who even as a child built models of racing cars. Who had won trophies for drag racing and swimming. The best driver I knew. The best swimmer I knew.

Then, sitting on that bench in the library courtyard, I realized what Frank had done. My hands gripped the edge of the cool stone bench as the knowledge slowly filled my brain.

Two women, laughing and chattering, came out of the library and down the stairs. I turned my face away from them as they passed by me and went out into the street. This was St. Thomas, not New York: if they had made eye contact with me, seen my panic, they would probably have come over to offer me assistance. I was not sure I would be able to speak.

Only one person could answer my questions, and she was in no condition to do so. But she knew; I was certain of that. She'd said as much that first time I'd met her, if only I'd been listening. Really listening. Those nine words, uttered so blithely; immediately retracted, qualified. And yet, taken literally, it may well have been the only truth she'd ever told me.

"Oh, my dear, of course! I saw it happen!"

What? I wondered. What on earth had she seen?

I rose from the bench and took a deep breath. I would have to pull myself together, control my trembling. I had to go to L'Escargot to meet Lee and Dennis, and I didn't want them to see my anxiety. They would be concerned and ask me questions I couldn't answer. Not now. Not yet.

With an effort, I drew myself up and left the courtyard. I walked around the library building to Main Street and turned in the direction of the Royal Dane Mall. I reined in my scattered thoughts and focused on one single resolve. I would find out the truth, if it was not already too late.

He had lied to me, not to mention the police. He

had misled me and distracted my attention from his own suspicions for as long as he possibly could. He had, at last, burst into tears and thrown himself into my arms. The next day he had taken his wife, the woman he loved, and driven her in the car across the island, out past the airport and Brewers Bay, faster and faster . . .

And it had all been a terrible mistake.

I sensed, even as I approached L'Escargot, that I was very close. If I thought about it for a few minutes, if I could clear my head and concentrate, the answers were there. They were at the tip of my mind, just out of reach. . . .

Before stepping forward into the restaurant, I paused in the alley and looked around me. This was where it had occurred, just over a week ago. Right over there I had stood, pinned to the wall by the large blond man while the native man with the knife had rounded the corner and confronted us. It was ridiculous, surreal, and yet it had actually happened.

I looked back at the entrance to the mall. No, my champion was not following me today. I had not been aware of his presence since—when? The day before Letitia Stewart's party. Someone was apparently satisfied that I was no longer in any danger. I would soon know whom that someone was.

Lee and Dennis were waiting for me, and they had been joined by Jenny Hughes. The three of them produced forced smiles as I approached. I said hello and dropped into a chair. Casual, Joe: that was the way to play this scene. I produced what I hoped was a nonchalant smile and ordered coffee, acutely aware of the oppressive silence that had suspended all activity the moment I had arrived in the crowded room.

Everyone had watched surreptitiously as I walked over to the table. As soon as I was seated, the lunchtime noise and bustle resumed. A small town is bad enough, I mused, glancing at the menu and realizing that I had no appetite for food. A small town surrounded by miles of ocean is infinitely worse. *There he is*, the room fairly shouted. *The third Musketeer.*

I looked over at Dennis. "Did you get the same treatment when you came in here?"

He frowned in disgust. "Vultures. I'm sick of everybody around here not minding their own business." Then, realizing what he'd just said, and to whom, he looked quickly away.

I was not offended. I turned to Lee. "Any news?"

"Not yet," she said. "I told everyone we'd be here if anything—happens. . . ." She trailed off weakly as the waiter lowered a fresh cup of coffee in front of her.

"I have someone waiting at the hospital—" Jenny began. Then she, too, glanced around at the rest of us and lapsed into silence.

They had not waited for me to order. Food lay before them, untouched. I had not eaten since I'd heard of the crash, and I would not eat now. The thought of food made me feel queasy. I lit a cigarette.

My sister regarded her omelette with distaste and pushed it aside.

"I'm sorry," she said, staring down at the table. "We're all being so polite and quiet, so civilized, and I really can't bear it for another moment."

We all watched her. I knew she would not look up to confront us: it had never been her way. She would state her opinion in a low, firm voice, and that would be the end of it.

Which was exactly what she did. "Now I'm the one not minding my own business. I never got to know the Jensens. I know that the two of you must feel terrible, and I appreciate that, but look at it all: Hubert, Helen, and now this. That beautiful young woman. How old is she, twenty-two? Twenty-three? It's pretty obvious who was behind it all—I'm sorry, Joe, but let me finish—and what he did is wrong. It's horrible. It doesn't matter who's good and who's bad: that's not for us to decide. Any of us. So, if he's dead, he's dead. If not—well, he's probably going to go to prison. Forgive me, but that's just where he belongs. Cutting people's heads off, driving off of cliffs—*no.*" She shook her head. "Maybe he thought violence was necessary, but that doesn't make it acceptable. Nothing will ever make it acceptable."

She nodded once, resolute, more to herself than to us. I looked over at the others, then back to her. I almost told them then. That her sentiments were right but her facts were wrong. That it hadn't been Frank. I was in the act of leaning forward, forming words, when something happened that changed everything.

Forever.

My sister Lee, whom I love more than I can say, shrugged her shoulders, pulled her coffee cup toward her, and slowly—slowly, slowly—reached for the creamer.

The creamer.

Just like that. No vast pronouncements or deathbed confessions. No pointing fingers and angry, loud accusations. Only Lee, reaching out with her hand. . . .

"Where's the cream? I'm sure it was here a few minutes ago. . . ."

Another restaurant. Another table. The creamer. A

small, perfectly ordinary gesture. It is in these that secrets are so often concealed.

That's how I figured it out.

I see it in my mind now in just that way. My sister reaches out with her hand and grasps the dripping blade. She raises the machete in front of her and tips it sideways. The warm, fresh blood flows sparkling down into the cup. . . .

I have relived that moment a thousand times. Describing it is relatively easy: experiencing it was the hard part. It began as a doubt; a small, new consideration. But as I reflected on all that had occurred from the day I'd received Tangera's letter until that instant, the bizarre suspicion grew and grew until it burst in a wave of shock that swept through my body. It subsided momentarily, only to be followed by another, greater one.

I knew.

Practically everyone had told me, unwittingly, by various words and deeds, from the very beginning. The truth had been there all the while, hiding in plain sight, like the cream in the restaurant. And I had not seen, had not wanted to see.

Lee and I had found the pitcher behind the rack of sugar packets. My sister had looked for it because she had known to look for it. It was tucked away out of sight. . . .

But she knew it was there.

The dog, bribed into eternal silence with poisoned meat flung from the darkness, from the other side of the high stone wall. The weapon, carefully chosen, grasped and clutched and moving silently, snakelike, around the side of the house. That furtive, secret journey, like the mongoose dance, unintended for other eyes.

"Oh, my dear, of course! I saw it happen!"

But somebody sees. Somebody knows. In St. Thomas, the moon sees everything: I know that for a fact. The bright full moon is watching. The moon, and one other . . .

The hostess arrived at the table and leaned down to whisper in my sister's ear. Excusing herself, Lee rose and followed the woman out of the room. As she reached the doorway, she was met by Bertram and Carlos, who were on their way in. Greetings were exchanged, and then the two men were shown to a table across the room from us.

I looked over at Dennis and Jenny. They were bent together, whispering, discussing Lee's sudden departure. They turned to look at me with questioning eyes.

I looked away. Bertram was waving from the other side of the room. I nodded to him. He looked a question. I shook my head: no, no word from Tangera. I noticed, even from the distance, that he was not in his usual buoyant mood. It wasn't merely concern for his friend in the hospital: he seemed to be angry or annoyed, I thought. In a moment, the reason became apparent. He flung himself down into the chair the waiter held for him and glared at his partner. A lovers' quarrel. Carlos, equally upset—or was that just his natural expression?—sat down and reached for a menu. I watched them, fascinated.

My interest, of course, really had nothing to do with them. I didn't care why they were quarreling: it was only a distraction, a bid for time. I didn't want to alarm my sister and my friends with what I had just concluded. I had to get away from them, away from everybody. I had to think about what I was going to do with my knowledge.

As I watched, Bertram turned his attention from Carlos to the waiter who hovered above them. The young, handsome waiter. Bertram collected himself enough to flash his brightest grin. The waiter then turned to Carlos and said something—asked him what he wanted to drink, probably—and Carlos, in a rare display of any emotion whatsoever, replied with a lazy, sexy smile. The waiter smiled, too. Bertram and Carlos, perfectly synchronized by long familiarity, lowered their gazes to each other. They frowned, obviously still not on speaking terms. Then, in unison, they looked back up at the waiter and smiled. The waiter smiled. Everybody smiled.

Of course, I thought as I stared at the three men across the crowded restaurant. That's what people do. That's how they behave. And I, like that young waiter, had simply gone on smiling, oblivious. I looked away, making a mental note to tell Bertram and Carlos, if I lived through this, that they had helped to solve the murder of Hubert Jensen.

My sister returned and handed me a slip of paper. On it was written the name of a doctor and a room number at St. Thomas Hospital.

"That was my housekeeper," Lee explained. "The message was left with her. Tangera has regained consciousness. She woke up about an hour ago. Apparently, the first thing she did was ask for you."

I was already out of my seat. My car was parked near the library. If I ran . . .

Lee grabbed me by the arm and bent her head to whisper, aware of the nearby tables. Dennis and Jenny leaned forward to hear her words.

"Joe, she says it's about the judge's death."

The first person I saw in the crowded waiting area in St. Thomas Hospital was Elsa. She sat with Willie on a long row of attached metal-and-plastic chairs, her hand gripping his tightly. The beach crowd surrounded them, and everyone was speaking in whispers or staring vacantly at the floor. A native family sat nearby in similar mournful silence. A young native man in a suit leaned against a wall nearby, obviously not a member of either group.

I had just emerged from the elevator and headed for the big desk before me when I noticed the people waiting, and my attention was arrested by the familiar face. When Elsa looked up and saw me, she rose from her seat and came over.

"Hi," she said.

"Hello. How long have you all been here?"

She turned to indicate the others. "They've been here since yesterday, on and off. I got here an hour ago. I figured Willie could use the company. He and Tangera are very close."

I nodded.

"Tell him she's awake," I said. "I have to go now; she's asked for me. I'll—I'll see you later."

She stood there, eyes widening, as I turned toward the desk. Then she went back to join the others. I noticed out of the corner of my eye that she leaned down to whisper to Willie and the beach people. They all turned to stare at me. The young man in the suit approached them. He listened to Elsa for a moment, then he walked over to a nearby pay phone.

The attractive, efficient-looking native woman in starched white was obviously in charge of the nurses' station on Tangera's floor. I ignored the gossiping younger girls behind the counter and spoke directly to her. She nodded briskly and pushed a button on the console in front of her. Almost immediately, the doctor whose name was on my slip of paper materialized next to me.

It was he who led me down the cold, silent corridor, talking to me in the low, oddly hushed tone everyone automatically adopts in hospitals. It was bad, he said. She was in traction, and there had been much internal trauma and hemorrhaging.

He had been summoned as soon as she awakened. She was unable to move, unable to feel anything in the lower half of her body. The pain in the upper half was considerable. She was told that the search was still on for her husband. Then she asked for me. She refused painkillers and all other medication. She would take them, she promised, as soon as she had seen Joseph Wilder.

As we arrived at the door, a young police officer rose from a chair next to it and faced us. The doctor waved him back into his seat.

"What's this all about?" I asked.

"Direct order," the doctor replied. "From the Commissioner. Don't stay too long, and try not to upset her."

I had to know. "Is she going to make it?"

He averted his eyes. "Her back is broken, in more than one place. There is other severe damage, as well. If she survives, she'll never leave a wheelchair. She'll probably never leave a bed. Please don't tell her that now. I'm sorry."

I couldn't think about it now: I had to get through this. "No offense, but why isn't Pierre Deveaux attending her? He's her doctor."

He shrugged. "I haven't seen Pierre for several days now. He hasn't shown up here, and he's not answering his phone at home. There's a rumor that he may have left the island." He began to move away.

I closed my eyes. Would it never end?

"Doctor," I called after him.

He turned around.

"Do you know where Deveaux lives?" I asked.

"Yes."

"I think," I said slowly, "you'd better send someone to his house."

He regarded me a moment, the import registering on his face. Then he turned and hurried away down the hall.

I glanced down at the policeman. He, like all cops holding such a vigil, was politely ignoring everything. I pushed the door open and walked into the room.

Nothing, not even photographs, would have prepared me for the sight. I had always understood "in traction" to mean an arm or a leg. Not all four limbs, and certainly not the torso. Or the head.

Her eyes and mouth were visible, and part of one side of her face. Everything else was hidden under layers of white gauze. She half-sat, half-lay on the large bed near the door. The other bed was empty. She was clad in a standard-issue blue hospital gown. Blue, I thought incongruously: the complement of orange, as far from it as possible. There was an impressive collection of bottles and boxes on the table next to her. I tried not to stare at the intravenous hookup or the tubes and wires connected to various parts of her face and body under the bandages. But it was impossible to ignore the sound; the tiny, rhythmic blip as the phosphorescent green streak swept across the screen of the large, bulky machine on the far side of the bed.

The curtains at the windows were drawn against the harsh glare of the afternoon sun. The only light in the room came from a small, dim lamp on the bedside table. I was grateful for the darkness.

"Tangera," I said softly.

She opened her eyes and looked at me. The green streak quickened. I went over to the bed and leaned down.

"Joseph . . ."

"Yes, I'm here."

"Joseph, he—he tried to . . ."

"Yes, I know."

"No, you do not—know. You do not understand. Frank thought I killed his fath—"

"Yes. Please don't exert yourself. Take it easy. You want to get well, don't you?"

Neither of us believed the joviality in my voice. All those acting lessons had not prepared me for this. Put me in a costume in front of several hundred strangers and I'll convince them that the earth is flat. But this . . .

She spoke again, and I had to lean closer to hear. ". . . not getting well . . . stupid doctor . . . have to tell you something."

I reached out as gently as I could and placed my hand on the side of that lovely face, the only visible part of her.

"Never mind," I said. "It doesn't matter."

". . . matters . . . please . . ."

My ear was next to her lips now.

"I saw," she whispered.

I pulled back and looked down at her. "I know."

The eyes between the bandages widened. The blip raced even faster.

Then I told her what she had seen.

I had not been aware that her body, broken and wrapped as it was, could be so tense. Yet, when I said it aloud, she relaxed slightly and lay back more comfortably on the bed. Gradually, the artificial sound that traced her heartbeat slowed to a calmer, more even tattoo.

So. That was that. I had been watching her eyes as I spoke, waiting for a change in their expression; some indication that I was on the wrong track, that she had no idea what I was talking about. It never came. She listened in accepting silence, and then her body told me the rest. I'd been hoping so much that I was wrong.

I leaned down very close to her. In a broken, halting whisper she told me the whole story. Everything she had done and seen and heard that night last July, from the moment she laced Frank's brandy bottle with codeine until she slipped undetected into the bed next to him nearly three hours later.

She had gone there to kill him. She had not climbed over the wall. She left her car down the road and walked through the iron gates and up the drive. She concealed herself behind the big tree on the patio, where she and I had twice stood together. She'd been lucky about the dog. Having only been to Haven View once before—that disastrous dinner party when she'd left the table and gone out to sit in the car—she had no way of knowing about the doghouse. Not to mention the crawl space: it was invisible behind the hedge. You'd have to know about it, and she did not.

Prince, in his doghouse at the back of the house, had remained unaware of her presence in the grounds.

For nearly an hour, she had watched Hubert through the open French doors, steeling herself. At one point she made some slight sound, causing him to look up from his desk and peer out over the patio. That's when he'd uttered that cryptic reference to mongooses, the one I'd later explained to her. She was just preparing to leave her hiding place with—a knife? A gun? A baseball bat? She never told me that part—some weapon, when she saw the figure coming out of the shadows at the side of the house. . . .

"*Oh, my dear, of course! I saw it happen!*"

Then she told me about the letter. My guess there had been right, as well. When she realized that Frank was not going to desert his crazy mother and leave Haven View, she looked around for other possibilities, her attention finally resting on Frank's rich writer friend from New York, who wrote such moving, sensitive stories of unrequited love. . . .

She sighed and closed her eyes. There were so many things I wanted to understand, things I knew I could never ask. She was tired and in great pain, and I didn't want to prolong this. I would ask the one question uppermost in my mind and leave.

I leaned down once more and spoke. "Was Helen Jensen murdered?"

I listened, waiting for the blip to quicken again. It did not. She took a long, rasping breath and exhaled.

"No. Heart attack. Really—"

"Okay," I said, holding up my hand to stop her. "You rest now. I'll send the doctor in. He's going to give you something to help you sleep, all right?"

She blinked, and I saw that now there were tears in her eyes. "What . . . you going . . . do?"

I shrugged. "Nothing. It's over. It doesn't make any difference now."

"Joseph?"

"Yes?"

". . . love Frank. Really. Tell him I love him."

I forced the smile to my lips again. "Tell him yourself. Sleep now. I have to go, but I'll be back to see you again soon." I reached carefully down and brushed her cheek with my fingers.

"Joseph?"

"Yes?"

". . . must tell you . . . vision does not seem . . . work for me anymore. Only others . . . saw you in . . . dream. You . . . at Haven View . . . danger . . . terrible danger . . . careful, please . . . hew . . . hew . . ."

"I don't understand," I said, bending closer. I caught one last, faint whiff of the citrus scent. Her lips brushed against my ear as she slowly pronounced the word.

"Hubert . . ."

"What about Hubert, Tangera?"

With an effort, she finished.

"Hubert will protect you."

I pulled away and stood next to the bed, staring down at her. In that moment, as her final words echoed through me, chilling me, I knew what I was going to do next. Her letter summoning me to St. Thomas had been written, it turned out, for entirely different reasons. That was of no consequence. Not anymore. I was here now, and it was what I had to do.

When I got to the door, I turned around to look at her. She was so small, so vulnerable, there on the bed with all those life-sustaining implements around her. I knew I would not remember her this way. Now, whenever I think of her, I see again that tall, laughing, impossibly lovely creature wafting across the patio in her bright orange beach dress, her hair still wet from the sea. Or sitting in the library, her arm brushing against my thigh, smiling as I sign the book for her. Or in my arms, dancing. I had been angry with her on that occasion, but I would not remember why. Only the music and the perfume and the feel of her slender, warm body pressed against mine.

I have so many memories of her, more than I have of most of the people I've known in my life. And I had only known her for—how long had it been? I calculated: fifteen days.

"You must be Joseph Wilder. How glad I am to meet you, at last!"

"Everybody calls me Joe."

"Then I shall call you Joseph."

"Good-bye, Tangera," I said, and I left the room.

I nodded to the policeman and walked down the hall to the elevator. Willie and the beach people still sat where I had last seen them, across from the weeping native family. The young man in the suit was once again slouched against the wall, watching me.

Elsa was gone.

I nodded to Willie and the others and pressed the button for the elevator. At that moment, the doctor materialized beside me once more.

"I did as you suggested," he said in his quiet hospital voice. "I sent one of the interns to Pierre's house. I didn't, uh, call anyone. Not yet, anyway." He glanced down the hall at the sentry next to Tangera's room. Then he leaned forward. "Mr. Wilder, do you think something is—wrong?"

The elevator opened and I stepped inside. Something wrong, I thought. Something wrong. I knew what they would find at Deveaux's house, and that was wrong. Tangera would probably not live out the hour, and that was wrong, too. Hubert, Helen, Bunky Tremayne:

wrong, wrong, wrong. Somewhere, in the restaurant or the hospital room, a nice, friendly, naive young man named Joe Wilder had disappeared forever. I would never fully trust anyone ever again.

Something wrong.

I smiled at the doctor.

"Let's just call it—a vision," I said, and the elevator doors closed between us.

If I hadn't been so preoccupied, if I'd bothered to pause and look around as I left the building and got into my car and drove away, who knows? The whole thing might have ended differently. It might have ended right then and there, in the parking lot of St. Thomas Hospital. But I had only my new destination in mind, so I didn't notice a thing.

I would finish it, confront the rest of it. Now. I would confirm the last part from the only one who could tell me the truth.

Frank.

I nearly pushed the accelerator through the floor.

13

DANCE OF THE MONGOOSE

Evening can come early in St. Thomas, especially in winter. Well, what we call winter, anyway: the months between December and March. The days are shorter, and the average temperature goes down about ten degrees, mainly at night. One Christmas when I was a teenager, the thermometer dropped into the low sixties for several days, and we all huddled in blankets and shivered. As a rule, though, the only way you can determine the season is by looking at a calendar. The long shadows I noticed in the driveway and the chill that edged the tropical air were not unseasonal, technically speaking. It was, after all, four-thirty on a January afternoon. But they were definitely unusual.

The gates of Haven View were closed, but someone—Lucien, presumably—had neglected to lock them. He hadn't locked them that night last July, either. But I wasn't taking that route. I left the car by the side of the road outside the walls of the estate. I gauged from memory the approximate location of the doghouse. Facing the eight-foot-high stone wall, I drew back my arm and hurled the imaginary steak. Then I leaped up, clambered over the top, and dropped noiselessly down onto the grass. Right on target: I was directly in front of the doghouse. Several yards beyond it was the kitchen courtyard. In the dead of night with everyone asleep, and maybe a ladder for the wall, a child could have done it.

The servants' cottage was to my right, about thirty feet from the back of the house. The faint sound of a television told me that Lucien and his wife were still in residence. I would have to be careful.

I made my way silently to the edge of the courtyard, keeping as much shrubbery as possible between me and the cottage. I watched my feet as I crossed the walkway, careful to avoid any loose cobblestones that might shift under my weight. I stopped at the base of the kitchen steps and turned to look at the hedge running the length of the house. Behind that hedge, invisible from the courtyard, was the crawl space.

At the top of the stone steps was the door to the kitchen. All other entrances to the house were from the veranda, at the front and sides. The shuttered sets of French doors and windows would be closed and locked, and the storm doors over them. The kitchen door, I remembered clearly, contained top-to-bottom frosted glass louvers. It was, to my knowledge, the only glass in the entire external structure. It was my best chance.

I removed the keyring from my pants pocket. Using the largest, flattest key, I carefully attacked the louver closest to the doorknob. By inserting and prying, I loosened the aluminum slat that held the glass in place and bent back the edges. The process took several minutes, and I constantly glanced over my shoulder at the door of the cottage. At any moment that door could open. . . .

At last the glass pane came loose. I slid it from its housing and reached through the opening to unlock the door from the inside. I entered the kitchen, carefully closing the door behind me. I set the glass louver down on the Formica counter and went through the swinging service door into the downstairs hall. The heavy door closed behind me with a soft whoosing sound and I was in sudden, complete darkness.

I stood in the hall for several moments, waiting for my eyes to adjust. The house had been shut and abandoned, and not one ray of sunlight penetrated. I held my breath and listened. Nothing: not a sound.

The now-familiar feeling had gripped me from the moment I'd crossed the kitchen threshold. Now here I stood in pitch darkness, all alone, the only soul in Haven View. Yet not alone; not alone at all. I couldn't see it, but the door to Hubert's office was there in the dark, about fifteen feet in front of me. I was reminded of the Brandt's party, when I had suddenly, inexplicably been certain that someone was watching me. At the time I'd thought it was Tangera, who had come over to join me a moment later. Now I knew the true identity of my malevolent observer. Now I knew a lot of things.

Until this trip to St. Thomas, I had never considered myself to be fanciful or suggestible. Now I wasn't so certain. Now I felt it on my skin, as I had at the party. There, in that empty house, I could feel the eyes.

I began to make out shapes in the hall. On my left was the door to the library. The staircase was a few feet in front of me. Next to the office door was a large, dark object against the wall: the table with the potted plant that held the key.

With a conscious effort, keeping my gaze away from the direction of the office, I stepped forward to the bottom of the stairs. Feeling the presence in every shadow, in every corner, I ascended. At the top of the stairs, I found a light switch, and the crystal chandelier above the steps came brilliantly to life. The sudden onslaught of light dazzled me. When the black spots before my eyes stopped dancing and swam away, I walked down the hall and opened the door of Frank's bedroom.

The overhead light I switched on revealed the shuttered windows and the still blue drapes. The clown in the painting above the bed grinned across at me as I stood in the doorway gazing at the room. Books, bedspread, carpeted wood floor, trophies, ship-in-a-bottle: yes. Even without the light, I could easily have made my way around.

I leaned against the doorframe, slowly expelling my breath. I had been holding the oxygen in my lungs from the moment I'd started down the hall. I'd half-expected him to be here.

Without so much as turning to look for it, with no need to guide my hand, I reached down into the shell.

The Secret Place bore secret treasure. Slowly, carefully, I removed the neatly folded envelope from its slick, cold, pink interior. I went over to sit on the bed and switched on the lamp.

It was the stationery of the law firm, exquisite white linen with the handsome, engraved return address: Hammond and Jensen, International Plaza, St. Thomas, Virgin Islands 00801. My name was written in large block capitals with a black fountain pen. I weighed it in my hands: there were obviously several pages inside. With a mounting sense of trepidation, I tore open the envelope, unfolded the letter, and began to read.

Haven View
January 12

Joe,

    I don't know if you'll ever read this. If you do, it means I went ahead and did it.

    It's late at night, and Tangera is asleep down the hall in "our" room. But I'm here in my old digs with a bottle of brandy(!) and a stack of paper. I'm sitting at the desk with that stupid ship in front of me. I can't stop looking at it tonight—I don't know why. And every time I glance up at it, I start to laugh. Maybe I'm a little soused. Who knows?

    Remember when the three of us put that thing together? We thought we were gosh-darned Leonardo da Vinci all rolled into one. ("All rolled into one"—what the hell does that mean?!) I've been thinking about stuff like that tonight. A lot. All the times we had when we were kids.

    Oh, well, enough of this nonsense. You're probably looking for some kind of explanation, not a trip down you-know-where.

    I guess what it boils down to is that I just couldn't deal anymore. Mother's gone—that's only now beginning to sink in. And after what you told me, or kind of told me, today, I don't know. I just don't know what to do.

    I told you that I hated him, and that's true. I still do. All my life I did whatever I could to get his attention. I really knew all that stuff you and Dennis were always helping me with—English and science and all that. Hell, I even knew algebra. But I couldn't let him know that. He was always so in charge, so on top of things. I thought maybe if he saw I could use some help—that was the fantasy, anyway. Well, we all know where that got me! So I went to Harvard and applied myself. He seemed more pleased with me, but by then, his abuse of Mother had reached such a point—well, it all went from bad to worse. He was doing all those things with Abel Brandt, building and planning. And he'd already set his cap on being governor. He ignored her and he ignored me and he went on hurting everybody.

Then Tangera arrived. Oh, God, Joe, I was so happy! It wasn't just that she was wonderful—so funny and sexy and attentive. She made me feel like I was somebody, you know? But I could also see that he would have a fit! Revenge at last, for me and for Mother.

You know what happened next. But you don't know this: Tangera didn't love me. God, Joe, it's almost funny. Like one of those stupid Greek plays we had to read for Adv. Eng. She married me for my money. And my "position." And a green card! She'd had enough of Martinique, it seems, and I think I know why. Mother let some things slip recently. He hired a detective, or something. He even went to our apartment once and threatened her with it—told her if she didn't disappear, I'd find out about some kind of "past," or something. Mother called her a harlot at the party last night. I guess that's what the detective came up with. Well, that's all water under the burning bridges. . . .

What you have to understand in all this is how I felt about Mother. He was a pig, and I soon saw the way Tangera worked. Shaking around the place, kissing up to men. Rich men. She doesn't have any female friends—did you notice that? Women don't seem to like her, and I'm beginning to see why. So, Mother was the only one who cared about me. I've never understood why he hated me. Why I've had so few friends in my life. Why I had to fall for an operator like Tangera. All I could depend on was Mother.

I'd made my bed with Tangera, so to speak. And it wasn't all bad. I was actually very happy. I felt good about myself, at least for a while. And I got away from him. He wrote me off completely. Tried to get Austin to drop me from his firm. Cut all communication. I used to call Mother in the daytime, when I knew he wasn't home. We'd talk for hours, but I couldn't come over and see her. He'd had us here once for dinner. Once. After that, he made it clear he had no use for Tangera. He never mentioned that it was because she's black, but I knew.

So there we were in that apartment downtown, and Tangera got bored. Running around with those creeps from the beach, carrying on. She wasn't the Great Lady she thought she'd become when she married me. You know, dinner parties and trips to Europe and all that. But she hung around and waited. For Father to change his mind. For me to resolve things with him. For him to drop dead and leave us everything.

I guess it wasn't happening fast enough for her. I guess that's why she killed him. That night, when he called, she asked me what he'd said. When I was finally drunk enough to tell her, she went nuts. "Disinherited!" She kept screaming that, stalking around the living room, throwing things. Then she suddenly seemed to collect herself. She said, "Oh, well, I guess we will just have to lump it." And she went and got me some more brandy.

I didn't suspect anything at first. I thought I'd just passed out and she'd put me to bed, and somebody else had gone to the house and killed him. One of those senators, or someone else he was blackmailing. I even considered Elsa. I still don't know what his business was with her. If you marry her and settle down—and you just might!—remember to ask her sometime.

But then I knew that it was Tangera. It was the nature of it—the passion. *Cutting his head off, like one of those other plays from Adv. Eng. You know, Oscar Wilde. Salome. "Bring me the head of—" whomever.*

Gradually, I just came to accept it. We moved in here, and I could be with Mother again. But it was really too late for her. All that booze and all those drugs, and losing him like that—she'd gone off the deep end. I wanted to protect her, take care of her. I didn't even mind that my wife was running off God knows where every day. I was even beginning to fantasize about getting rid of Tangera. Divorcing her. If I don't go through with Plan A, I still might. That's Plan B, between you and me and the lamppost.

I thought about ditching Tangera and taking care of Mother for however long she had. Deveaux had told Tangera and me about her heart. She didn't have long, you see. The high blood pressure and all that stuff in her system. And Father. Hearts break, Joe. They really do. That's not just a figure of speech.

And then, when Mother was gone, I'd get me a boat. Not that dinky Sunfish, thank you very much! Something nicer, just for me. I'd sail off into the proverbial. Just me. Nobody else.

Well, I guess you've figured it out, but first let me explain something. What you saw on the veranda that night. When they were young, when he first brought her here from Boston, their relationship was different. They even used to do that—what you saw. There was this old Victrola they'd found in the marketplace downtown, and they'd crank it up late at night and play old records and dance on the veranda. Naked. Of course, it was long ago, before I was a gleam, about the time that photograph was taken. It's funny to imagine them doing that, with the wine and the Victrola and everything.

Then he gradually lost interest in her and went off to be a lawyer and so forth. But once, just once, the day he became a judge, they had a reunion. I must have been ten years old, and I remember waking up and hearing the music at about four in the morning. I sneaked down the stairs, just like you did, and there they were. That song was the big hit then, "The Girl from Ipanema." They played it over and over, and they danced and danced. God, Joe, I'd never been so happy! Well, it only happened once.

Then it was back to the neglect and the abuse and the torture.

You know, it's really too bad she didn't just marry Deveaux after Father was gone. That might have solved some things. Sometimes lately, since the murder, she had what I guess you'd call episodes. You know, late at night after a lot of drinking and pills and whatever. One night a few months ago I was awakened by the music. "The Girl from Ipanema." I went down and found her, all alone, dancing. She was in a fugue state, or whatever they call it. She was dreaming that he'd come back to her, and that he loved her again.

Then Tangera killed her. At the party. She put something in one of those drinks, I'm sure of it. When Eunice came running in to wake us this morning, I knew. Tangera saw her as an albatross, one more thing standing between her and the Jensen millions. I don't know why I didn't see it coming, now that I think of it. I don't know how she did it, but Tangera induced that seizure.

And today you dropped your little bombshell. Oh, Joe, I'm so sorry! I don't know what she did, or tried to do, but you're okay. That's the important thing. She got you down here, didn't she? She called you or wrote to you—yes! You two were talking about a letter on the patio the day you arrived. "Oh, please, come help Frank," right? All the rich men around here are either married or gay. Or drunks, or drug addicts, or criminals of one kind or another, or all of the above—this island is a virtual barnyard of black sheep. So she took to importing a rich man—you! I guess you were supposed to fall in love with her and take her away from all this. She hadn't planned on your being a loyal friend. And she for sure hadn't planned on your seeing through her. You did, didn't you? You figured out that she killed Father. Did you actually tell her that? I hope not. Or did she have one of her "visions"?

I've gotta laugh at that. Ha ha ha ha ha! I used to believe that hooey about her clairvoyance. She's about as clairvoyant as this stupid ship in this stupid bottle!

God, that was fun! Building the ship, I mean. Oh, well. . . .

So that's where it stands now. I didn't kill them, but I caused their deaths, if you think about it. And I might have caused yours, too. I was the rocket scientist who fell in love with her, who didn't see her for what she is. And now it's up to me to do something about it. I'm not going to turn her in to the fuzz, or anything. This whole thing is bad enough without that. Besides, I have no proof of any of this. I just know. I mean, who else could it have been?

So: Plan A. I've got a lot of cash with me. It's sitting here on the desk next to our masterpiece. His money—isn't that ironic?! I called the bank after you left today, and when it was ready, I went down and picked it up. I also transferred a lot of money to— well, I won't bother you with those details. Besides, I don't know if this is gonna work. My little conference with Austin this morning was about my new will. I told him where it was, if "anything should happen." And I know a certain Musketeer who's in for a big surprise!

Do you remember what your mom did that time

with that boyfriend of one of your sisters? (Must have been Marla—I don't think it was Lee.) When he cut up that native guy who tried to rob him? The cops were looking for him, and in those days white boys didn't want to be locked up in Fort Christian for fighting with a native: they might never be seen again, you know? So he ran to your house. You and your sisters were away at the time—New York, or someplace. Anyway, the rumor was that your mom patched him up and kept him hidden for a couple of days, and then she hired some maverick pilot to get him off the island. He just kind of disappeared. Did your mom ever tell you about it? I'm not really sure she was involved, but that's how I heard the story. It sounds like Linda Wilder—something she might do. I've always envied you having her for a mother.

Anyway, that's Plan A. It can be done. It's been done.

Tomorrow morning I'm gonna put this cash in a bag and stash it in the 'vette. Then I'm going to get Tangera and take her for a little drive. And one of two things will happen. I've already picked the place, that hairpin out by—well, if you're reading this, it's history.

Hey, maybe I'll buy the farm and she'll be okay, and she'll become the Lady of Haven View, after all! Wouldn't that be a scream?! Some strange kind of justice. Hubert Jensen's house and all his millions in the hands of a black hooker!

But that's not the plan. She killed my mother.

If they found both of us (as you read this), then I guess it didn't work. Otherwise . . .

I don't know if we'll ever see each other again,

*but I want you to know how much your friendship
has always meant to me. I've only been able to count
on two people in my life, and you're one of them.
Even Dennis didn't stand the test of time. He got
busy with his life, and Father became his big political
enemy, and he stopped coming around completely.
You're the one, Joe. You are my only friend. Don't
ever forget that, no matter what happens.*

*Enough of this. My hand's about to fall off, and
it's time to get some sleep. I'd better be alert if I
want to make like a stunt driver.*

*Good-bye, Joe. I love you, and I thank you for
loving me.*

Frank

I folded the letter carefully, placed it back in the envelope, and set it down on the bed next to me. There was
a large, heavy, cut-crystal ashtray on the night table. I
pulled it over onto my knee and lit a cigarette. Long drag,
hold, exhale. Then another. The blue smoke hung before
my face in the quiet room.

I glanced at my watch. It was a few minutes after six.
There was no way to see through the shuttered window,
but I knew that it would soon be dark outside.

In the lamplight, the intricately cut pattern in the
crystal formed prisms. I raised the ashtray up before my
face and stared into its shimmering depths, hypnotized
by the flashes of red and blue and green. And orange:
brilliant, vivid orange.

Tangera. Frank thought she'd killed his parents, but
she had not. Whatever crimes she'd committed, murder
had not been among them. Helen's heart attack had been

natural. Hearts break, Frank had written. He was right about that.

Frank. I imagined him now, moving away from the island and from me, in some plane with a maverick pilot. Or in a boat, alone, his sail catching the wind as he glided away toward some unknown horizon.

And me: what would I do now, with my knowledge? The answer to that one was easy enough. Nothing. Nothing at all. I would leave this house and forget about the whole thing. But first . . .

I stood up and walked over to the desk. I placed the ashtray next to the ship in the bottle and crushed out the cigarette. Holding the letter up before me, I removed the lighter from my shirt pocket. The edge of the envelope smoked for a moment, then it burst into flame. I put the lighter back in my pocket and dropped the burning paper into the ashtray. Leaving the door open, I walked away down the hall.

I paused at the top of the staircase, looking down. When I had come up here, the lower floor had been dark. Now a shaft of weak, late afternoon sunlight lay across the downstairs hallway. A cold breeze, a draft, came up from below, whipping past me and down the hall toward Frank's room. The light was pouring in through the wide open door of Hubert Jensen's office.

Past shock, past caring, past everything, I slowly descended the stairs.

"Where are you taking me?"

"Hush! Just come on!"

"Oh, my dear, of course! I saw it happen!"

I paused in the middle of the flight, listening. Listening . . .

"It's over, as far as I'm concerned. He was a disgusting man, and now he's dead."

"I'd almost forgotten how the weather can be in this part of the world."

"Yes. It can be deceptive. Sometimes the rain will come out of nowhere. When you least expect it."

"It was a Friday night, actually Saturday morning."

"I just handed the phone to somebody and went on to my next move."

I stood there, my hand on the banister, staring down at the open door.

"Where's the cream? I'm sure it was here a few minutes ago. . . ."

"Where are you taking me?"

"Hush! Just come on!"

Of course, it was the judge who had the final word. When I reached the bottom of the stairs, I looked over at the closed door to the library. I had found him there that day.

"You seem like a very capable young man. . . . No false modesty, but no fear, either. My son should have your wits. . . . Yes, a very capable young man. . . ."

And there was no fear, no hesitation. Not this time. I simply moved forward across the hall and into the office. I walked to the center of the room and stopped. I looked at the French doors, then I turned to face the urn on the shelf next to the picture.

"Hello, Your Honor," I said.

Silence. The books, the desk, the leather chair. The beautiful faces grinning out at me from the photograph. The silver urn gleaming in the last light of day. No sound except the beating of my heart and the wind in the trees outside the French doors. They had been open that night.

They were open now.

I felt the eyes before I saw them. In one sudden, chilling instant, I knew that I was no longer alone in the room. I turned around. My eyes met those of the figure standing quite still in the doorway that had been empty only seconds before.

"What the hell do *you* want?" I demanded. "Haven't you caused enough trouble already?"

The eyes, as angry as mine, stared back.

"You know, don't you?"

"Yes," I said. "Tangera saw you. She was here that night."

"I thought as much. But it doesn't matter now. Tangera's dead—or will be, soon enough."

I took a step backward. The back of my leg collided with the judge's desk. This is really too much, I thought.

"Look," I began. "I have no intention of telling anyone—" I stopped in mid-sentence when I noticed the machete.

There was no time. An arm was raised. The blade flashed. In that last wild moment, I wondered at how quickly it comes. There was no time to scream, no time for anything. I would never be heard. I would never be saved. Instinctively, I brought up my hands to protect myself. I fell back against the judge's desk, and it and I were sliding backward across the polished wood floor. The desk smashed into the leather chair; the chair smashed into the bookcase.

With a deafening crash, the silver urn toppled to the ground. The lid went flying off, and a huge cloud of dust and ashes filled the air.

Everything stopped. Poised and ready to strike, the machete froze in midair. I lay back across the desk, looking up at the wild, horrified eyes that stared down past me at the urn on the floor.

Then the moment passed. I heard the awful, anguished cry of a woman and saw the machete coming at me, toward my neck.

The explosion that followed shook the desk, the room, the house itself. The arm flew upward. The hand flew open. The machete flew away. The blood flew everywhere, raining down on the desk and spattering the shelves and the white stucco wall behind me. The hot, sanguine red liquid smashed into my face, my hair, my open mouth. I could taste it as I screamed. The heavy weight crashed down on top of me, cutting off my scream, knocking all the air from my lungs. I lay there, pinned to the desk as the blood poured over me.

Somewhere, on the other side of the room, the machete clattered to the floor.

Then, in one long, graceful move, the torn and gory carcass that had just been Dennis Grey slid down my legs and landed on the floor at my feet.

I sat up, clutching the edge of the desk for support. Through the cloud of ashes and the fog that suddenly seemed to be filling the room, I could just make out the two figures that now stood in the doorway. I watched as the man named Milton reached over and gently removed the gun from Jenny's hand.

She came forward and knelt beside Dennis. She studied his still, upturned face for a moment. Then she rose to her feet, raised her head, and looked at me.

It seemed to take forever. For some eternity of time we stood there, she and I, alone in the world, staring.

Slowly, so slowly, the dazed expression in those lovely eyes was replaced by another. Sorrow, I suppose, or something beyond sorrow. Beyond desolation. I don't know if there's a word for it. Whatever it was, it was in my eyes as well.

Then Milton came running toward us through the mist. He seized her arm and pulled her out to the veranda. She stood there watching as he came back in and bent down to grab Dennis's legs.

"Help me!" he shouted up at me.

That's when I snapped out of my trance. I focused on his desperate face as the acrid stench began to fill my nostrils. The stench of the fog that wasn't fog at all. I looked up, my gaze drawn by the crackling sounds above our heads. Already the office ceiling was black. I reached down for Dennis's arms. We carried him out through the French doors and put him on the patio.

Jenny came over to kneel beside him and gently place his head in her lap. Milton ran off across the patio, shouting into his transmitter as he moved.

There was another body lying on the patio next to the driveway. Milton bent over to check for vital signs. As I watched, the large blond man from the blue Mustang slowly stirred and rose to a sitting position. He groaned, raising a hand to his bleeding head.

The flames were bursting from the roof and pouring out through the shutters of the upstairs windows. With a mighty crash, the office ceiling collapsed and several fiery beams fell down into the room. After a moment, a second explosion came from the other side of the house, from the direction of the kitchen.

Lucien and his wife arrived from nowhere, shouting and gesticulating. The wife took in the conflagration and the dead body on the patio and dropped to her knees in the driveway, clasping her hands together in fervent prayer.

From somewhere far away came the sound of sirens. I stood there, numb with astonishment and soaked with blood, watching the fire engulf Haven View. After a while, my gaze traveled up the column of thick black smoke into the dusky sky. And there was the moon, not yet bright, pale blue against dark, looking down upon the burning mansion, knowing everything.

14

LAST WALTZ

I never told anyone about the letter. Not even Lee, and certainly not the police. What I've recorded is a paraphrasing; the letter not as it was, but as I remember it.

Two days after the fire, I was called into Police Headquarters at Fort Christian on the Waterfront. I waited for a long time in the ancient red stone structure that had once protected the harbor from enemies and marauding pirates. I'd been there for an hour when the man I knew only as Milton arrived and sat next to me in the crowded reception area. He, too, was giving a statement.

As we sat there, he told me about his associate, the blond man from the blue Mustang, whose name was Charles Lannigan. At about the time I arrived on the island, Jenny had asked Milton if he knew of a professional security man who could be very discreet. Milton, on the advice of a trusted associate, brought in Lannigan from New York. Even he, Milton, had not been told the identity of the person from whom I was being protected. Jenny told only one person: Lannigan. But even Lannigan did not know why he was to protect me from her own fiancé. The huge blond man had been treated at the hospital for a mild concussion and released, and he had returned to New York. The police did not know—*must not know*, Milton stressed as we waited—of Lannigan's existence.

Milton also told me what I'd failed to notice in the hospital parking lot as I rushed off to Haven View. Dennis was there in his car, having followed me from the restaurant after Lee's bombshell about Tangera having information concerning the judge's murder. Lannigan—alerted by Jenny—was following Dennis. That's how we all got to Haven View. But Dennis had been prepared for Lannigan's arrival, and that was my fault. It was I who told him of the man's existence, at Letitia's party.

"Bodyguard? What bodyguard?"

Lannigan never made it as far as the house. What Dennis didn't know was that he was in constant contact with Jenny and Milton. When his transmissions abruptly stopped, they raced to Haven View, arriving in the doorway just as Dennis raised the machete. Jenny screamed, and Milton raised his gun to fire—not at Dennis, but into the air. Then the urn had crashed down, startling Milton. In that frozen moment, Jenny had grabbed the gun from him and fired. The irony was not lost on me: Tangera's final prediction had been accurate.

"Hubert will protect you."

Jenny had relaxed the surveillance on me after the accident and Frank's disappearance. She thought I'd conclude that Frank murdered his father and stop asking dangerous questions. When Tangera woke in the hospital with vital news, the chase was on.

Milton assumed, and I agree, that after he had killed me, Dennis would have returned to the patio to finish off Lannigan.

Dennis. I imagined him opening the office door downstairs with the key he'd seen Frank use two days before and waiting for me as I sat in the bedroom upstairs reading Frank's letter, resetting the scene of his earlier crime. I've made a guess as to why he chose the judge's office. Some sense of the dramatic, of everything coming around, of justice being finally done. And for Dennis, who loved his island and his family and his timeless, tropical way of life, it must have appeared to be justice. Hubert Jensen had tried to destroy St. Thomas. He'd called Dennis's parents niggers, to their faces, at Letitia's house. He'd threatened everything Dennis held dear. He would have become governor: everyone agreed on that. And then the phone call had arrived to Clayton Hughes at his Friday night chess game.

"*It was a Friday night, actually Saturday morning.*"

"*It's been a tradition with us, every Friday night for the past two years . . . we lock ourselves in a room together, just the two of us.*"

Condominiums. Jetport. Gambling.

"*I just handed the phone to somebody and went on to my next move.*"

Hughes, exasperated, had handed the phone to Dennis—the only other person in the room—and gone on to his "next move." Queen takes bishop, perhaps . . .

I regarded Milton as he spoke, studying the proud, handsome face of this native Virgin Islander. He had been born here, and his parents before him. St. Thomas:

the actual, ultimate intended victim. This man reminded me of Dennis. I knew, looking at him, that there are things worth dying for, worth killing for. Lee said that violence is unacceptable, and she's right. But what about violation? The cold, systematic rape of a place, of a way of life? The world is full of Hubert Jensens, and Dennis's unholy act had only been a temporary measure. How can St. Thomas and all the St. Thomases of the world be protected from those who would obliterate them? I have no answer for that. Dennis thought he did, but he was wrong.

Dennis. Every time I'd seen him on this visit, he'd been inviting me somewhere: his wedding, the Inaugural Ball. Encouraging me to stay when he was obviously desperate for me to leave—desperate enough to hire the kid with the knife to scare me away. Not really a mystery, I suppose. What better way to deflect suspicion from oneself than to appear eager for the detective to remain. I remembered my lunch with Abel Brandt and his creepy partner, realizing that I should have told Dennis about their new development plans. If he'd perceived me as an ally rather than a threat—well, who knows. . . .

My name was called by the desk sergeant. Just before I left Milton in the waiting area, he leaned forward and whispered to me. I nodded and went into the office of the lieutenant in charge of the investigation.

I lied my head off, and they allowed me to do so. The scandal was too close to the governor's office, and they were eager to close the books. When they asked me about the fire and how I came to be in the house that afternoon, I told them I had some hunch that Frank, in shock and on automatic pilot, might have returned there after the accident—provided, of course, that he had sur-

vived it. I told them I'd wanted to be sure. I'd gone everywhere, I said, even to his bedroom. I had a lit cigarette
with me, and I thought I'd put it out in the ashtray. The
draft caused by Dennis opening the office doors downstairs might have blown the burning ash over to the gauze
curtains. . . . I shrugged and looked around at them all.
It was only half a lie, really. That's probably exactly what
happened, only it hadn't been the cigarette. At last I informed them—with clear eye and steady voice—that
Milton had shot Dennis to prevent him from murdering
me. They thanked me and said I could go.

I nodded to Milton as I passed him and went out of
Fort Christian. I had followed his whispered instructions:
our stories would match.

Tragedy begets tragedy, and soon it becomes your world:
a vast landscape of disaster as far as you can see. You are
lost, unable to breathe, in miles and miles of sorrow.

They found Pierre Deveaux, just as I'd known they
would. He'd injected himself with something that was
supposed to make him go to sleep and not wake up, but
it hadn't been that easy. Asphyxiation, aspiration—one of
those words. He'd choked on his own vomit. Inspired by
Helen, he'd died with a photograph on the bed next to
him, but it was not a photograph of her. The woman in
the picture was Celeste Deveaux, who'd died of leukemia
at the age of thirty-two.

Some relative of Helen—a cousin, I think—came
down from Boston to claim her body. She's buried somewhere in Massachusetts with the rest of the Bennetts.

Helen. Throwing the glass to the floor. That part has
always bothered me, that moment at the reception.

"As if I didn't know who killed my husband!"

Did she know? And, if so, how? Maybe she was awake that night, looking out of her bedroom window. Or coming down the stairs in a trancelike state, with some idea of dancing with her husband on the veranda. I suppose she could have seen something—but why didn't she report it? No, it doesn't make sense. I have chosen to think, rather, that her tirade at the party was an act of grandstanding, a last bid for attention. Even if that attention was negative. Lonely people have been known to do that.

Tangera had refused to dance with Dennis at that party. She was polite, it seemed to me, but cold. Moments later she'd danced with someone else. No fraternizing, I guess. He, of course, had only suspected her knowledge at the end, when she'd asked for me at the hospital. So, naturally, she and I would have to die.

Well, Tangera died. The doctor later informed me that she drifted off to sleep soon after I left the hospital. She never woke up. About an hour later, the steady green blip became one long, sustained green line.

I spent one more week in St. Thomas. I lay on beaches and sailed and snorkeled. I took a good, long look at everything—old and new, quaint and offensive—committing it to permanent memory. I called American Airlines and made a reservation to return to New York on January twenty-first, the day after the Inaugural Ball. I'd say good-bye to everyone there.

Jenny Hughes refused to see me. She was in seclusion at Government House and was granting no interviews, least of all to me. I was burning to ask her one question: how did she know Dennis had killed Hubert? As it turned out, I would wait nearly seven years for the answer.

Thinking about Jenny makes me think about Elsa. I

don't know what it is to be a woman, and I can't understand what goes on in the mind of a woman who is hopelessly, perhaps obsessively, in love. Jenny was protecting me from her lover, even as she was protecting his secret. She wanted to get married and have children, and she wanted to work with special kids. For these things, she was apparently willing to remain silent about what she knew. When women love someone as Jenny obviously loved Dennis, their field of vision becomes surprisingly narrow.

It can be argued that women love more deeply and passionately than men. I only have to think of Jenny. And Elsa.

Elsa. The morning before the ball, I went back to the library on Main Street and sifted through some more newspaper files. I found what I was looking for, a coroner's inquest from January, six years ago. The man testifying was new to the island: he'd never seen those people before. He'd received the phone request that very morning, from the husband. He'd gone to do the job that afternoon. As he worked, he heard voices from the next room, voices raised in anger.

It was just as I had feared. The old Joe Wilder would have fallen apart. The new, improved Joe Wilder took it in his stride. He could handle it. He could handle anything. When I left the library and went back to Lee's house, there were several phone messages for me, all of them from Elsa. I didn't return her calls.

On my last night in St. Thomas, I went with Lee and Paul to Governor Hughes's Inaugural Ball at Bluebeard's Castle Hotel. We were seated at a large round table in one of the dining rooms with what I can now look back and refer to as my supporting cast: Bertram and Carlos,

Biff and Honey, Letitia Stewart. Across the room I saw Abel and Abby Brandt at a table with a crowd of other wheeler-dealer developer types, including the business partner from New York, Mr. Whoever. There were about four hundred people spread out over two dining rooms and the large, torchlit terrace on the cliff below them.

Clay and Iris Hughes arrived to much fanfare and applause. They made the rounds in the rooms, shaking hands and accepting congratulations. They didn't stay long, as the festival was spread out over several of the island's hotels, and they had to appear at all of them. Jenny was not with them. When they stopped at our table, I noticed the strain on their faces, particularly as they greeted me. They were polite but abrupt, and they moved quickly away. I could think of nothing to say to them that might make a difference.

There was not a lot of good cheer at our table. I looked around at everyone, knowing that we were all feeling the loss. Bertram was particularly subdued, which I could understand. Without Tangera, it didn't seem like much of a party. I thought of her other great friend and glanced around the room. Willie Whitney was a few tables away, looking uncomfortable in a jacket and tie, sitting in mournful silence with the beach crowd.

And Elsa. She was next to Willie, looking beautiful in a strapless white gown, her shiny gold hair caressing her bare shoulders. Our eyes met, and she smiled and nodded. I turned my attention back to my own table. A few moments later she arrived next to my chair. As my group observed us, she leaned down to me.

"Hi, Joe. Did you get my messages?"

"Yes."

"But you didn't call me back."

"No."

"I understand you're leaving St. Thomas tomorrow."

"Yes."

She reached down to take my hand. "Come dance with me."

There was no way to refuse, not with everyone watching. She led me out of the room and down the steps to the terrace. We walked through the dancing couples to the railing at the edge of the cliff.

The music of the steel drum band filled the night. The huge panorama of lights and black mountains and dark, shimmering ocean lay before us; behind us shone a thousand chandeliers. The torches flickered, casting the crowded terrace in constantly changing shadows. The full moon watched from above. For the last time, Elsa Tremayne stepped forward into my arms and we began to dance.

I looked out at the lights as we moved, wondering how long St. Thomas would be this perfect. Already, Abel and Mr. Whoever and all the others were making plans. . . .

Forget it, Joe, I thought. Just enjoy it while it's here. Let it go, relax, and dance in the moonlight. Dance one last time with this beautiful woman, the last woman you may ever love.

This woman, who murdered her husband.

I closed my eyes and held her close. If I forgot, if I didn't think about it, maybe I could go through with it. Stay here with her, take her to New York—whatever. Change my outlook, my whole point of view, until I was the kind of person who could accept them. Frank. Dennis. Tangera. Elsa. Accept them all without having to consider my own outmoded, inconvenient morality.

No. I knew I couldn't do it. There would always be my questions, and where there are questions there is distrust. And love and trust, the new Joe Wilder knows, are symbiotic.

I have never considered suicide, and I don't know what goes on in someone's mind at such a desperate time. There must be a million things that would occur to me if I knew that today would be my last day on earth. But there is one thing that would never, under any circumstances, enter my head.

I would not hire someone to tune my piano.

I'd gone to the library to find the man's testimony, and my last hope had been dashed. It wasn't a regular appointment of long standing: Bunky Tremayne had called the piano tuner that morning.

Bunky, whose best friend knew nothing of his alleged state of mind.

"He just kind of hung out, drinking, using, messing with women. . . . Elsa says that in those last couple of weeks he started threatening to—do it. . . . He didn't mention it to anyone else, not even me. Just her. . . . According to Elsa, he just disappeared one night. . . . She found him. . . . He never said a word about—what Elsa said he was planning. . . ."

Elsa says. Elsa said. According to Elsa.

Okay, I had thought. An accident. Tequila, downers, swimming. It was entirely possible.

Until I considered Hubert Jensen.

"I didn't want to scatter his ashes on that beach. . . . His other favorite place. . . . Sitting at the end, on that damned rock of his . . . two, three nights a week, right up until he died. . . ."

And the phone calls.

"The fourth phone call was to Elsa Tremayne."

And her uncharacteristic behavior with Frank.

"Tangera got all bent out of shape. . . . 'That woman was making a pass at you,' she said. . . . The more I think about it, the more it seems that maybe she was coming on to me. After I'd married Tangera. Besides, there was something going on between her and Father. . . ."

He must have been on his rock that night, staring out at the ocean, when something had happened. Something that had allowed him to use Elsa as a pawn in his game. She wouldn't have done it just to get Bunky's debt to him canceled. She would have worked like a slave to pay back every cent. No, she was afraid, as only Hubert Jensen could make someone feel afraid.

"Get my son away from the nigger and I'll forget I saw you put your drunken, doped-up husband in the water and hold him under. . . ."

Then the last phone call, the night he died: "Forget it, I'm disinheriting him. You're off the hook—for now. . . ."

And the message she'd left at Frank's office the next morning, before she could possibly have learned that the judge was dead: "Must see you. . . ."

And the meeting, months later, when she'd told Frank it no longer mattered. . . .

And the fact that her flirting with Frank had ended as mysteriously as it had begun, the minute Hubert was gone. . . .

I had, just days ago, seen a woman shoot her lover. A woman who loved him—and hated him—so much that she'd kill him before she'd watch him destroy himself, and her, and everyone else. . . .

There on the terrace, dancing with Elsa, I didn't know any of these things to be facts. But I was considering them, and that was bad enough. I would never question her. And I knew that if she was aware of my suspicions, she wouldn't say anything, either. We'd both remain forever silent. We'd pretend that this was a lovely time that now was over, and I'd go back to New York pretending I was not—had never been—in love with her.

I never loved them, any of those people. Frank. Dennis. Tangera. Elsa. If I tell myself that often enough, I may come to believe it.

I opened my eyes on the torchlit dance floor. The steel band came to the end of its tune. I held her close to me a few seconds longer. Then I let her go. I let all of them go.

I smiled and thanked her for the dance. She regarded me quietly for a moment, then she leaned forward and brushed my lips lightly with her own. I walked away and went up the steps to the dining room. Just before I entered, leaving that woman and that island forever, the new Joe Wilder turned around for one last look at her.

She stood there gazing up at him, watching him go, alone among the moonlit dancers.

It's snowing again outside in Hudson Street. I've just been over at the window watching the flurries and the hurrying passersby, remembering. It had been snowing that day seven years ago, December twenty-third, when the whole thing had begun.

Jenny Hughes came to see me recently. She's just moved to New York, and she says she's here indefinitely. She lost her father three years ago, just after he completed his term of office. His replacement, another Democrat, has his hands full: Abel Brandt and his confederates are still going strong. Jenny's mother is still living there.

She looks very well, all things considered. She got the degrees she wanted, but a few years of working with challenged children have convinced her that she is not the altruist she thought she was. She's up here looking for a new line of work.

I haven't mentioned it to her yet, but I may be able to help her find one.

We talked about it all over a bottle of wine, everything I have recorded here. I think it was her arrival on my doorstep, breaking our seven-year silence, that convinced me to write it all down. At any rate, she seems to have recovered from the worst of it. It was she who brought up the subject of St. Thomas, asking me how I'd figured it out, and I told her about the creamer in the restaurant.

My sister and I had been discussing the machete from the concealed crawl space, invisible behind the bushes under the kitchen steps at the back of the house, when she suddenly began foraging around for the pitcher. I explained that it wasn't until I saw the action with the creamer repeated, at the table in L'Escargot, that I realized the crucial fact of the case.

"Whoever it was knew the house. They knew where the doghouse was, and where the tools were kept."

Like the creamer, you had to know the machete was there in the first place. Who knew that? The residents of the house, of course: the family and the servants. Once you eliminated them, which I had by that time done, there were only two people who knew about the machete, as far as I was aware. Tangera had been to the house exactly once, for dinner, and she'd spent half her time there waiting in the car. Elsa and Willie and Biff and all the others, as far as I knew, had never even been to Haven View. Even if they had, a rudimentary tour wouldn't include the doghouse and the crawl space. So, two people. I knew *I* hadn't killed Hubert Jensen, which left only one person. Once upon a time, in a game of hide-and-seek, it was I who had shown it to him.

"Where are you taking me?"

"Hush! Just come on!"

Jenny listened in silence and nodded. I didn't want to belabor it, bring up too many painful memories, but I did finally ask her the question I'd wondered about for so long: how did *she* know Dennis killed Hubert? Her answer, after all this time, was amazingly simple.

It was her steak, from her refrigerator.

After the famous Friday night chess games with her father, Dennis would always come to her apartment in downtown Charlotte Amalie and spend the night with her. On that evening, she'd fallen asleep waiting for him. She was awakened at one point in the night—about one-thirty, according to her bedside alarm clock—by sounds from her kitchen. Dennis was getting something from the refrigerator. Midnight snack, she thought, and she fell asleep again. Later—about three, by the clock—she heard him come in the front door. She got up this time, and she found him in the living room, removing his clothes. He kissed her and apologized for playing chess so late. Before she could ask him about his being in the kitchen ninety minutes before, he dropped his clothes in the bedroom hamper and went into her bathroom. Moments later she heard the shower running.

The next morning, she'd gone to her refrigerator and noticed that the steak she'd been thawing for Saturday's dinner was missing. Later that day, when she heard the details of the judge's murder—including the presumed time and the poisoned dog—she began to suspect. She was suspicious enough to go to the hamper and inspect his clothes. There was a small, dark brown stain on the cuff of the right sleeve of the shirt he'd been wearing the night before, and a similar one on his pants.

Thus began her nightmare: her inadvertent involvement, her decision to remain silent, and her frantic attempts to keep me safe when I arrived on the island and proceeded to ask all the wrong questions. Dennis never knew she knew: he died not knowing.

Now, so many years later, all I could do was smile at her, thank her for my life, and send her on her way with a kiss on the cheek and a promise that we'll get together soon. And we will. I have to tell her the rest, the one last thing I haven't told her—or anyone else, for that matter.

It is this: about two months after I left St. Thomas, Austin Hammond arrived in New York on business. Part of that business was to see me. Over dinner at 21, he gave me what was—after St. Thomas—the second biggest surprise of my life.

I have one more month to wait. If in that time Frank Jensen does not reappear, I will inherit fourteen million dollars.

It had not occurred to me, that odd chain reaction of wills that resulted in my great expectations, until Hammond leaned across the table at 21 and handed me a copy of Frank's revised last will and testament. He had left everything to me.

I've had seven years to think about it, and I know what I will do. I've already taken the first steps. I've used my show business connections to secure an enrollment at

Juilliard, and I have set aside money for George Powell's education and training. I have also arranged for him to study with a retired, world-famous concert pianist who lives above Carnegie Hall. Of course, all of this depends on their assessment of his talent when they meet him, but I don't think he has anything to worry about. He has just celebrated his seventeenth birthday, his mother writes from the island, and soon he will be ready. Maybe, just maybe, one single positive thing will come of all this.

I will pay for George myself. As for Frank's money . . .

I went to the bank the other day and opened an account. It is there, waiting for Frank's legacy. My mother's flair for the dramatic has been passed on to me. On the line indicating the title of the account I wrote three words, finishing with a flourish of my pen:

The Mongoose Fund.

When the last snake is vanquished, the legend goes, the mongoose dances under the full moon. If St. Thomas has taught me anything, it is that the world is full of snakes. I stood by then, watching helplessly as lives were destroyed, the lives of people I loved. I will not stand helplessly by again. With Frank Jensen's money, the new Joe Wilder will do what he can to see that what happened to Frank and Tangera and Helen and Dennis and Jenny—and Elsa—does not happen to anyone else.

I am waiting. One day, I will dance beneath the moon.

But that will be another story.